Also by Sherry A. Burton

Tears of Betrayal

Somewhere In My Dreams

The King of My Heart

"Whispers of the Past," a short story.

SURVIVING THE STORM

by

SHERRY A. BURTON

Surviving the Storm (c) Copyright 2014

by Sherry A. Burton

First Printing June 13, 2014

Published by Dorry Press
Photo by Hobbs Studio
Edited and Formatted by BZHercules.com
Cover by LLPix Design

For more information on the author and her works, please see www.SherryABurton.com

A Special Thanks...

To my husband, Don, thank you for everything you've done to bolster my self-esteem. Your love and support have given me the strength, confidence, and encouragement to follow my dreams.

To my family and friends for helping to spread the word.

Many thanks to my early readers, Tina, Tracie, Jane, Kathy, & Dianna for their comments and corrections. To my proof readers, Brandy, Becky, & Trish, for taking that one final look.

To my fans, I couldn't do this without you!

To the Writers' Police Academy, and all the work they do to help writers "get it right." It was at the 2012 WPA conference where my "voices" took notes and moved this storyline in a new, and exciting direction.

Lastly, to my "voices," without whose help I would not be where I am. Thank you for giving me such amazing ideas and, most importantly, thank you for picking me!

TABLE OF CONTENTS

CHAPTER ONE

March 28, 2005

Abby turned onto Dumas Street and glanced at the GPS on the dashboard to get her bearings. The final destination flag popped on the screen. She giggled. It was something she tended to do when she was nervous. Just over a mile until she reached the end of her journey, only three minutes from the new life she'd chosen. Butterflies took flight in her stomach. She was really going through with this. She was going to marry a man she didn't love.

She gripped the steering wheel tighter in an effort to control her trembling fingers, as she silently sought to justify her decision. Dang it, she thought, I married for love once and look how that turned out. She shook her head. That was a memory she didn't care to revisit at the moment. *Jacob loves me and he will make me happy. He will keep me safe.*

"He always has," Abby said aloud.

It had been that thought that had propelled her onward since leaving her home in Indiana. She leaned forward in an attempt to urge the car to go faster. After traveling on the interstate for hours, the current twenty-five MPH speed limit felt as if she were crawling.

Abby blinked several times in an effort to convince herself that what she was seeing was real. Trees lined the street on either side. Single-family craftsman homes, with perfectly manicured lawns, sat equal distance apart, looking like a Norman Rockwell painting come to life. Perfection. The epitome of the south. Her heart fluttered as she struggled to remain calm. This was going to be her new home. A new fairytale life. A fairytale? Was that even possible? Still, didn't she deserve a little happiness after all she'd been through? In a short period of time, she'd lost her husband and both her parents in horrible accidents.

"Brian." Her breath caught as an image of the man she'd married flashed in her mind. Handsome, funny, charismatic...dead. She gripped the wheel harder. Dead by his own hand. That one was brought on by his choice. Not an accident. No, she would not mourn him. That marriage had been a mistake. She had given him her heart – which he had promptly broken in two.

She replaced the image with one of Jacob. Twenty-one years her senior, Jacob was everything that her first husband was not. Suave, sophisticated, well spoken. She had known him all her life. He'd been relentless in his pursuit of her, infuriated when he'd learned she had eloped with Brian. Jacob had taken it personally, as if she'd betrayed him. Still, he had been there to pick up the pieces when Brian had overdosed. Once again, Abby shook off the memory and replaced it with one of Jacob holding her, telling her she deserved better. He'd tried to convince her to leave with him that night. But it was too soon. At Jacob's insistence, she had gone back to her maiden name, Turner, but she had stayed in her apartment, knowing she needed time to think. Jacob made it hard to concentrate on anything but him, sending her flowers, gifts, and romantic e-mails, telling her he'd waited all his life for her, begging her to marry him. She smiled, picturing his face, strong jaw line, and soft, wavy brown hair that was always combed to perfection. He kept himself in shape and it showed. He looked at least ten years younger than his actual age. Only the soft creases along his eyes and the slight graying at his temples betrayed his true age of fifty-two. Jacob thought the gray made him look old. Abby thought it made him look distinguished and sexy. She bit at her bottom lip. It was hard to imagine she was just months away from becoming his wife.

"Abby Annette Buckley." She tried the name on for size and smiled.

"Abigail Annette Buckley," she corrected, using her full name. Jacob preferred Abigail over Abby, saying that Abby sounded too childish.

"Mrs. Jacob Buckley." Yes, that had a nice ring to it. She took a deep breath. Everything was happening so quickly. She maneuvered the car to the curb, shifted into park, and stared straight ahead. She needed a moment to get a grip on her emotions before she arrived. "Come on, Abby. You've made it this far," she reasoned.

She eased her fingers from the wheel, flexing to relieve the tension of grasping the wheel. "You can almost see the house and Jacob is going to be worried enough."

Rolling her shoulders, she cursed her cell phone battery for dying. Guilt nagged at her, since a part of her was glad. Jacob had been calling her constantly to make sure she was okay. More proof that he cared, even if it was a tad annoying.

"It'll be fine, Abby. It's not like you're marrying Jacob tonight, or even next week. Your lease was up. You and Jacob are getting married, so this is the next logical step. People move in together all the time." She glanced around, making sure she had not been seen talking to herself. Appearing crazy would not be the best first impression to give her new neighbors.

Staring in the rear view mirror, her eyes roved over the boxes that filled the confines of the car. She'd brought everything she owned with her. At least everything she had left. Jacob's house was fully furnished, so he'd convinced her to sell what little she did have. All of the rest of her belongings fit neatly into her 2002 Dodge Intrepid, leaving just enough room for Ned's birdcage in the back and her cat, Gulliver, in the passenger seat beside her. She gazed over her shoulder and sighed.

Putting the car back into gear, she returned her attention to the road, refusing to dwell on the fact that at the age of thirty-one, everything she owned fit neatly within the confines of her car.

An eager meow came from the depths of the carrier beside her.

"Don't worry, big guy, Jacob will grow to like you." She reached through the grate to pet the black and white cat. Jacob had balked at her bringing her animals. It was one of the few arguments they'd had. He had relented when she made it clear they were a package deal. If Ned and Gulliver were not invited, then she would make other arrangements for the three of them.

9

"You will arrive at your destination in five-hundred feet." She glanced at the navigator, turned on her blinker, and began searching the house numbers. She knew it was the right house the second she saw it. She recognized it from the pictures Jacob had e-mailed her. It was a neat white house with burgundy shutters. *He was right,* she thought with approval, *it is the nicest house on the street.* While the other homes were nice, none were as well kept as this one was. From the perfectly manicured yard to the neatly edged sidewalk, it was picture perfect. Neatly trimmed shrubs sat just in front of the porch. Large earth-colored planters rested at the base of the steps. Each was filled with bright yellow flowers so perfect that Abby wondered if they were even real. The house looked new, when in actuality it was probably over a hundred years old. All the houses on the street were the same single-story craftsman. A small window sat just above the roof of the porch, which spanned the width of the house. White painted brick pillars supported the overhanging roof. Large double windows paralleled each side of the doorway. It looked quaint and safe, nothing like she had pictured when she had first envisioned New Orleans. Actually, even though the houses were close together, it still had a small town feel, something that pleased her.

As she pulled into the driveway at 421 Dumas Street, Jacob burst out the front door, worry etching his eyes. Relief washed over his face as he hurried down the sidewalk. His wavy brown hair, normally combed to perfection, was disheveled. His broad shoulders remained tense as he approached. When he opened her door, the panic in his normally smooth voice was evident.

"Where have you been? I expected you hours ago. When you didn't answer your phone, I thought you had changed your mind. I tried to call over and over, and it kept going straight to voicemail," he said.

"I didn't drive all this way to be fussed at the second I opened the door," she said curtly. Abby was taken aback by his intensity. Jacob was always the epitome of control. Taking a deep breath, she forced a smile and eased her way out of the car, not an easy task since she'd been driving nonstop for hours. "My phone died and I ran into construction."

He pulled her into his arms, kissing her firmly on the lips, as though still not believing she was there. His lips were soft, yet demanding. Abby responded to his kiss, feeling herself melt into his strong embrace. She had never in her life been held like this, like she meant something, like she was a lost treasure suddenly found. Yes, she could get used to this. She was here, she felt safe and needed. She'd made the right decision.

"I'm sorry, Abigail. I was worried. I'm so glad you made it safely." He breathed the words into her ear before releasing his hold on her.

"No, I'm sorry. I didn't mean to worry you. After the phone died, I couldn't find the charger. I must have packed it in one of the bags." She didn't tell him that she'd enjoyed the brief reprieve.

His brown eyes narrowed, flashing with golden specks. He ran a hand through his hair, leading Abby to realize why his hair had been out of place. He must have really been worried. She felt guilty. She should have taken the time to stop and find the misplaced charger.

11

His gaze swept to the car. When it returned to her, his expression was softer. "You should have stopped and called."

"You're right. I should have." She rubbed at the worried crease that remained in his forehead.

"I thought I was going to have an anxiety attack the whole way here. I thought the snow in the mountains yesterday was bad. I figured today would be easier since I was heading south. First, I ran into construction. Then it rained so hard that I had to pull over for a while. After it passed, I felt like I couldn't get here fast enough. I'm lucky I didn't get a speeding ticket." This seemed to appease him as his shoulders relaxed for the first time since her arrival.

Jacob clutched her to him once more. "I was worried. My stomach has been in knots. I was scared something had happened and you wouldn't be able to come. I should have insisted that you fly."

As she felt the need in his embrace, her decision to come was reaffirmed. "I had to drive. How else would I have gotten everything here?" She had sold nearly everything she had as it was. She was not about to leave her car and what little personal items she had left.

She pulled back, flashed him a smile, and tucked her long, red hair behind her ear. Cupping his face, she met his eyes.

"I'm here now." Her words held promise.

A soft mew interrupted the tender moment.

"Oh, I nearly forgot about Gulliver and Ned." Turning her attention to the animals, she returned to the car and opened the passenger side door. As she pulled the carrier from the seat, she did not miss the tension that suddenly returned to Jacob's shoulders. One thing was for sure, while Jacob was truly happy that she was here, the same could not be said when it came to her animals.

She took a deep breath and readied herself for another argument. "I need to take the animals inside; I'm sure Gulliver would like to get out and stretch his legs."

Jacob closed his eyes briefly. When he opened them, he smiled, showing gleaming white teeth. "If I have to have the animals to have you, then we might as well take them inside."

Unfortunately, Jacob's smile did not reach his eyes. Abby let out the breath she'd been holding. Okay, it was clear he was not happy about having the animals here, but at least he was not going to fight her on it. She balanced Gulliver's crate while hoisting the bulky birdcage out of the back seat. Once she had both securely in hand, she turned and followed Jacob up the narrow sidewalk.

His walk was stiff, as if struggling with something. He stopped at the door and held it open as she approached. His nostrils flared as his eyes shifted to each carrier in turn. He held the door, but did not make any move to help her with the cumbersome load. It did not help matters that both cat and bird were voicing their discontent. She turned her body sideways and managed to maneuver both animals through the doorway. She offered him a feeble smile as she passed. His mouth twitched as gold flecks mingled with the brown in his eyes. Abby had barely entered the house when her feet refused to continue. She stood planted in place. She'd seen this room before…but not in this house.

CHAPTER TWO

Lowering the animal carriers to the floor, she studied her surroundings in fascinated disbelief. This was not the room she'd been – expecting, the room she'd seen in the pictures Jacob had sent her. No, this room was straight out of the Pottery Barn magazine that she'd shared with him. She peered around the space, her mouth agape. A leather couch, the color of chestnuts, sat under the front window. Draped across the center was the red plaid throw, exactly as it had been in the picture. Matching pillows sat nestled in each corner of the couch. A red tweed wingback chair, with matching ottoman, rested against the far wall. It was flanked on each side by dark mahogany bookshelves. A leather recliner in the same hue as the couch was on the opposite wall. The red and cream striped curtains were also identical to the ones that had graced the pages of the magazine. As she scanned the rest of the room, she saw the same red-pillared candles, rustic lamps, even the woven area rug that had covered the shimmering hardwood floors in the clipping. She turned toward Jacob, who was leaning against the doorframe.

His eyes met hers. "Do you like it?"

Did she like it? She loved it. Jacob had sent her pictures of his home, telling her it would be her home, and she could decorate it the way she wished. The thought had thrilled her. She'd spent hours pouring through magazines, finding the perfect pictures and sending them to him for his approval. While she loved the room, she couldn't help but feel a tinge of remorse. She had thought "she" would be the one who did the decorating. "Yes..."

He straightened to his full height. "I thought it was what you wanted."

Oh crap, she'd been in the house less than three minutes and already sounded ungrateful. Here he had gone to all the trouble of making her feel welcomed and she was moping like a schoolgirl. She forced a smile to her face and peered upward. At five-foot-three, she felt slightly intimidated by his six-one stature. "Of course I love it, Jacob. It is exactly like the picture I sent you. What's not to love?"

He crossed the room in three easy steps, stopping close enough for her to feel the heat of his body. He held her gaze as he traced the edge of her jaw line with his fingers. She nearly melted at his touch. His fingertips brushed across her lips before he lowered his hand. He moved past her and started down the hallway.

"Good, then I think you will approve of the rest of the house."

The first room was right off the living room. He opened the door and motioned her inside. The room was freshly painted pale lavender. It held a four-poster bed and was the image of yet another magazine picture she'd sent him, right down to the shower curtain in the en suite bath. Her fingers lolled against the soft comforter at the end of the bed. It was even prettier than the picture. She was tired from the trip and the bed looked inviting.

Jacob turned to her, his face intent. "This is your room. I hope you like it."

She snatched her hand back in surprise. "My room?"

His expression softened. "Only until we are married."

His statement startled her. It wasn't as if they were teenagers. "I guess I assumed we would be sharing a room."

"You will not share my bed until you are mine." His tone left little room for argument.

But something in his words raised a red flag. Something in the way he had said the word "mine." What the hell was that supposed to mean? The hairs stood up on the back of her neck as she took a step backwards. "Excuse me. What do you mean 'yours'?"

A smile played on his lips. Gold flecks danced within the brown of his eyes. He caught her hand and pulled her into him. His hand gripped her jaw tenderly. Lifting it to meet his, he leaned toward her. When he spoke, she felt the heat from his breath on her lips. "You are such a firecracker, Abigail. I love the blaze in your eyes. I want you more than anything in the world. I want to bury myself in you and listen to the sounds of our desire. I want to fill you with my essence and watch you glow in the aftermath. I've thought about the things I want to do to you for so many years that I ache just being in the same room with you, but I'll not touch you before the time is right. I'll not have you until we are married."

Abby felt her knees go weak as his mouth closed on hers. It had been a kiss such as this that had sent her over the edge the night she'd finally agreed to become his wife. She had known him for years. He'd been a friend of the family, but he was older and she'd never paid him any mind until then. Sure, he had pursued her for years. He'd lavished her with presents when she was younger, and professed his love for her on more than one occasion. It had nearly broken his heart when she'd married Brian. Her father, who had been Jacob's ally, had pleaded with her to get an annulment, saying she didn't know what she had cost him.

She closed her eyes, remembering her parents. She missed them dearly, her mom anyway. The ironic thing was that her husband, Brian, had not turned out to be the man she had thought. She hadn't even known he'd been using drugs until the day she'd found him dead from an overdose. She was all alone now. *No, not anymore,* she thought, leaning into Jacob's kiss. He pulled her close. She could feel his need pressed hard against her, a weight that held the promise of more. But more was not forthcoming. He pulled away abruptly and motioned for her to follow as he left the room.

He led her through the hallway and past a half bath. As she followed him through the house, she saw that each room was as she'd dreamed it would be had she done it herself. He led her into the master bedroom. The walls had been freshly painted a steel gray. Bright white trim and white picture frames stood in stark contrast to the dark walls. She ran a slender finger along one of the frames. Each remained empty, waiting to be filled. At least he had left that for her to do. It was uncanny how much the room looked just as it had in the photo she'd e-mailed him a few short weeks ago. It was apparent he had gone to great lengths to see the magazine photos come to life. It should have made her very happy, but something nagged at the back of her mind. He stopped and stared at her expectantly.

"Oh, Jacob, it is stunning," she offered after she realized he was waiting for approval. *Just how I would have done it*, she added silently.

He nodded before continuing the tour. He paused in front of a closed door. "This used to be the kitchen before I had the addition added to the back."

He squared his shoulders and drew himself up.

"This is MY office." The sentence came out as a warning. He led her further down the hall without bothering to show her what lay beyond the closed door.

She cast a glance over her shoulder, her curiosity piqued. She was still glancing backwards when she ran into him, unaware he'd stopped. His mouth was tight when he spoke. "There is nothing in there that concerns you, my dear. I will tend to business and you will tend to the house."

She opened her mouth to speak, but he pressed on before she could protest. "I have waited for you all your life, Abigail. I watched you grow and knew the stunning woman you would become. I knew, given the fire in your eyes, you would be a challenge. But trust me, it is my job to take care of you and I take my job seriously. A man of my age…feels the need to be the provider. I assure you I have the means to take care of you, so please let me do so."

While part of her wanted to protest, the idea did have some appeal. She was tired. The past seven months had left her emotionally drained. With Brian's and her parents' deaths in such quick succession, she was a wreck. Jacob loved her, and if he was old school enough to want to take care of her, then why not let him? Would it be so bad? Why did people work anyway? For the money, right? If she didn't need the money, then why should she work? She could devote herself to being a housewife and making Jacob happy in return. She was a great cook. If she didn't have to work, she could make him elaborate meals. Would it be so terrible to be a housewife? Maybe even a mom someday? Did he even want kids? They hadn't ever discussed them. What if he didn't? Would she be content just being Jacob's wife?

"Would you like to see the kitchen?" Jacob asked, pulling her out of her musings.

Part of her wanted to say there was no need. She already knew exactly what it would look like. She'd sent the picture as soon as she found it. Bright white cupboards, speckled gray granite countertops, and stainless steel appliances. Twelve by twelve travertine tile would line the floor, and touches of red would be dappled throughout the room by way of small appliances and linens. She had little doubt she could stand in that very spot and see the room he was about to show her. She struggled not to let him see her disappointment. He had gone to great lengths to make her happy. Too bad he didn't realize he'd stolen some of her joy by not allowing her to be a part of it.

She forced a smile. "I would love nothing more than to see my new kitchen."

Sure enough, the room matched the vision in her mind. It was perfect right down to the red dishtowels.

She walked to the counter and admired the deluxe red mixer that sat on the counter, just waiting for her to whip up something divine. "It's lovely."

It was, too. The whole house, with the exception of the office, which she'd not been privileged to see, was decorated exactly as she would have decorated it, if given the chance.

So if it was so perfect, then why did she feel so disappointed? It must be the drive. The thought pacified her. That was it. She was simply worn out from the long drive. With the construction, the rain, and the unexpected blanket of white in the mountains, it had taken longer than expected. She needed a shower and a full night's sleep and then she would be as grateful as she ought to be. She had a man who loved her and a house straight out of a magazine. She was well on her way to living the American dream. After nearly a year of hell, she was going to be living in the perfect house, on the perfect street. She was going to be a housewife and serve perfect meals to a man who adored her, who had just assured her that she would never want for anything. What more could a woman ask for? Suddenly, she felt a bit like Cinderella being released from the grasp of her evil stepmother and the thought made her giddy. She wanted nothing more than to return to her pretty lavender room, and to look under the bed for the glass slipper, which she just knew had to be there.

CHAPTER THREE

Abby jerked awake. She fought to remain still against the instinct, which begged her to run. She was certain it was footsteps that had awoken her. Disoriented, she tried to focus in the unfamiliar room. Her pulse raced, yet as her eyes roamed the moonlit room, she saw no one. Gulliver's soft mews calmed her.

As her vision became adjusted to the muted light, she caught sight of the cat at the foot of her bed. The tall bedpost reminded her of the picture she had selected from the magazine. She relaxed; she was in Jacob's house. Her house, she quickly amended. She searched the realms of the room, wondering if Jacob had relented and come to her after all, but a quick survey told her that she was alone. Maybe it had just been a dream. Silently, she drummed her fingers on the duvet to get the cat's attention. The action, which normally led to the immediate insertion of a cat head under her hand, evoked no such response. The cat remained where he was seated, tail twitching, head tilted toward the ceiling.

Abby turned her glance upward, half expecting to see what had captured the cat's concentration, but saw nothing. Then she heard the sound again, heavy footsteps coming from above. But from where? There was no second floor. The roof? Was someone walking across the roof in an attempt to shimmy down into her window?

You're on the first floor, brainiac, she reminded herself. If someone wanted to come in through the window, they would not have to climb onto the roof. She shot a quick look to the window. Seeing it was tightly closed, she breathed a sigh of relief. Closed, yes, but she hadn't thought to make sure it was locked before she'd went to bed.

Moving the covers aside, she scooted out of bed, tiptoed across the short distance, and verified that the window was indeed locked. More steps, these stopping directly overhead. Gulliver growled a feline warning toward the ceiling. Abby hurried to the end of the bed and placed a trembling hand on his head to soothe him. He hissed his dismay.

"Easy… don't panic," she whispered, wondering if she was trying to calm the cat or herself.

Ned ruffled his feathers under the covered cage. Abby ran a nervous hand through her hair. Great; all she needed was for the bird to start squawking or, worse, calling a cheerful hello to the intruder. Intruder? Surely not. Couldn't they have waited at least until she'd settled into the house before breaking in. She didn't even know where Jacob kept his knives.

Jacob! She looked to the door, wondering if she should wake him. Maybe she'd only imagined the footsteps. She stole a look at her cat, whose glowing yellow eyes were still trained on the ceiling above. No, she had not imagined them. She clutched her robe from her bedpost, pulling it on as she crept toward the doorway. She left the room, taking care to shut the door so Gulliver would not follow.

She eased her hands along the wall, wishing for a nightlight. The hardwood floors felt cool against her bare feet. Feeling her way in the dark, she found the entrance to the master bedroom. Finding the door open, she peered inside. Darkness greeted her.

"Jacob," she whispered into the air. "Jacob, wake up," she called slightly louder.

She groped her way into the room, bumped into the foot of the bed. Keeping her hands on the bed for guidance, she traveled the length of it. *Seriously, hasn't he ever heard of a friggin' nightlight?* she thought, fighting panic. Her hands found the pillow, but no head lay on top of it. She lunged across the bed, expecting to find him on the other side, but felt nothing more than empty space. Great, a psycho was traipsing around on top of the roof and she was playing hide 'n' seek with her future husband.

She pulled herself off of the bed and once again felt her way out of the room. Her eyes were becoming adjusted to the darkness enough to allow her to see shadows. She peeked around the door with mixed emotions. She was grateful to find the hallway empty, but at the same time wondered what had happened to Jacob. A sudden thought struck her. What if it was Jacob on the roof? Picturing him in his tailored suits and manicured nails, she dismissed that thought instantly. He was not the type of person that would be found climbing on the roof in the middle of the night. Instead of finding comfort in the fact that he was not on the roof, her realization had the opposite effect. If Jacob was not on the roof, then who was?

Abby's breath quickened as she felt her way along the wall. The muted sound of a door shutting stopped her cold. Within seconds, a dim light lit up the hallway where she stood waiting. The light, she realized, was coming from under a closed door at the far end of the hall. Her mind fumbled to recall the layout of the house. Jacob's office. Her heart quickened as she made her way toward the lighted room and gripped the doorknob. She was startled by the fact that the knob didn't budge. Locked? Why? She remembered his look when telling her this was *his* office. It was enough to send chills rushing up her spine. Why would he need to lock a door in his own home and why was she not privy to what was inside? If they were to be married, shouldn't he trust her? Didn't she deserve to know what lay on the other side? Her emotions were now in a tug-of-war: one wanting to pound on the door and demand to be let inside and the other wishing to respect his privacy.

The light under the doorway disappeared, bringing her back to the moment. She collected herself just as the door swung open. Jacob, not knowing she was there, walked right into her, sending her sprawling onto the floor. She could see his mouth agape, even in the dark. He was still dressed, his hair perfectly coiffed, revealing that he had not yet been in bed.

"What the hell?" he said, reaching for her.

"I...was..." she said, trying to catch her breath.

"Spying on me?" he asked with an edge to his voice that she'd never heard before. He reached behind him and closed the office door before switching on the hall light.

Blinking in the sudden brightness, she shook her head in denial. "No, I wasn't spying on you. I was looking for you."

"Well, you found me." His voice was condescending. "I told you this was my office and you are not allowed in."

He was mad at her? What the heck? She hadn't done anything wrong and didn't deserve this tone. She thrust up her chin, feeling tightness grip her jaw.

"I was not being nosey," she assured him through gritted teeth.

"No?" His mouth quivered as if he found her bravado amusing.

"No!" she repeated rather loudly.

They stood appraising each other. Jacob's mouth twitched, the veins in his neck flexing with each breath. Finally, Jacob closed his eyes and blew out a long breath. When he opened them, his demeanor had changed.

"Let's start over. Tell me what you were doing in the hall."

She hesitated briefly before deciding to accept the truce. It was late and she had never seen him like this before. Maybe it was merely a misunderstanding. He was probably just as tired as she was.

"I checked your room, but you weren't there. I heard a noise. I thought I was imagining things, but then Gulliver heard it too." Her words were slow and deliberate as she tried to curb the anger in her voice.

He let out another sigh. She narrowed her eyes, convinced he didn't believe her. That was it. She didn't need this. Maybe she'd been wrong about coming after all. He caught her by the arm as she turned to go and pulled her into him.

"There, there. Is that what got you so upset?" He ran his hands across her back as he spoke. His voice was soft, caring; his embrace solid, protective. This was the Jacob she knew.

She fought to remain angry, but found it hard to do when he held her this way.

"What noise?" he asked, his voice tender.

"Jacob, there is someone on the roof." Her voice trembled, remembering her fear.

He pulled away from her, cocked his head, and looked at her as if she'd lost her mind. "The roof?"

"Yes, the roof. I was sound asleep and I heard footsteps. Gulliver heard them too." She hoped that by adding the cat's corroboration, he would believe her. She set her chin, peering up at him. She had not imagined it.

Jacob's jaw tensed. Abby wondered at the look that passed over his face. He appeared angry. With her? When he spoke, his voice belied his anger. "I'm afraid I must apologize. I was up in the attic, putting away your suitcases. I didn't realize the noise would wake you."

"The attic?" she repeated, looking upward. Of course the house had an attic. She'd seen the window above the porch. But where were the stairs? She hadn't seen them when he'd given her a tour of the house. She was just about to ask him where they were when he pulled her into him once more. His mouth came to rest on hers, parting her lips with his tongue, seeking out her own in return. She leaned into him, urgent need replacing her anger. The kiss united them for several moments before at last Jacob pulled away abruptly.

She opened her mouth to question his sudden departure, but he placed his hand to her mouth to silence her, his fingers tenderly wiping the kiss from her swollen lips.

When he spoke, his voice was heavy with desire. "You're just tired from your trip and let your imagination run away with you."

He walked the length of the hallway with her, stopped just outside her bedroom door, and brushed the hair from her face.

"It's late, Abigail. Go back to bed." His breath was hot against her face.

Abby felt embarrassed at her panic. She should have realized there would be a simple explanation. She watched as his eyes traced her thin robe, making her aware of his desire.

"You could come to bed with me. I would feel safe if I wasn't alone," she offered, hoping he would finish what he started.

The door behind her rattled, causing her to jump. Looking down, she saw Gulliver's paw reach under the doorframe. The paw turned, extended claws clutching onto the outside of the door, causing it to rattle once more.

Jacob stiffened beside her, the spell broken. "I told you, I will not share your bed until you are fully mine."

A soft mew, followed by another rattle. Jacob scowled at the paw that snaked underneath. "Besides you are not the one sleeping alone."

He turned and walked back the way they'd just came. He turned off the hall light, entered the master bedroom, and closed the door without so much as a backwards glance. Abby stood staring in disbelief. Finally, she opened the door to her own bedroom, scooped up her furry friend, and crawled back into her bed. She lay there for hours, feeling a bit like a child being sent back to her room after having a bad dream. It was her first night in the house with her future husband, and she was suddenly wondering if she'd made the right decision. She'd seen a new side of Jacob tonight, a side she didn't care for. Between the secretive room and his reaction to Gulliver, she wondered at his response. She'd known his dislike for the animals, but his reaction left her a bit unsettled. She drifted off to sleep on a wave of emotions, listening to the sounds of Gulliver's reassuring purrs.

CHAPTER FOUR

Abby awoke, feeling like a brick was weighing down her chest. She opened her eyes and smiled. That brick was Gulliver, who lay sprawled out across her chest. He meowed a protest when she lifted him from her bosom. He stretched out beside her and rolled to his back, turning his purr motor on. She rolled onto her side to face him, passing her hand up and down his belly, much to his delight. He purred contentedly as he wiggled his torso from side to side.

The room was cool, proving that even the Deep South could succumb to winter's chilly blast. She wondered if the heater was on, then questioned if the house even had a heater. It was New Orleans, after all. She scratched the cat's belly with more vigor, causing him to scoop up her hand and chew on one of her fingers, purring as he did so.

"Are you hungry?" she asked, prying the digit from between his teeth.

"Hello?" The scratchy voice was tentative.

Abby jumped up and pulled the cover from the oversized birdcage. "Good morning, Ned."

The Quaker Parrot responded with a flutter of green wings and a perfect imitation of a kissing sound.

"Give us a kiss," he said, leaning closer to the bars of his enclosure.

Abby pursed her lips, mocking him. Opening the cage, she offered the bird a finger, which he eagerly accepted. She hefted the parrot to the top of the cage, where he busied himself with his morning pruning.

She pulled back the window coverings to allow in more sunshine and winced at what she saw. The ground was only a few feet away, leaving her feeling embarrassed at how she had overreacted during the night. If anyone had wanted in, they would have opted for breaking a window, not climbing onto the roof. She remembered the look on Jacob's face when he'd sent her back to her room.

She blew out a huff. He'd sent her back to her room. Treated her like a child. The memory was met with anger. She pulled herself up to her full five-foot-three stature and felt the heat build in her face. She chided herself for allowing him to get away with it. Not normally one to back down, it angered her to have permitted someone to get the better of her, even if that someone was her future husband. She was not a child to be reprimanded. She was a grown woman. *If we are going to be married, we will have to get a few things straight.*

Donning her robe without bothering to tie the sash, she picked up her brush and began pulling it through the length of her fiery red hair. As she brushed, her anger festered. *Who does he think he is? Just because he's older does not give him the right to treat me like a child.*

She tossed the brush onto the bed, threw open the door, and was met by the smell of bacon. Oh, how she loved bacon. How could she be mad when he was cooking bacon? Shit! She followed the aroma to the kitchen, her anger waning with each step. Gulliver ran in front of her, obviously just as eager to find the origin of the smell.

Jacob was standing in front of the stove, a spatula in hand. In a black mock turtleneck and matching black slacks, he seemed out of place at the gas range. The silver at his temples mingled with his wavy brown hair, giving him that distinguished look that she adored. He looked up when she came into the room. A smile brightened his face, making him appear suddenly younger, and reminding her of what an attractive man he was.

"Well, good morning, sleepyhead. I was wondering if you were going to sleep your life away." His voice was smooth as liquid gold.

Gulliver brushed against his legs and, for an instant, she thought he was going to fling bacon grease at the feline. He tempered his anger so quickly, she wondered if she'd imagined it.

"I guess I had to make up for the sleep I lost during the night," she countered. "If someone hadn't been traipsing around in the attic all night, I might have been able to get up earlier."

"I was not traipsing. I was putting away your luggage," he countered.

"And just how was I supposed to know that? You scared the crap out of me."

"I didn't mean to wake you. I forgot that section of the attic goes over the guest room," he said firmly.

"When I came looking for you, your office was locked," she accused.

His nostrils flared. "My office is always locked, Abigail."

"You don't trust me?"

"I don't trust anyone when it comes to my work."

"Including me?" She felt a bit hurt.

"Including you," he said without hesitation.

"Yet you expect me to marry you?" What was a marriage without trust?

"I do," he replied, his voice even.

What an arrogant ass! "Maybe I don't want to marry someone who does not trust me."

"Such an idle threat, my dear," he said, turning a strip of meat.

"Excuse me?" The smell of bacon lingered in the air.

"Let's face it, my dear. There is so much we each have to learn about the other. While we've known each other most of our lives, how well do we actually know each other?" He flipped another slice of bacon before continuing. "Of course, I assure you, I know much more about you than you of me."

This caught her off guard. "How do you figure?"

He laughed. "Because I've wanted you much longer than you've wanted me. I've watched you since you were a child. I've seen you grow into a stunningly attractive woman. I know what makes you smile and what sets you off. I could tell by the color of your hair and the fire in your eyes that you would fight me to the end. You like to do things your way, and I mine. We will be like oil and water, but we are a good match, Abigail. You will come to see that in time."

"You seem so sure." She had no doubt that he loved her. She only wished she loved him the way he wanted her to.

He smiled a confident smile. "I *am* sure, Abigail. You will come to see that I am the only man for you. I will show you what it means to be married to a real man. You will learn to respect the vows you recite."

She felt her face heat up, knowing he was referring to her marriage to Brian. Jacob had warned her not to marry Brian, and while he'd never rubbed her nose in the fact that she didn't listen, he'd just made it clear he thought her first marriage was a mistake.

Crossing the room, she snatched up a can of cat food, pulled on the tab to open the metal lid, and emptied the contents into Gulliver's dish. She was still bending over the dish as the cat raced to her side and began eating, even before she was finished.

Standing upright, she caught Jacob staring at her with hunger-filled eyes. It was obvious he'd gotten a full view of her bosom as she was emptying the can. *Like what you see?* She didn't say it out loud. She was still angry with him. She pulled the robe closed and tied the sash around her midriff. She was not going to have him leering at her when she was still angry with him. A smirk fleeted across his face, letting her know he was fully aware of the game she was playing.

"The bacon is nearly ready. How do you like your eggs? Soft or hard?" he asked, letting the innuendo dangle in the air.

She fought hard to keep a straight face. "Hard."

Then, feeling brave, she added, "If you can get it that way."

He circled the small island, taking the longest path to the refrigerator, ensuring he would have to brush against her as he passed. He smelled divinely of fresh-cooked bacon. She edged further away, not giving him the satisfaction of her touch. She had her pride and could not be bought with distinguished good looks and bacon. She narrowed her eyes in an effort to remind him that she was still angry.

He pulled the carton from the fridge, never taking his eyes off of her. His gaze was so intense, she could feel her breath quicken. What was this hold he seemed to have over her? It had always been like this whenever he was near. It was as if he could see inside of her. As if he knew things about her that even she did not know. She wondered what it would be like when they finally made love. Would he be able to take her places she'd never been? Shit! Why was she letting her mind go there? She was mad at him, and she had every right to be mad. Yet, he was wearing down her defenses. *No, it is because you are hungry,* she reminded herself. *I am hungry,* she agreed...*hungry to be loved. To feel safe. To be needed. I am hungry...for bacon,* she thought on a sigh.

He tore his gaze away. Moving in the opposite direction, he returned to the stove. Casually, he gripped the fork and removed the last of the bacon from the pan, setting the floppy slice onto the paper-towel-laced plate. Silently, he lifted another, cooler slice and held it aloft for several seconds before taking a bite, closing his eyes in apparent ecstasy. She felt her mouth water as he savored the strip. Damn him for knowing her weaknesses.

Seeing her watching, he smiled. Picking up a second slice, he turned to her, a glint in his sparkling brown eyes. He removed the skillet from the stove before closing the distance between them, pressing her back against the counter. She kept her hands behind her, gripping the counter for leverage. She turned her head away, showing him he could not possess her that easily.

She struggled as he gripped her jaw and turned her face towards his. Bending his head, he placed his mouth on hers. All the while, his hand lingered on the side of her face. She tightened her lips, refusing to yield to his kiss. He bathed her lips with his tongue before pulling away. The corners of his mouth twitched. She could feel his fingertips pulse against her neck, leaving her with little doubt he was enjoying the game.

He held the bacon in his free hand, waving it as if it was a red cape before an indecisive bull. Would she charge or retreat? his eyes seemed to ask. He brought it to her lips; holding it just under her nose. The smell caused her mouth to water. Damn the man. How was she supposed to resist freshly cooked bacon when she was famished? He locked her gaze once more, willing her to give in to him. No, she couldn't let him get away with the way he had treated her. His eyes narrowed, he pulled the bacon away and took a bite, chewing fully before swallowing. He leaned forward once more. This time, he was successful in prying her lips apart. He took pleasure in his feat, kissing her until a soft moan escaped from deep within. When he pulled away, she could taste the bacon on her mouth. She flicked her tongue across her lips, retracing his salty kiss.

He raised his hand and offered her the other half of the strip. Her mouth watered and she took the peace offering. A triumphant smile crossed his face as she put it in her mouth.

Without a word, he returned to the stove, set the skillet back on the flame, and opened the egg carton. His chest puffed like a matador who had won the battle. He had waved the cape and she took the bait. She had met his challenge, had given in far too easily. Seeing the victory in his eyes, she had the sinking feeling she was going to pay dearly for that salty slice of pork.

CHAPTER FIVE

Abby stood in front of the mirror, drying her hair. She aimed the dryer at the strands while she ran the flat brush through the length. Once she gave in to the bacon, the old Jacob returned, smiling, joking, and making her feel at ease.

Breakfast had been uneventful, pleasant even, with Jacob playing the doting host, waiting on her hand and foot. She smiled, remembering how he'd whisked her plate away the second she was finished, placing it in the dishwasher and telling her that today it was his job to wait on her. "After we are married, you will be the woman of the house. Until then, you are my guest," he'd said when she protested. He was courting her and she rather enjoyed all the attention.

She caught another clump of wet hair with the brush, letting the hot air circulate as the bristles moved through to the ends. She was nearly naked with the exception of a pink lace bra and matching panties. She bent at the waist, flipping her hair so she could dry the underside. It wouldn't be long before they would be married. She marveled at that. What would it be like to be Jacob's wife? What would it be like to share his bed? Other than kissing, they had never been intimate. She knew he wanted her; she had seen it in his eyes so many times. So what was he waiting for?

His claim of not wanting her until they were married came to mind. But still it was not like they were virgins. She'd been married. Once again, her thoughts went to Brian. The one man she had ever really loved. The one man she had thought she would spend the rest of her life with. He was the one man who had completely let her down. Her father had been correct when he'd said Brian had not been the right man for her. Her thoughts moved on to her father. What was it with the men in her life? She thought of the casualness of their father-daughter relationship. He had always seemed so distant. She tried to think of a time when the man, her dad, had actually told her he loved her, but she couldn't pinpoint even one single time. The realization made her feel hollow, as if she were somehow broken.

She felt her lips quiver, but refused to give in to the tears that threatened.

Her thoughts returned to Jacob, the only man she had ever been able to count on. She aimed the dryer at another section of hair. She had no doubt that Jacob loved her. He had professed that love on more than one occasion. Then why the delay? A thought hit her. *Maybe he's impotent and he doesn't want me to know so I won't back out.* She paused, aiming the dryer down. Would it matter? *I've survived this long without sex and have done just fine. It's not like I spend every waking minute thinking about it. Or Jacob either, for that matter.* The thought pained her. As much as she wished she were, she was not in love with Jacob. *Don't start,* she chided. *We have been through this before. You married for love the first time and look where that got you.* She stood up, her damp hair forgotten.

As she rose, she caught an image in the mirror. She flipped the dryer off and spun around. Jacob was standing near the windowsill, watching her. How had he entered her room undetected? How long had he been watching her? His brown eyes were blazing as they traced her nearly naked body. She ignored a sudden urge to wrap her arms around herself to shield against his gaze. Instead, she let her eyes drift to the bulge in his pants. *Not impotent,* she thought with relief, making her realize that she did indeed have needs, even if she'd let them grow dormant. They weren't dormant at the moment, she realized, raising her eyes to meet his. *I'm ready. Take me now,* she willed as she held his stare.

"You should learn to lock the door if you are not dressed." His voice was intense.

Well, that was not the comment she'd expected to hear. "It was shut. You should have knocked," she retorted with a bite.

He raised an eyebrow at her tone. "I knocked. You didn't answer."

"I was drying my hair," she said, stating the obvious.

"It didn't look like a lot of drying was going on. The dryer was aimed at the floor."

So he had been there for a while. "I was drying the water from the floor," she answered lamely. She dared a peek at his crotch. Yes, he was still awake. She decided to see how interested he really was. She crossed over to where he stood, leaned in, and kissed him softly on the lips. She heard his intake of air as her breast touched his chest. She pushed into his manliness, confirming her earlier deduction. Jacob had no problem getting or maintaining an erection. She reached up, kissing the length of his jawline. His breath quickened, but he did not reach for her. He closed his eyes, as if trying to remain in control. She could not believe how brazen she was acting. This was so unlike her. But now that her body had come alive, she yearned for release. She reached for his maleness with her hand. A moan escaped his lips as she slid her hand along the fabric, feeling its length.

He ran a hand through his hair, his breath coming even faster.

She moved her fingers upward, unfastened his belt, slipping her hand inside. He was pushing into her touch. She felt him pulse in her hand as her mouth found his. She licked the tips of his lips as he had done to her so recently, beckoning him to open his mouth. He responded to her demand, his tongue meeting hers, matching her intensity. She removed her hand from his pants, grabbed his waist, and pulled him closer. He broke the kiss, his mouth moving down to her chest. He buried his face in the space between her breasts, moaning with delight. She held the back of his head, urging him to continue.

His hands roamed her backside, dove into the waist of her panties, cupping the roundness of her flesh.

Releasing her nipple, he nuzzled her neck, breathing hot air into her ear. "It's been so long, my cherry blossom. I knew if I waited long enough, you would return to me."

"I haven't gone anywhere. Make love to me. I need you, Jacob." The words sounded husky to her ears.

He pulled back suddenly, blinking as if he just woke up and was trying to figure out where he was. She reached for him, but he evaded her touch.

"You're playing a dangerous game, Abigail," he warned. His hands dipped inside his slacks, adjusting the contents.

She was stunned. He had seemed so willing only moments before. Now he was rejecting her. "Game? What game?"

"You sit here in your underwear, teasing me, using your body like a seductress. A man has needs, Abigail. I'm trying to stay in control, but you make it hard to be strong. "

He was making her feel like a wanton tramp, yet he was the one who'd invaded her privacy, the one who had looked at her like a wolf eyeing its prey. "Tell me about it. I have needs myself. Correct me if I'm wrong, but I do believe it was you who walked in on me. You were staring at me as if I were lunch, if I remember right."

"Yes, but I kept my distance. I told you: I will not have you until you are mine, Abigail. That is the way it has to be."

"Why, Jacob? Why does it have to be that way? It is not like we are virgins. At your age, you had to have had sex before." Although, as the words came out of her mouth, she realized she had never seen him with anyone else, nor had anyone ever mentioned him being with anyone else. "And you know I was married to…"

He cut her off. "Don't say his name!" He moved back as if she'd struck him. "I will not have you speak of the man who soiled you." His words were venomous.

"Soiled me? Is that what you think?" She suddenly felt dirty. What had she been thinking coming here? She reached for her robe. She needed to cover herself against his accusations. He snatched it out of her hands and pulled her into him. She fought him as he held her.

"I didn't mean it, Abigail. I'm sorry. So very sorry. Please forgive me," he begged. "It is just that I hate him for what he put you through. He hurt you. Why did you have to run away with him? I loved you. I've always loved you. You were supposed to be mine."

She eased her struggle, not knowing what to do. How could he profess to love her when he hated her for being with another man? How could she marry a man who'd just accused her of being unclean?

"But if you can't look at me without thinking of him, then how can you love me?" Her words came out on a sob. What had she gotten herself into? She thought he loved her. But now she was beginning to wonder. Was it enough that he wanted her? She had hoped that his love would be enough. That she would grow to love him in return, but was that even possible? Could a relationship last that was not grounded by the roots of love? How could it?

She let out another sob. "But?"

He covered her mouth with his, kissing her until she stopped fighting him, before finally pulling away. His eyes pleaded with her to listen. "Have no doubt that I love you."

He trailed kisses along her neck as he spoke, his words so intense she could barely breathe. "You will be mine and only mine. I will wipe away his memory when you are finally my wife. I will make sure I am all you think about, Abigail."

Was that what was spurring his mood swings? Was he trying to compete with a dead man? It would explain his defensiveness. The thought brought her comfort. This was the Jacob she knew. The Jacob she cared for. This was the man she had convinced herself she could fall in love with.

"You don't need to prove yourself to me, Jacob. I'm here and I'm not going anywhere."

"I want you to want me, Abigail. I want you to choose me like you chose him. I will not settle for anything less."

"I'm here," she repeated.

He held her as if he thought she would disappear. "That is not enough, Abigail. We will not share a bed until you are my wife. I must be certain that you will not leave."

His voice broke. "I could not bear to lose you too."

So he'd been hurt before. That must be what was fueling his actions. He was afraid she would hurt him as he'd once been hurt. The knowledge of his pain pulled at her. They were not that different after all, both wanting the same thing. Both wanting to feel safe in the arms of love.

She made herself a promise never to hurt him. In turn, she believed he would offer her the same unspoken promise. She sank into him as he held her. His words held the promise of the future. She was here. She was safe. She was slowly allowing him to wipe away her fear.

CHAPTER SIX

Abby and Jacob walked leisurely through Jackson Square. It had been two weeks since her arrival and Abby was thrilled to be taking her first tour of the city. The temperature had warmed to the high sixties, allowing them to leave their jackets in the car. It was just before noon and the smell of onions and peppers cooking amongst sausages and hot dogs filled the air. People of all ages, races, and creeds mulled along the sidewalks, each caught up in the ambience of the historic city. Abby had never been to a place where she'd heard so many languages spoken within just a few short blocks. As they walked the streets, Jacob pointed out the occasional landmark, telling her the history or significance of each attraction as he knew it. Abby hung on his every word as she looked from building to building, soaking in the charm of the Big Easy. She remembered hearing it was called the City of the Dead.

"Why is it called the City of the Dead?"

"It's the cemeteries," Jacob said.

"What about them?'

"New Orleans is so marshy that they couldn't bury the dead below ground. They used tombs and crypts and buried the dead above ground. The graves are all lined up in rows and since they are all above ground, they look like mini cities, thus the name City of the Dead."

"It sounds rather creepy," she said, rubbing against a sudden chill.

He shook his head. "On the contrary, the cemeteries are pretty amazing to see. We could go sometime, if you'd like."

"I think I'll pass for now. Cemeteries give me the creeps. Knowing I was even closer to the dead than normal would really freak me out."

"It's not the dead you have to be afraid of, Abigail."

"I know. I just think I've had my share of death lately."

"I can't say I'm sorry," he said.

"Wow, that's pretty harsh," she said, peering up at him.

"It's the truth. I'm sorry you've been through so much, but in the end, it is what brought you to me."

It was true. If not for the events of the past six months, she would not be here now. "Funny how life has a way of steering a person in a different direction," she said softly.

"It's a pity it had to come to that, but you're here now and that's all that matters."

They continued in silence for a bit, each caught up in their own thoughts. Jazz filled the air from several street bands, their sounds wafting through the square, wrapping around them like a warm hug.

Street hustlers beckoned to passersby, preying on the weak and less informed. Fortunetellers, faith healers, and women dressed in colorful costumes called out in unison, no doubt expecting to be compensated for the services they rendered. Jacob steered her clear, calling them vultures, leeching off the unsuspecting tourist. He didn't seem to have any higher opinion of the peddlers selling their wares from vending carts.

They approached an old man who was hawking walking puppets. As they passed, the guy maneuvered an orange-feathered ostrich, held up by fishing line and operated by two crossed sticks, closer to Abby. The man had the bird give her a quick peck on her ankle. She gasped and barely dodged out of the way as the bird attempted to get a bit fresher.

Clutching her arm possessively, Jacob scowled at the man, causing him to retreat in the opposite direction. Abby shot the man a quick look as they continued on, flustered by his audacity. She glanced at Jacob, noting the tension that had suddenly appeared in his jawline.

"You're not jealous of a little bird, are you?"

"The bird was not operating itself," he said tersely.

Abby gave Jacob a quick kiss on the cheek.

"Don't worry. I'm not interested in that dirty old bird, or the ostrich either," she said, smiling her best smile for him.

Jacob's face relaxed and he released her arm, clasping her hand in return. "Are you happy that you came?"

She tilted her head toward him. "Today, or New Orleans in general?"

He frowned. "Is there a difference?"

"Yes, no... maybe." *What the hell kind of answer is that, Abby?* she wondered.

He stopped in the middle of the sidewalk and turned to face her.

"What the hell kind of answer is that?" His question mirrored her own.

She shrugged her shoulders, smiling her apology as people skirted around them. Stepping out of the way of the crowd, she motioned for him to follow. Once clear of the walkway, she explained herself.

"I wasn't sure what I was getting myself into, either way. I've known you all of my life, but I don't really know anything about you. And I have never been to New Orleans either. All I have ever seen were the parties and parades on TV. Have you ever watched a Mardi Gras episode of *Cops*? It looks rather scary."

He laughed an easy laugh. "Luckily, the crazies only come out at night."

The words had no sooner left his mouth when they were passed by a man in a tutu, with a cat sitting on his shoulder. They watched as the man waltzed down the street, curtsying to the occasional onlooker.

Abby suppressed a giggle. "You were saying?"

"Looks perfectly normal to me," Jacob said, nonplussed.

He resumed walking and tightened his grip on her hand. She was about to say something, when he startled her into silence with his words.

"I know you don't love me. So why did you come?"

She stumbled, only remaining upright because of his grip on her hand. *Think, Abby. Think. Just be honest.* She swallowed hard and struggled to regain her composure.

"I…" How the hell was she supposed to answer the question?

"So I was right," he pressed.

"I want to love you." Her voice was meek, but her answer seemed to placate him.

"You will learn to love me, Abigail. You will see that I only have your best interest at heart."
His eyes took on a faraway look "I always have."

She followed as he maneuvered her around a crowd that had stopped to watch a little monkey dance to a tune from his handler's accordion. When she hesitated, Jacob led her to an opening where she could watch. Abby smiled at the sight of a capuchin monkey wearing red and white striped pants, a yellow shirt, and matching cap. The little monkey was black and white and stood about knee high. He would dance for several seconds, then venture as far as his leash would allow, taking various coins from bystanders and tossing them into his trainer's cup.

Jacob slipped a dollar into her hand and nodded for her to give it to the monkey. She did and was rewarded with a tip of his hat in return. Instead of tossing the bill into the cup with the change, he smiled broadly before shoving it into the pocket of his own pants. This thrilled the crowd, who in turn reached into their pockets in search of cash. They watched the scene for several minutes before moving on.

"Are you having fun?" Jacob asked, searching her face.

Of course she was having fun. It was a glorious spring day. She was strolling through the streets of New Orleans with the man she was going to marry, a man who didn't seem to be bothered by the fact that she didn't love him, and she was giving money to dancing monkeys. What was not to love?

"I am having a blast," she answered with enthusiasm.

Leading her out of way of the passing crowd, his face turned serious. "You didn't answer my question."

"What? I just said I was having a blast."

"I meant the one I asked earlier. I want to know why you finally agreed to marry me, even though you've admitted you do not love me." There was no hurt in his voice. He'd asked a simple question. A simple question that did not have a simple answer.

"Love is highly overrated." She took a deep breath, hoping the rest of her answer didn't provoke a fight. She looked around. The streets were alive with people. This gave her comfort, as she felt certain that Jacob would not want to have an argument in such a public place.

"I married for love the first time." She saw his nostrils flare, but stayed the course. "I thought Brian was my soul mate. We could laugh together. We had fun together. He lied to me. No, he didn't lie, he just didn't tell me the truth," she corrected.

Jacob's face remained stoic, so she pressed on. "I didn't know he was using drugs or I would never have married him. It was a side of him I never knew. Never even imagined. Drugs, Jacob. Not just pills; he shot heroin into his veins! Who does that?"

She closed her eyes, taking a moment to steady herself before continuing.

"Do you know how hard it was to find him after he overdosed? He was foaming at the mouth. The syringe was still in his arm." Her voice wavered as she recalled the image.

Jacob finally broke his silence. "He did not deserve your love. He would have broken your heart eventually anyway."

She tucked her hair behind her ear and cast her eyes downward. "Will you?" Her words came out on a whisper.

"Only if you give me reason to."

Her head jerked up. "Meaning?"

"You don't have to love me, but you do have to respect my wishes. You will not betray me or cause me to doubt you. As long as you follow the rules, everything will be just fine," he promised.

"Rules?" She was not sure she liked the sound of that. What...was this some sort of a game?

He sighed, as if talking to a child. "Yes, rules. Every marriage has rules. Think of your dalliance with Brian. He did not follow the rules, so you are no longer with him."

It did not escape her that he'd referred to her marriage as a dalliance and not a marriage. Of course, it had been Jacob that had insisted she file for an annulment immediately following Brian's death. He had swooped in, helped her to pick up the pieces and protect her reputation. It wasn't the first time he'd been there when she was in trouble.

She had a faint recollection of Jacob pulling her out of the house fire when she was only four. He was passing by, saw the flames, raced into the house, and rescued her. She didn't remember much of her life before then, but her parents had welcomed Jacob into their lives from that day forward. They told her that Jacob had been sent from above to save her, and that she should always be grateful to him. Maybe that was why she was so willing to place her fate in his hands. He had saved her once; couldn't he do it again? Her parents had loved him – well, her father anyway. Didn't daddies always want what was best for their little girls? If he was good enough for her dad, shouldn't he be good enough for her? Would it be so awful to spend the rest of her life with Jacob? Especially since he was so willing to love her unconditionally. Well, as long as she followed the rules. That part bothered her slightly. She recalled her father's disappointment after she eloped with Brian; she'd never been one to follow the rules.

She screwed up her mouth, debating. "I'm not very good at following the rules."

A smile fleeted across his face. He took her into his arms, kissing her with passion. When at last he broke the kiss, he took hold of her flaming red hair, brought a handful to his nose, breathing in its essence. Gold flecks danced within the brown of his eyes.

"I don't doubt it for a second, Abigail. With hair this color... spunk is sure to follow."

"And that doesn't bother you?"

"I look forward to the challenge."

CHAPTER SEVEN

They strolled along Bourbon Street at a comfortable pace. The aroma of spicy cuisine floated through the air. Abby's stomach began to rumble. She tilted her head, trying to detect which one of the restaurants was responsible for the smell, but determined it was a mixture of them all and quite possibly some of the adjoining houses as well. Abby was amazed at the detail in the buildings. Even though they were nestled together, they all stood out as individuals with their bright reds, blues, greens, purples, and yellows, each adding charm and ambiance to the well-known street. She wondered what it would be like to live here on one of the most famous streets, in a house that shared a wall with a restaurant or tavern. Even in the daylight, the French Quarter was different than she imagined, but in a good way. While there were crowds, they were not rowdy drunks or women baring their breasts.

"It's a lot different than I imagined," she said, admiring the architecture of the old buildings.

She pointed at the intricate detail of the cast iron balconies. "I thought there would be women on the balconies, flashing everyone that walked by."

She noticed several fully clothed ladies sitting on the balcony of a bright blue house, chatting quietly while enjoying their beer. A part of her ached to join them. As if somehow sensing this, they waved a hearty hello and offered her a beer, which she regretfully declined.

"There is so much more to the area than what you see on TV," Jacob said, following her gaze.

They veered around an elderly couple, smiling their hellos as they passed.

"The area is relatively quiet during the day. After the sun goes down, things pick up a good deal, but the real partying is generally saved for Mardi Gras, then it is pretty much anything goes," Jacob said with a conspiratorial whisper.

Abby tucked her arm through the crook of his. She felt more relaxed than she had in months. In the time since Brian's death, she'd felt so lost; then, when her parents died so soon thereafter, she hit rock bottom.

She shuddered, remembering the call saying they'd succumbed to carbon monoxide poisoning during the night. She sighed suddenly, missing them both immensely. She'd felt so alone that morning. When Jacob just happened to come by, she'd melted into his embrace. He'd held her until her tears were spent, telling her over and over she was not alone. That she still had him. She'd clung to him, knowing that he was the one person that had always been there when she'd needed him. She tightened her hold on his arm and leaned into him. She might not be *in* love with him, but she did love him. Surely that would be enough to make the marriage work.

Jacob laid a hand on her arm. "Are you cold? I don't want you getting sick on me."

His concern was genuine and it made her heart swell. She'd not had anyone fuss over her in so long. Yes, she could get used to this.

"No, I was just thinking of my parents. I wonder what they'd think if they knew I'd finally agreed to marry you."

His face tightened. Eyes narrowed, he turned to her. "You don't think they would approve? I can assure you I am the best man for you."

His reaction made her laugh. For all his confidence, he sounded like a jock trying to prove himself. "I think Daddy would have been ecstatic. He had been singing your praises as long as I can remember. He was furious when I…"

She paused, not wanting to bring up Brian twice in one day. "He thought I should have married you a long time ago."

He relaxed slightly. "I am not sure your mother felt the same way."

Jacob was right. Her mother had not been his biggest ally. She had tried to act calm around Jacob, but Abby always felt there was something her mother wasn't telling her. She had seemed so relieved when Abby eloped with Brian. She'd never actually said what had bothered her about Jacob, but Abby knew her mother had never approved of his advances.

"I think maybe she was worried about our age difference."

His jaw clenched. "She loved you too much. It clouded her judgment."

What a strange thing to say. How on earth could a mother love her child too much? She was just getting ready to voice the question when someone slammed into her left shoulder, knocking the air out of her lungs. She tumbled forward as Jacob tightened his grip on her other arm to keep her from falling.

"He has my purse!" she shrieked as the teen dashed down the street.

Jacob pressed her against the brick wall.

"Don't move," he ordered and was gone before she could protest, rounding the corner after the retreating boy.

Abby stood glued to the spot for several moments, watching incredulously as throngs of people passed by laughing and joking. If anyone had seen what had just transpired, they were not making mention of it. She wondered if they actually had not seen or if things such as this were so commonplace, they went unnoticed. All of a sudden, the wonderful city seemed a bit daunting. As her adrenaline wore off, fear set in. Jacob had been gone a long time. What if something had happened to him? She'd just admitted to herself that she did actually love Jacob, at least in her own way. She suddenly felt very much alone in the crowd full of people. She had lost everyone that she cared for; what would she do if she lost Jacob too? She swallowed hard, realizing just how much she needed Jacob. He was her only friend, all she had left.

Tears started to trickle down her cheeks. She had to call the police. Panic ensued as she realized her cell phone had been in her purse. She wrung her hands together, wondering at her next move.

She took a tentative step in the direction in which Jacob had gone. Seeing that her legs would actually cooperate, she continued. Her mouth went dry as she turned the corner. The street was deserted. Still, she knew this was the direction in which they'd both run, so she continued numbly down the street. She came to a cross street and stopped, looking in both directions, seeing no one. She hesitated, wondering if she should turn around. The town, which had felt so welcoming only moments before, now felt foreign and unsafe. Her tears fell unbridled. She was alone.

From a doorway, a woman's voice called out to her. "Come here, honey chile."

Abby felt compelled to heed the woman's call as if being summoned against her will. She found herself moving in the direction of the elderly Cajun woman as if answering a siren's call. The woman was small framed and even shorter than Abby. Her face was heavily lined with wrinkles set in deep, sun-roasted skin. Her dark eyes were hooded with heavy eyebrows.

"Give me your hand, *bebe*," she said with a thick French Cajun accent.

Abby felt her hand rise involuntarily. The woman's hands were even more wrinkled than her face; however, the aged hands were soft as silk. She held Abby's hand palm up. Her tongue clicked as a gnarled finger traced the lines on her outstretched hand.

Abby glanced around, hoping to see Jacob, but he was nowhere in sight.

"I have to go," Abby said fearfully.

Her words fell on deaf ears.

The woman's hands began to tremble. "You've lost much. Your destiny is controlled by others."

Abby's gaze returned to the woman as she felt her feeble grip tighten.

"The life you live is a lie. All you know is not true." The woman's voice grew thick as she spoke and Abby had to strain to understand the words.

"You seek what you've lost, but this is not the way."

Abby struggled against the firm grip.

"Jacob?" This was not the way to Jacob? She was sure he had come this way.

The woman spat in the street beside her. "Heed my warning, honey chile. A storm is coming."

Abby glanced up toward the clear blue sky. The hairs on her neck stood at the ominous warning. "I...I have to go," she stammered. "I have to find Jacob."

Once again, the woman spat before speaking. "*Il est le fils du diable.* Eva Radoux knows all... *L'homme a un coeur noir.*"

Her tone sounded venomous. Abby did not know what the woman had said, but she knew from her tone the lady had been agitated. Terrified, she pulled her hand free and took off running in the direction she'd just come. The woman called after her, begging for her to come back. Abby kept going, too frightened to oblige.

She rounded the corner onto Bourbon Street and saw Jacob standing along the wall where he'd left her. He was turning his head from side to side, while pushing his hands through his hair. She had seen him do this on numerous occasions when he was anxious. Seeing her, relief washed over his face. She ran to him, sinking into his arms, sobbing uncontrollably.

"I was so worried. I thought something bad had happened to you. I tried to find you, but you were gone," she blubbered into his shoulder.

"I told you to stay here," he breathed into her ear. "I came back and you were gone. You had me so worried. You should have listened to me, Abigail. You don't know this city like I do."

"I did, but then you didn't come back right away. I went looking for you, but there was this old lady. She was telling me things. She had my hand and wouldn't let me go. She scared me."

He stiffened and pulled away from her. "Where? What old lady?"

"There was an old lady on the street and she read my palm. Then she spit in the dirt and said something. I didn't understand what she said, but it sounded like she was upset. I tried to get away, but she seemed mad. She told me my destiny was controlled by others. "

Jacob's nostrils flared. "What else did she say to you?"

"She called herself Eva Radoux and said something. I think it was in French. She said, '*Il est le fils du diable*' and I think the second thing was *'L'homme a un coeur noir,*'" she said, concentrating.

His eyes narrowed.

"Do you know what it means?" she asked on a sob.

Jacob shrugged his shoulders, his eyes moving past her in thought. "My French is not all that good, but I think she was warning you that you were going to marry an old man. I didn't catch the kid who took your purse. Maybe she was right."

For the first time since the ordeal began, Abby laughed. She had been scared out of her wits and all the woman was worried about was her marrying someone a bit older. She pressed her hand against Jacob's graying temple.

"I'm not worried about my purse; it can be replaced. I was more worried about losing you. When I couldn't find you, I was so afraid something bad had happened to you. It made me realize that I really do love you, in my own way."

Any misgivings Abby had had about marrying Jacob dissipated the second she thought she'd lost him. The old woman was right; she had lost so much. She'd seen the look of worry on Jacob's face. He'd been afraid he'd lost her too. She might not love him the way that she'd loved Brian, but she did love him and he loved her as well. She had seen it in his eyes when she returned. It was obvious they cared about each other. It was a beginning. They had a foundation on which they could build. She studied him. He was attractive, self-assured, and just being around him made her feel safe. With sudden clarity, she realized he was what she'd been searching for. She heaved a huge sigh of relief as she realized that she was right where she belonged.

CHAPTER EIGHT

Abby awoke to the sound of Ned whispering under the covers of his cage. Easing out of bed, she crossed the room and lifted the covering.

"Good morning, Ned," she said, opening the door to his enclosure.

The Quaker Parrot wasted no time in hopping onto the open door. In quick succession, with the aid of his beak, he made his way up the steel bars. Once he had successfully traversed the cage, he climbed onto his rooftop play yard, voicing joyful murmuring sounds along the way. Seemingly pleased with himself, he stretched his wings outright and flapped them several times. His wings being clipped, the display was only for exercise, not an attempt at liftoff. He tucked his wings neatly back into place and bobbed his head at Abby in greeting.

"You sure are the merry little man this morning," Abby said, cooing at the friendly bird.

Ned grabbed a peanut with one claw, enthusiastically munching away the outer shell, eager to find the treasure within.

Not wishing to be left out of the festivities, Gulliver jumped onto the dresser to get a better view.

The bird ducked his head up and down and called to the cat in greeting. "Nice kitty."

The cat, having obviously seen this display before, ignored the bird, meowing impatiently in Abby's direction. She reached down, tracing her hand along his back. Gulliver arched against her palm, purring with delight. Ned bobbed his head, imitating the feline's purr.

"Isn't it a bit risky letting that bird out with the cat so close?" Jacob said over her shoulder.

She jumped at the sound of his voice.

"No, they play together all of the time," Abby said, shaking off the intrusion.

Jacob reached a hand toward the cat, which hissed, jumped off the dresser, and bolted from the room.

A frown formed on Jacob's face as he watched him disappear down the hallway. "I don't think your cat likes me very much."

"I think he's picking up on the fact that you don't like him," Abby said, turning to face him.

"The cat is smarter than he looks," he said, not bothering to correct her assessment.

"Besides, he is not the only one you scared. I didn't hear you come in either," she said.

His look turned incredulous. "Would you prefer I knock?"

She shrugged her shoulders. "Well, it was your idea to sequester me in here away from you. Maybe knocking wouldn't be such a bad idea. I mean, what if you'd walked in and found me naked? We couldn't have you rising to temptation now, could we?"

His eyes roamed the thin gauzy material of her gown, which hugged her body and left little to the imagination. A smile played at the edges of his mouth as his gaze stopped at her breasts. His mouth twitched as he lifted his eyes up to meet hers. When he spoke, his voice was like liquid fire.

"I don't think I could see much more of you if you were standing in front of me in your birthday suit."

She peered down and saw what had caught his attention. Her nipples obviously were happy to see him, and to have him see them in return, as they stood pert against the flimsy fabric of her gown. She brought her arms to her chest, suddenly self-conscious as his eyes continued to bore into her.

He shook his head in protest. "Modesty doesn't become you, Abigail. You are a woman of great passion, not a mouse who tiptoes away unseen."

The hunger in his eyes was electrifying. In the few days since their outing, she had been having vivid dreams of him making love to her. The dreams had been so intense that she often woke breathless and hungry for his touch. She lowered her arms at his challenge. He held her gaze as he stepped closer, cupping her face with his palm. The heat of his touch raced through her, warming her from within. He traced his fingers along her jawline, trailing alongside her neck, the motion sending chills through her body. She turned her face towards his, hungry for his kiss. His lips were on hers in an instant. Insistent. Demanding. She felt herself melt into him, wanting him, needing him. He pulled her in, holding her as if he was afraid to let her go. Slowly, he allowed his hands to explore. She felt a pull from deep within as he continued to explore her mouth with his. Damn, he was a good kisser. The heat from his hands left tingling trails along her skin as his palms roamed deliberately across the fabric of her gown. She could feel her need rising as she gave in to his touch. The passion was short lived as Jacob pulled away from her, leaving her somewhat bewildered at his sudden withdrawal. His breath was labored, showing that he was just as worked up as she. He traced a finger over her lips, then placed the finger into his own mouth, sucking the moisture from the length of it. The simple gesture made her quiver with desire.

"Your passion is like fire in my veins, Abigail." His voice was breathless. "I cannot control myself when I'm around you. I want to bury myself in your depths and explode into you like a volcano. The fire you ignite in me is as bright as the red in your hair. It pains me to have you this close and not be able to take you at my will."

His words melted across her, confusing her senses. He wanted her and she was willing, so what was the big problem? "I'm afraid I don't understand what the problem is. I feel the same way as you. It's not as if we are obligated to others, so why pull away? We are both consenting adults. Why not give in to the passion we both feel?"

He shook his head. "I can't take that chance. I need to know that you are my wife. When I make love to you, I need to know that you truly belong to me. That you're not going anywhere."

She started to speak, to ask him if it was an age thing, but hesitated. She remembered how upset he'd been at the palm reader's dig about his age. Maybe he just didn't approve of sex before marriage. She opted for a different approach. "I have accepted your proposal. I'm here, Jacob. Isn't that enough of a commitment?"

His eyes took on a faraway look. "People break promises all the time. They tell you what you want to hear when it suits their needs. I am not prepared to take that risk. Not with you, Abigail."

Abby was struck by the pain in his voice and knew he spoke from experience. "Who was she?"

Her question seemed to catch him off guard. "She?"

"The woman who broke your heart," she said softly.

He searched her face for several moments before answering. "Her name was Clarice. We were to be married many years ago. We were both so young. She was to be mine. We made love and talked about our future plans. We were going to do amazing things. She gave herself to me completely, or so I thought. But then something changed. I wasn't sure what it was. At first, I thought maybe she was just getting nervous. You know: pre-wedding jitters. The next thing I knew, she had eloped with someone else. She betrayed me with a guy she had only known a very short time."

Abby winced at the anguish in his voice. His words struck so close to home. At least that explained why he was so upset by her own elopement. Not that she had promised him anything prior to marrying Brian, but if he cared for her as much as it seemed, then maybe her actions had brought back unpleasant memories of what had happened to him. No, she couldn't blame him for being angry at her decision to marry Brian, when obviously the suddenness of it mirrored his own lost love.

He opened his mouth as if to continue, then stopped. He turned his head away, but not before she saw the pain that was etched across his face. He walked to the door, then pivoted to face her. Now that distance separated them, he had recovered his composure. "She does not matter anymore, Abigail. She made her choice years ago. The woman is dead to me. That part of my life is buried."

He paused in the doorway a lopsided smile on his face. "It's funny how things work out, don't you think? If it were not for her choice, I would not have you now. I really am a very lucky man....I've been given a great gift."

Abby wanted to run to him, to explain that she knew how he felt. While she had not been jilted, she now wished she had been. It would have been easier in the long run if Brian had betrayed her with another woman and not drugs. At least she could have wrapped her brain around that. Even if it was not exactly the same, she was in fact betrayed by the person she'd loved. It was another thing she and Jacob had in common and something she felt drew them closer together. While she had come in hopes that he would help her mend her broken heart, she now knew she was here for more than that. She was here to help mend his as well. Any doubts she'd had up to this point were gone. If anything, she was more ready to marry Jacob after learning of his heartbreak. It was time they both found their happy place. It was time to mend their broken hearts.

"Jacob... I don't want to wait any longer," she said anxiously.

"No, I told you, not until we are married," he said, turning to leave.

"Wait, you don't understand. That's what I am talking about. I want to marry you... now," she said with conviction.

"Are you sure?" His voice trembled.

"Yes, I am." She smiled at the wonder in his voice.

He turned and left the room without further comment.

For several seconds, she stood questioning what had just happened. Had he not believed her? Should she follow him and beg him to marry her? She'd heard of being left at the altar, but being left at the proposal?

Gulliver came sulking around the corner, leapt onto the bed, and sought comfort in her touch. Scooping him up, she cradled him close.

"You had better find a way to get along with Jacob, big guy. It looks as if we will be staying. I think so, anyway," she said, looking towards the vacant doorway.

The cat meowed in response.

"No back-talking, young man," she said as if his meow had been a refusal to get along. "I know he has his moments, but he really is a great guy. I know it's hard to believe, but he and I have a lot in common. We've both had our hearts broken. Now it's time for us to move ahead and be happy. You want me happy, don't you, pretty kitty? I want you to be happy."

"Here, kitty kitty," Ned called from atop his rooftop perch.

She smiled. "See... even Ned wants you to be happy."

Placing the cat onto the dresser, she went in search of Jacob. Seeing him come out of his office, she paused.

"There you are. I was wondering where you went," she said, still bewildered by his sudden departure.

"I went to make the arrangements," he said, as if that solved the puzzle.

"The arrangements?"

"Yes, for the wedding. Everything is set for tomorrow at ten."

She stood there blinking for several moments before realizing he was serious. "Tomorrow...where? How? I have to buy a dress."

Taking her by the hand, he led her back to her room. Opening her closet, he pushed aside several hangers before stopping at a simple yellow sundress. Pulling it from the rack, he held it to her for approval. "There; see? The perfect dress for a simple ceremony, don't you agree, Abigail?"

Her words froze in her throat as she nodded in agreement. She loved the dress, and it was the perfect choice for a simple wedding ceremony. She still had the pictures to prove it, as it was the same dress she'd worn when she had married Brian.

CHAPTER NINE

Theirs was a simple ceremony, *too simple,* Abby thought, given the impressive size of the stately southern home. The manse, which was located in the historic Garden District, belonged to the preacher Jacob had hired. She was not sure how Jacob managed to get such an impressive venue on such short notice, but she was quick to discover that Jacob had a way of getting the things he wanted. Having made the arrangements in an obscenely short order, they were married less than twenty-four hours from when she'd agreed to wed him. Now all that was left was to sign the marriage certificate and have their witness verify it. It was the witness that they were waiting on. The one who didn't witness anything, due to car trouble, and was now in a cab, speeding to their location. Abby had questioned the legality of it, but Jacob had assured her it would be fine. No one would know but them and they were not about to say anything.

They were standing in the expansive library, where the ceremony had just been held. Dark mahogany bookcases lined three of the four walls. Books were neatly lined on the custom shelves, which were built around the massive floor-to-ceiling windows. At the back of the room was a stately desk that matched the rich color of the shelves. An immense mirror was the focal point of the library, which in itself was hard to believe, since the whole room looked like it was straight out of *Preservation Magazine*. Situated behind the desk, Abby wondered if it was placed there to make the enormous room appear even larger or to allow the happy couples to view themselves during the simple ceremonies. Focusing on her and Jacob's reflection, Abby decided it must be the latter.

Jacob had his arm around her waist and was making small talk with the reverend about the weather. Abby found herself mesmerized by their reflection in the broad mirror.

Teetering on three-inch heels, she stood half a foot shorter than Jacob, who was, as usual, impeccably dressed. Today, he rose to the occasion, in a tailored three-piece suit. Medium gray, it drew out the silver from his temples, making him look even more distinguished. She bit at her lip as she studied her own image with critical eyes. Her red mane was piled high upon her head, each strand tucked securely into place with dozens of hairpins. Delicate white baby's-breath flowers were nestled into the mix, giving her both an elegant hairdo as well as much-needed height. Between the shoes and hair, she looked a good half a foot taller than she actually was. Not being keen on excessive makeup, she'd stayed true to herself, only highlighting her brilliant green eyes with eyeliner and mascara. She hated foundation; it was no use wearing it anyway, as it always failed to hide the mass of freckles that went with being a fair-skinned redhead. Today, her cheeks were flush with color. Between the flush of the moment and the added sun she'd gotten since her arrival to New Orleans, the freckles stood out even more than was usual, making her look girlish.

Much to her dismay, she was wearing the pale yellow dress that Jacob had plucked from her closet. She'd tried to protest, but he had been quite adamant. He'd said yellow was the perfect color for her, insisting that this was the dress she would wear. She had attempted to tell him the reason the dress was not appropriate, but Jacob had cut her off every time she'd tried. It was as if he had his heart set on her wearing the dress, and since no one was around to tell him about the dress' original use, she had finally given in. It was, after all, a very pretty dress, and he was right; it was the perfect complement to her pale skin and golden freckles. Abby let out a sigh as she realized the intensity of the freckles made her appear much younger than her thirty-one years.

She was not a child, nor was she sheltered. At thirty-one, she was entering her second marriage, a marriage that was starting off exactly as the first had, in a hurried ceremony, wearing the same simple yellow dress. She sent out a silent prayer that this marriage would be different from the last one. The image in the mirror blurred until she saw not Jacob standing beside her, but Brian. Dressed casual in khaki pants and colored shirt, he was the direct opposite of Jacob. His tousled blonde hair sticking out in various directions, a boyish grin staring back at her as they vowed to love each other till death did they part. If only she'd known that death would come sooner than expected.

She chewed at her lip with increased vigor. She should not be thinking of Brian, not today. *It's the dress,* she thought with sudden contempt. She gazed at her reflection and smiled; the dress was not to blame. It was just as innocent as she was. She had not known Brian's history any more than Jacob knew the history of the dress he had insisted she wear. Simple as it seemed, the dress held many secrets, and simple as it might be, it did flatter her, dipping seductively in the front, thus accenting her breasts.

She shifted on her heels, vying for a better look at her bosom. While not overly abundant, she had been blessed with a nice rack, which she felt made up for her short stature. She used to tell her mom that if she couldn't have her height, she was grateful that she'd at least inherited her boobs. Her breasts had been the only family resemblance she'd inherited. At five-foot-three, she was shorter than either of her parents, and bore little resemblance, neither of them sharing her flaming red hair. Her mom had a smidgen of freckles, but nothing like Abby's own roadmap, which the kids in her class made fun of, often asking to use her to play Connect-the-Dots. She pictured her parents' mousy brown hair and tall frames. Her father more gangly, her mom tall, a bit on the chunky side, no doubt the added weight helping to add to her voluptuous bosom. No, she definitely had not gotten her looks from either of them.

Her father had often made jokes about her being the daughter of a pizza deliveryman, something her mother never found overly amusing. Her mom insisted that she took after her great aunt Rena, but Abby herself had never seen a photo of her aunt to prove the resemblance. There were no photos of any of the relatives, but then again, there were none of Abby before age four. The fire had destroyed everything the family had owned. At the memory of the fire, she shuddered and leaned into Jacob, whose conversation with the reverend had turned to sports.

Abby remembered the fire vividly. She'd been trapped in her room, heard her mother's screams as she tried to get to her. Abby had suffered some smoke inhalation, but Jacob had broken the window and rescued her before the flames had reached her. She was only four years old then and Jacob had been twenty-five. That realization caught her momentarily off guard. The man she had just married was old enough to be her father. Maybe the fortuneteller had been right. Maybe Jacob was a dirty old man.

Jacob looked up and caught sight of her in the mirror. A frown creased his brow. She felt herself blush. Had he read her mind? She smiled at his reflection. The frown disappeared as he answered a question from the reverend about the stock market. He tightened his hold on her as the conversation moved off in a different direction.

She relaxed and wondered at the man she was now married to, the man who was always there when she needed him. As she matured, it was obvious that Jacob was interested in her. She'd just turned eighteen the first time he proposed to her. At thirty-nine, she'd considered him far too old for her.

It struck her funny how her perspective had changed over the years. Their age difference had seemed vast back then, but now at age thirty-one, a twenty-one-year age gap did not seem beyond reason, especially when he looked at least ten years younger than his age. She studied the gray at his temples. It was the only sign of his true age, adding to his features to make him look distinguished, not old. Jacob caught her looking and released his hold on her. Something in his body language worried her. While his voice remained casual, tension was evident in his shoulders.

There was a knock at the door and the reverend excused himself to answer it.

Abby watched the man leave before turning her attention back to Jacob. She was surprised to see the tight set in his jaw. She reached a hand to him, but he evaded her touch. She pulled her hand back, wondering at what she'd done wrong, but refrained from asking. She was still pondering Jacob's mood when the reverend returned to the room with another man following at a fast clip.

The burly man looked to be in his sixties. Brown unruly hair fell across deep-set walnut-colored eyes. His face was pitted as if he'd been plagued with an overabundance of teenage acne. His suit looked a size too small, had a tear at the lapel, and a dark stain on the right forearm.

She watched as Jacob took in the man's appearance and shot him a questioning look.

The newcomer made eye contact with Jacob by way of a head nod and quirk of a smile. This seemed to convey something significant as Jacob visibly relaxed.

The man hurried to the table, signed his name on the line marked "witness," and left without uttering a word.

The reverend nodded his approval and handed them the certificate that deemed them officially married.

Abby wondered why go through all the trouble to begin with. She looked at the signature, Steve Merrick, laughing at the absurdity of it. "Why not just sign a fake name and be done with it?"

The reverend's eyes grew wide as if she'd just committed a mortal sin. "Oh no, the certificate has to be legal. It is a sacred bond. You must take your vows seriously. You do remember them, don't you?"

Abby recalled the words he'd just recited to them.

The reverend looked at her in earnest. "Well, Mrs. Buckley?" he asked, using her new name.

"For better or worse, in sickness and in health. To love, honor, and obey," she answered, feeling like a child being quizzed on an exam. She was not sure if she'd recited them in the correct order, and didn't particularly care at the moment. What had started off as a simple impulsive reciting of the vows now seemed to be something of a joke.

Jacob reached for her hand, brought it to his mouth, kissing the back of it tenderly before releasing it. "You forgot until death do us part. But given my age, I guess you can breathe easy on that one, my dear."

He smiled, but it didn't reach his eyes, leaving her to wonder if he was in fact teasing.

Jacob turned his attention to the reverend. "Don't worry, reverend. Abigail has promised to follow all of the rules."

A chill raced up her spine as she remembered their previous conversation on following the rules. The way he said it made her scalp tingle.

His comment seemed to have the opposite effect on the reverend, whose smile returned as he ushered them hurriedly to the door. "The missus will be waking shortly."

This remark confused Abby even more. Why not let the missus sign the certificate if she was already here, and who the heck was the guy that had come and gone without a word? She looked to both men, wondering if she should voice that thought out loud, but decided against it.

Once outside, Jacob walked ahead of her and opened the car door. She was bending to get in when he pulled her up and into his arms. "Mrs. Buckley, I have waited all of your life for this moment. You have made me a very happy man today."

"You have a strange way of showing it," she shot back. She was not expecting a fairytale, but she hadn't expected the Godfather secrecy either.

The smile left his face. "Mrs. Buckley, I do hope you are not sassing your husband on your wedding day."

She set her chin. "And if I am?"

He brought his hand up, cupping her jaw firmly. "I would hate to have to spank you."

She tried to pull away from his grip. "You wouldn't dare."

He bent, gave her a brief peck on the lips, and released his hold. "Only if you give me a reason."

CHAPTER TEN

Abby placed the pile of clothes neatly into the dresser drawer and surveyed her new room. She'd just spent nearly thirty minutes transferring her things from the guest room to the master bedroom she would now share with Jacob. Even though she'd known him most of her life, she felt queasy. She was both nervous and excited at the prospect of consummating the marriage. The fact that they'd been home for over an hour didn't help. She'd half expected him to hoist her up, carry her over the threshold, and straight to the bedroom. When he did neither, she found herself disappointed. Instead, he'd left her to move her things into the master bedroom before heading to his study, closing the doors securely behind him. She had heard his voice through the closed doors and stopped briefly to listen. She could tell he was on the telephone, but could not hear what was being said. Still, she wondered what conversation was so important that it came before bedding your long-awaited bride. He was so relentless in his quest for her and yet his actions since tying the knot were more business as usual. She wondered at that. He was older and presumably more experienced than she was. He had been pursuing her for as long as she could remember, yet they'd never more than kissed. Maybe he was just as nervous as she? She shook her head at the thought. Jacob had said he had waited all her life for her. Surely during that time he had imagined what it would be like for them to be together. What if she didn't live up to his expectations? She had only been with one man and that relationship was so short lived.

An image of her first time with Brian came to mind. He had not even waited to reach the motel, pulling over on a side road and telling her he had to have her now. They'd fumbled at first, but their passion had built for so long that the first time did not take long. Later, after they reached the motel, he had taken his time, had been so eager to please. She felt her breathing increase at the memory. He had taken her so gently and made sweet love to her over and over. She had loved him so completely then.

The bedroom door slammed shut, causing her to jump.

"You're thinking of him, aren't you?" Jacob hissed.

When she didn't answer, he approached, pushing her backwards onto the bed. His mouth was on hers in an instant. Firm, demanding, prying open her mouth with his tongue. His need was apparent against her thigh as he pressed his weight onto her. His hands took hold of hers. She didn't resist as he brought them over her head and held them in place. With his free hand, he pulled back the fabric of the dress, exposing her right breast.

She lay mesmerized as his eyes changed from a simple brown to blazing mahogany. She tensed as flecks of gold appeared to dance in the midst. Gold in Jacob's eyes was not a good sign, as it meant he was upset. His eyes spoke volumes as his mouth remained silent. He released his hold on her and she started to lower her arms.

"Leave them," he said firmly.

She gripped the covers as he traced the insides of her outstretched arms with his nails. Up and down in slow deliberate strokes, the nails brushed across the skin, uncomfortable but not painful. His fingers traveled the length of her arms for a fourth time, stopping just above the groove of her armpit. Without warning, Jacob took hold of the bodice of the dress, ripping it from her bosom. She felt her body respond as he cupped and caressed her exposed breasts. She cried out as he lowered his mouth to her nipple, rolling the end with his tongue, flicking and sucking each nipple in turn while his hands continued to caress her fleshy mounds. When he'd had his fill, he straddled her, and tore the remaining fabric of her dress further, exposing her to him. His hand slid under the waistband of her panties. She moaned as his finger slid easily into her slippery folds. She was amazed at how much his intensity had excited her. Even in his urgency, Brian had never ravished her this way. She pushed the thought from her mind. There was nothing slow and gentle to Jacob's touch. He thrust his fingers inside her once more and she moaned in response. His eyes continued to blaze as he pulled her panties off and tossed them over his shoulder. Abby lowered her arms, reaching for his belt. He didn't resist as she set his erection free, stroking him tenderly.

After a moment, Jacob pushed her hands away, hurried out of his pants, and straddled her once more. She moaned as he slid a hand between her legs. She closed her eyes, enjoying the sensation. Jacob's hand withdrew. A second later, he penetrated her in one determined thrust. The unexpected sensation was a cross between pleasure and pain.

"Oh, Jacob!" she called out, not sure if she was asking him to stop or keep going.

His hands scooped up her hips as he plowed into her over and over. She felt the tension building within her with each stroke. She climaxed without warning, screaming out his name a second time. He slammed into her a final time before shuddering his release. She threw her arms around his neck, wanting him to stay connected for a bit longer. This was so different from anything she'd ever known. There was nothing tender about the way he'd taken her, no gentleness in his touch. It was so raw, so carnivorous, so unlike anything she'd ever felt with Brian. A tear trickled from the corner of her eye as she clung to her new husband. Her heart swelled with love for him and for the way he had made her feel. Somehow, he'd known what she been thinking. Somehow, he'd known exactly what she needed. In his quest to take her, he'd pushed Brian from her mind and made sure it was his name she called out. It was a fresh start with a husband who could make her come alive. The fears over what it would be like between them ebbed. She'd just begun her new life as Jacob's wife and, for the first time in a long time, she felt hope. She felt loved. She felt like she belonged.

Jacob raised his head to look at her. His brown eyes, no longer flecked with gold, were set in a pool of tears. He brought a hand to the side of her face. "Oh, Abigail.

My dear, sweet Abigail. I have waited so long for this. You are mine now. You finally belong only to me. I don't have to share you with anyone else."

His words came out choked and sincere. He was a man who'd waited patiently for his prize and now, in his vulnerable state, he looked at her as if he'd won the lottery. Just looking into the depths of his eyes, Abby was sure he loved her more than anyone ever had. She was lucky to have Jacob in her life. He had kept her safe when everyone else had let her down. She was not sure what the future held, but she knew one thing. She was going to enjoy being Mrs. Jacob Buckley.

The elation she felt was short lived. Jacob disconnected, rolled off of her, and sat on the edge of the bed, his back to her.

Abby sat up, the shredded dress hanging over her shoulders like a shawl. The dress was destroyed, clinging to her body by thin strips of fabric encircling each shoulder. She toyed with the tattered remnants of the dress and giggled. "So much for my wedding dress. I think it's safe to say that I won't be wearing it again."

The words had no sooner left her mouth than Jacob rounded on her. His palm connected with her face, sending a searing pain across her cheek. It happened so quickly that it took her a second to realize that Jacob had struck her. Her hand flew to her face instinctively to help alleviate the sting. She sat frozen in place, blinking back tears of disbelief. Her mind raced. What had she said? What was she going to do? Had she imagined it? No, the fire beneath her hand was real. Jacob had indeed struck her.

She watched as he rose from the bed and casually walked to the bathroom. He reached the door and turned to face her. "You've worn the dress to two weddings. There won't be a third. You hurt me, Abigail. Throw away the Goddamn dress and keep your drug addict ex-husband out of our bedroom."

She opened her mouth to respond, but thought better of it when he leaned forward. She pulled the sheet up around her and swallowed her words. Jacob turned, entered the bathroom, shutting the door behind him without further comment.

Abby hurried out of the remnants of the dress, not sure how Jacob had known she'd worn it before. Why had she kept it? Why hadn't she objected more when Jacob had insisted she wear it? But if he knew, then why did he insist she wear it in the first place? Did it matter? She should have put her foot down and refused to wear it. Maybe it was a test to see if she cared for him enough to tell him the truth. She remembered the way he looked at her after they'd married. He must have been hurt that she'd agreed to wear it. The more she mulled it over, the more she believed she had failed him. He'd given her a chance to come clean and she had opted to deceive him. Not really, but that must be what he thought. It was the only reasonable explanation. Of course he was upset. Could she blame him? How would she feel if she were in his shoes? How could she have been so insensitive?

Still, did that give him the right to strike her? Would she have done the same thing in his place? No, of course not, but he was from a different generation. However, that didn't give him the right to strike her. She would have to tell him she would not tolerate such behavior. Yes, she'd be sure to tell him as soon as he calmed down.

Abby's lip quivered as she recalled how alive he'd made her feel only moments before. Turning on the dress as if it were somehow to blame, she wadded it up and threw it in the wastebasket. The remnants peeked out of the can as if taunting her. In a huff, she pulled on her robe, reclaimed the tattered dress, carried it through the house, and discarded it in the outside trashcan, slamming the lid as if closing a tomb.

Feeling the need for fresh air, she walked along the perimeter of the backyard, pausing to look at a ceramic planter, overflowing with early spring flowers. Alongside the bright new flowers were dead ones, long past any sign of life. Lying in heaps, they overshadowed their new sweet-smelling descendants. She stopped, taking the time to pull the lifeless flowers from the planter. Returning to the trashcan, she tossed the dried bulbs into the bin with the dress. The wilted flowers floated down, coming to rest on the grave of the freshly discarded dress. Seeing the spray of flowers on top the dress helped her to see her mistake. The flowers were as dead as the dress, as dead as Brian. Jacob was right: neither the dress nor her memories of Brian belonged in her new life. She had screwed up by hanging on to both. Closing the lid, she hurried back inside to ask Jacob's forgiveness. After, of course, he would apologize for striking her.

CHAPTER ELEVEN

Gulliver met her at the door, meowed his relief at finding her, and followed her down the hallway. A quick search of the house came up empty. Jacob was nowhere to be found.

Abby peered out the side window and was surprised to find his car gone from the driveway. Even though she'd been outside, she had not heard him leave. She retraced her steps to the kitchen to see if he had left a note. Her eyes swept the impeccable kitchen and found nothing. Jacob must still be upset with her. It was the only reason she could think of that would have him leave without bidding her goodbye. What if he didn't come back? She dismissed the thought immediately. Of course he would; this was his home, not hers. Her eyes drifted to the diamond ring on her left hand, reminding her that this was now her home as well.

She returned to the master suite, showered, traded her robe for a simple teal sundress, and ran a brush through her silky red hair. Gulliver nudged her calf, his purr so intense it vibrated all the way up her leg. Abby hefted the cat and went to the guestroom to check on Ned.

The bird was in his usual spot, perched on top of his cage. It was Abby's custom each morning to uncover the cage and open the metal door, thus allowing the bird access to his roof top play yard. Gulliver jumped onto the bed and made his way to the top of the dresser to get a better view.

"Here, kitty," Ned sang out when the cat came into view. Gulliver meowed his reply. Abby stretched out a finger, waited as the bird clambered on top, and lowered the bird onto the cat's broad back. The bird went to work pruning the cat's back while the feline purred his enjoyment.

She remembered Jacob's surprise at seeing the two unlikely friends, feeling or perhaps hoping, it unsafe to leave the two alone together. She laughed at the absurdity of the comment. No, she had no fear of leaving them alone. It had been that way since the day she'd brought the bird home five years ago. She had opened his cage, but remained ready to spring into action if she needed to intervene. Ned had hopped out of the cage, climbed down the ladder, and walked past the cat without incident. When the cat had finally decided to investigate, the bird had tilted his head to the side, and greeted him with a simple hello. Surprised, Gulliver had relaxed and meowed a soft reply, obviously deciding he could not eat anything that spoke to him. Ned had then climbed onto Gulliver's back and, with his beak, began grooming places the cat could not reach. They'd been fast friends ever since, Gulliver only taking exception when Ned became overzealous in his grooming. Even then, the only response from the feline was a much firmer meow.

Abby left the duo to their grooming and wandered through the house. She paused at the closed office door, contemplated opening it to have a peek inside, but decided against it. Jacob was already mad at her. She didn't want to upset him further.

Deciding to make amends, she made her way to the kitchen. Surely a cake would be a welcomed truce offering. She pulled the ingredients out of the pantry and busied herself in her task. She cracked the contents of eggs into the bowl and stood staring at the empty shells. It occurred to her she'd only been married a couple of hours and was already walking on eggshells. This was not how she'd envisioned her marriage, much less her wedding day. She turned on the mixer, sending the contents shooting up in a spray of white. Decreasing the speed, she hurried to clean the mess.

When she finished mixing the ingredients of the cake, Abby placed it in the oven, set the timer, and started washing the dishes. She'd returned order to the kitchen and had just finished a mental checklist of what was in the pantry when the timer rang. The aroma sifted through the air as she placed the round pans on the cooling rack.

That task completed, she stepped onto the screened sun porch and felt a blast of heat. The humidity was already starting to build and hung heavy in the air, making breathing difficult. It was just past one; she'd been married less than four hours. Jacob was nowhere to be found and they had already had her first marital spat.

Could what happened really be construed as a spat? It was not an argument, as Jacob had been the only one to actually speak. Still, she had given him reason to be upset. Not that she'd meant to. Her fingers traced the flesh where he'd slapped her. Yes, it was essential that she have a chat with her new husband. She was not going to be one of "those" women. The ones she'd seen on *Oprah* talking about their abusive husbands.

A sigh escaped her. Surely the cake would appease him, and then they could talk and discuss the rules. She wondered if he would be surprised to find out that she too had rules. Wasn't the way to a man's heart through his stomach? Maybe she should fix a nice dinner. She remembered seeing the herbs along the property line. There was chicken in the fridge. Her mouth watered as she anticipated rosemary chicken.

She found the rosemary bush, but it was not where she'd thought. It was just on the other side of the property line. Still, it was a large bush and she only needed a small amount. Surely the owner wouldn't mind her taking just a few tiny sprigs. Looking towards the neighbor's house, she felt emboldened. No one was outside; maybe they wouldn't be the wiser.

She tiptoed into the yard, stopped at the rosemary bush, then laughed at the absurdity of tiptoeing in the grass. Choosing the piece she wanted, she set to work breaking the stem. It was harder than she thought; the stem refused to be plucked in a single twist. She worked the narrow sprig back and forth, wishing she had a pair of scissors so she could snip and go in a hasty retreat. When the branch finally let go, her fingers were sticky with rosemary sap and smelled of the fragrant bush. She cast one last glance at the still quiet house, then retreated to her own backyard, letting out a long sigh of relief.

"You know, in some countries, people get shot for less," said a voice that bordered on feminine.

Abby turned toward the voice, but didn't see anyone. She shielded her eyes from the sun. Only then did she see the silhouette of a person sitting on a bench under the shade of a large magnolia tree. "I'm sorry. I didn't see you sitting there."

The man's voice rose an octave. "You're sorry you didn't see me, or sorry you stole my rosemary?"

Abby eyed the stolen twig in her palm. "Both, I guess." She extended her palm in his direction. "Would you like it back?"

"Sugar, if I'd wanted rosemary, I would have clipped it myself. And I would not have mutilated the poor bush in the process."

She swallowed her objection. She was in the wrong and arguing the point would be senseless. It was obviously her day to piss people off. "I didn't think to bring scissors."

"Oh, so this wasn't a planned heist?"

Heist? What was with this guy; it was just a sprig of herb. "Well, I did come with the intention of getting it, but I thought it was on my property."

The shadowed figure sat back, crossed his legs, and looked from Abby to the house behind her. "*Your* property?"

"Yes." It wasn't a lie. She was Jacob's wife.

The man's demeanor changed in an instant. "Are you telling me you bought the house? I didn't realize it was on the market. That's splendid."

"It's not. Wasn't." She shook her head to clear her thoughts, wondering at his sudden friendliness. "I didn't buy the house. I married the man who lives here."

Even shielded by the shade, Abby could see the look of surprise that danced across the man's face. Wide eyes were replaced by a worried brow. He rose from his secluded bench and approached her. As he came into the sunlight, it was clear that his femininity was not limited to his voice. His face was thin with high cheekbones and well-arched brows. Sandy blonde hair stood atop his head in short, edgy spikes. He had long, dark lashes. She asked herself, *could he really be wearing eyeliner?* He blinked. Yes, he was most assuredly wearing eyeliner. He was an attractive man, but would have made a beautiful woman. His body was dancer lean under a tightly fitting pink t-shirt. Sinewy muscles rippled along lean, golden-brown arms, which boasted long, well-manicured fingernails. She wondered at how he'd gotten so tanned, since he seemed to prefer lurking in the shade.

"Keep the rosemary. Consider it a wedding present. Although," his mouth turned up devilishly, "if you are using it to fix dinner for your husband, I would prefer you use the azalea bush."

"Azalea? Isn't that poisonous?" she said, remembering something she'd read.

He placed his fingers to his lips and blew her a kiss. "Only if you're lucky, darling."

He rolled his eyes upward and waved off the comment. "I wouldn't tell him that you spoke to me. He won't approve."

"What... why not?"

"You're cute as a button, but not very fast on the draw there, are you, love?"

What the heck did that mean? Wait...had she just been insulted? She planted her feet in an attempt of looking taller than her five-foot-three stature. "I'm not stupid."

He pursed his lips together while his darkened eyes studied her. "Now don't go letting your freckles pop. I never said you were stupid; I merely said you were a bit slow."

She felt the heat rise in her face and was pretty sure he was on point about her freckles getting ready to pop. She tossed the rosemary at him. "What the heck. It was just a bit of rosemary. I didn't know I'd be hassled by a queen on a power trip."

His eyes widened. He placed a hand on his hip and shook a lightly painted nail at her. "I see what you are doing. You come over here, mutilate my poor rosemary bush, and now I'm the bad guy? Come on, Ginger; you are the one with the sticky fingers."

"I am not..." She stopped mid-sentence, realizing her fingers were indeed sticky from rosemary sap. *Great. I think this has to be the worst wedding day in the history of wedding days.*

She still felt the heat in her cheeks at the insult, but knew he was right. She'd known the bush was not on her property, but she'd ignored the boundaries and took it anyway. She fought to maintain control. The last thing she wanted was to start weeping like a baby, even though, at the moment, she felt entitled to a good cry. She pulled herself up and managed a forced smile. "I'm sorry I took your rosemary without asking. It won't happen again. And please don't call me Ginger. My name is Abby."

He searched her face as if wanting to gauge her sincerity. He started to speak, but stopped his face transfixed over her shoulder. Then she heard it, the sound of a muffled car door from the driveway at the side of the house, announcing Jacob's arrival.

The man, whose name she hadn't gotten, scooped up the rosemary and pressed it into her hand. "Go now, and hurry," he urged, pushing her towards the house.

She turned back, confused by his urgency.

"Abby… remember…don't tell him you spoke to me," he pleaded before disappearing into the shade of the magnolia tree.

CHAPTER TWELVE

Spurred on by the panic in her neighbor's voice, Abby made it to the kitchen mere seconds before Jacob. She stood at the sink, rinsing the rosemary as he entered the room. Her body surprised her by tensing as he neared. She forced her shoulders to relax. This was silly. She'd known Jacob all of her life. She had no reason to be afraid of him. She turned to face him, hoping she looked more relaxed than she actually felt.

She spoke first. "I got worried when I couldn't find you."

"I had an errand to run."

She smiled in an attempt to look non-accusing. "You didn't tell me you were leaving."

"I'm used to living alone."

She tore off a paper towel and placed the rosemary on top to dry. "I was worried," she repeated.

Jacob's eyes drifted to the twig, then to the window. "I don't recall us having a rosemary bush."

She swallowed. When she spoke, she somehow managed to keep her voice even. "We don't. I borrowed some from the neighbor's bush."

His eyes narrowed. "You spoke to him?"

So the guy was right: Jacob was not happy. "No, there was no one around, so I just took a small branch."

Jacob's face relaxed slightly. "You stay away from him and you stay out of his yard."

She decided to play dumb. "Let me guess: he is a male model and you're afraid he will sweep me off of my feet."

Jacob barked out a laugh. "The only thing our neighbor would model is ladies' panties. I'm sure his highness does lots of sweeping, but more of the domestic kind. The little fairy likes to sing and dance while he is working in his yard."

This must have been why the man had been so adamant about her not telling Jacob they'd spoken. He and Jacob must have had words before. "Oh, you mean he's gay?"

"As the day is long."

"Well, then there are no worries about him sweeping me off my feet," Abby assured him.

Jacob closed the distance between them, brought her hand up to his mouth, and placed a firm kiss on her wedding ring. "I am the only one who is allowed to sweep you off your feet and I'd rather hoped I'd already done that."

She felt as if she'd just been given a warning. She met his eyes, not quite ready to rehash what had happened earlier. "I am all yours...Jacob."

"Good. I'd hate to have to return your present." He reached into his pocket and withdrew a small velvet box.

Excitement rippled over her. He must have felt guilty about his earlier actions. "My present?"

"Yes, I felt bad that you're not having an extravagant wedding," he said, handing her the box.

She gaped at the velvet box, wondering what lay inside. Jewelry from the looks of the case, but judging by the size of the box, it was not a ring. She opened it and blinked to see if the gift was real. "So you thought I would be mollified with a cell phone?"

"I know how upset you've been since yours got stolen with your purse," he cajoled.

"That's true. You didn't by chance find my license and car keys to go with this, did you?" She thought about her car sitting in the detached garage at the back of the driveway, the only tangible thing she owned, not that it did her any good if she couldn't even unlock the thing. Her license, keys, and phone had been in her purse when it was stolen. She had a car, but no license or keys to enable her to drive it.

"Now what do you need with a driver's license and keys?" he said, placing his own keys onto the hook by the back door.

"Well, it helps if you have those things if you want to drive a car," she said mockingly.

The smile left his lips. "I detect a note of sarcasm."

"I'm sorry. I just feel so dependent on you." Her eyes flitted to the counter and saw an opportunity. "I can't even go to the store to get rosemary without you taking me."

He seemed to consider this. "The store is only a couple of blocks away. I doubt you'd get pulled over if you do the speed limit. You can drive my car."

"And if I decide to get a job? Then what? How do I prove who I am? Or get to work every day?"

His head snapped up. "We've been over this. You are not getting a job!"

"How else am I supposed to meet people?"

"What kind of people do you hope to meet?" he asked evenly.

She could tell by his tone that she'd said the wrong thing. "I was just hoping to make a few friends in the area."

"You have me ...what do you need with friends?"

"I need girlfriends, Jacob. Someone to tell my secrets to."

"You will tell your secrets to me."

She giggled at the thought.

"I was not being funny. Anything you have to say, you can say to me."

She swallowed another giggle, which was hard because she tended to giggle even more when she was nervous. This was getting ridiculous. "Are you trying to tell me I am not allowed to have any friends?"

"Not at all, Abigail. My friends are your friends."

"What friends? I've never met any of your friends." She knew she should stop while she was ahead, but couldn't. Her mom always called her tenacious. She blamed it on her red hair and told her she was too stubborn for her own good.

"You met the reverend today, and Merrick."

"Merrick?

"My best man?"

"Best man?" She remembered the signature on the wedding license. "You mean the guy that showed up late for the vows wearing the ill-fitting suit covered in stains? He didn't even talk."

"He's the quiet type," he said by way of explanation.

"Sounds like a good friend," she said smugly.

"The best kind. He doesn't talk back." Once again, the words came out as a warning.

"I've never been the yes-man type," she reminded him.

He snatched her by the hair, causing her to call out. When he spoke, his words were warm against her cheek. "I'm counting on that."

"Let me go. You're hurting me."

His grip tightened as he pulled her down the hallway by her hair. He led her to the bedroom, pushing her down on the bed. He was undressed and on top of her before she could react. He smothered her with kisses. "There's no use fighting me, Abigail."

He pinned her hands. She fought his grip and he smiled, gold flecks dancing within the brown of his eyes.

Her emotions were mixed. Part of her wanted to scream and tell him to get off of her. The other part wondered what she'd done to infuriate him so. If he was so angry, then why was he so turned on? He was turned on! She could feel him hard against her leg. It occurred to her that this afternoon's lovemaking session had also been brought on after he'd gotten upset. Was this his way? Could he only get turned on if he was angry? It occurred to her that the slap was not an impulse brought on by the heat of the moment. The thought frightened her.

He released his hold on her. She felt him tugging at her underwear and tried to push his hands away. It was not supposed to be like this. Brian had been so warm, so gentle, so unlike Jacob. She pushed Brian from her mind. He was dead and he'd hurt her in a different way. She forced her attention to return to Jacob, who was prying her legs apart with his knee. She tried to fight him, but she was no match for his strength. There was no ease in his approach. No pause to allow her body to acclimate to his assault. She clawed at his back and he slapped her hard across the face. She screamed out in pain and he slapped her again, causing yet another scream. That only seemed to spur him on. His breathing increased as he continued to pump in and out in a relentless attack, finally finishing in one painful thrust. He pulled out of her as quickly as he'd entered.

She lay there, not knowing how to react to the assault. It wasn't supposed to be like this on your wedding day. Who was she kidding? It wasn't supposed to be like this ever.

He kissed away a tear as it slid down her face. "You're so beautiful, Abigail. You're everything I could have hoped for and more. I am so happy you didn't disappoint me. You make me come alive."

She heard the words he spoke and tried to rationalize what had just happened. One minute they'd been having a discussion, the next he'd been so overcome with lust that he'd forced her to the bedroom. How could that be?

He wiped her remaining tears, kissed her nose, and rolled off of her. "You've made me a happy man today. It won't be easy for you, but you will learn to control your temper. I knew when I first saw your flaming red hair all those years ago that you would have spunk. I knew you would be mine one day. It took a bit longer than I had thought, but you came to me, Abigail. You came to me as I knew you would."

His hand slid to his back. He brought it up and studied the blood from where she'd scratched him. "We will have plenty of opportunity to work on your temper. You are like an exotic, wild cat, just waiting to be tamed."

He reached for her hand. She was too tired to resist. He brought it to his mouth and kissed her ring once more.

She turned her head away from him. He leaned in and whispered in her ear, "You were worth the wait. We are bound now, Abigail. Till death do us part."

She didn't move when he left the room. She heard the shower turn on and had a fleeting thought to run. She had no keys. She remembered Jacob's keys hanging on the back hook. She could take his car. Where would she go? This was her home now. She'd given up everything when she'd moved here and what little she'd had had been taken from her. She had no license, no keys, no wallet, not even a single dollar to her name. She didn't even have a credit card to buy gas. He was right. She'd come to him on her own. He had not forced her. Even the marriage was because she had told him she was ready. There was no out. She batted at the tears that were streaming down her face. Her wedding ring glinted in the light from the ceiling, drawing her attention. Jacob loved her. He told her so many times and he'd never touched her in anger before today. She just had to stop provoking him. He was right; she had to find a way to control her temper. Then everything would be okay. A chill passed over her. She grasped the edge of the blanket, tugging it over her. Curling her legs into a ball, she cried herself to sleep.

***

"Hey, sleepyhead."

She opened her eyes. Jacob was lying next to her, smiling. It must have been a dream. She started to move and her body objected. The pain was real. It had not been a dream. His hand approached and she felt herself flinch. The hand came to rest beside her face in a tender embrace. She opened her mouth to speak, but he placed a finger to her lips. She heeded his warning.

He lifted her. She had no strength to refuse. He carried her to the bathroom and lowered her gently to the waiting tub. She had not even heard him fill it with water.

The water was hot, but not scalding; the bubbles parted as she entered, quickly covering her as she sank into their depths. She felt her body begin to relax. He ran soap along her shoulders, washing her as if she were a child. She felt the tears, but made no move to brush them away. As gentle as a mother's touch, he cleansed her.

He handed her a glass of wine and a small white pill, which she swallowed without questioning, washing it down with the wine. He lit a candle before leaving the room, shutting the door behind him. Her mind floated as carelessly as the bubbles in the tub, making her wonder what she'd taken. At this point, she didn't really care; it was the first time today she'd felt fully relaxed.

Just as the water cooled, Jacob returned, reached for her hand, and helped her from the tub. She groped for the towel, missed and tried again, this time succeeding. Jacob took it from her, patting the moisture from her body.

98

He led her to the bedroom, toward the bed. She was vaguely aware that he had changed the sheets. Candles flickered on the dresser. She froze. Surely he did not expect to repeat the earlier performance. He pressed his hands to her shoulders and eased her downward.

Her mind warned her to panic, but her body felt too relaxed. Her body could not take another pounding. She thought about running, but knew her legs would not cooperate. "What did you give me?"

"Shhhh." He lowered himself to her, kissing her tenderly. He started at her neck, worked his way down to her breast. While he was treating her so tenderly, she wondered if indeed this was the same man she'd been with earlier. His hands and mouth worked simultaneously. Her back arched as she responded to his touch. A soft moan escaped from her. How could her body betray her this way?

He took his time, was so gentle that just his touch brought more tears. He took her to new places. Places she had never been. Not even with Brian. Jacob entered her so carefully that even her bruises didn't hurt. He was slow, giving. This was what she'd imagined it would be like with him. He waited until she told him she was ready, then gave her the release he'd withheld previously. This was how a wedding night should be. This was how love felt. When he was finished, he held her, professing his love to her. She closed her eyes, wondering yet again if she were dreaming.

CHAPTER THIRTEEN

Abby awoke to a stream of sunlight beaming in through the window. She glanced at the clock on the wall. It was after ten. The clock – this was not the guest room; she was in Jacob's room. Her thoughts were like cobwebs in a dusty attic, threads she could see, but just could not grasp.

In a panic, she sat up against the painful protest of her body. She winced, her insides begging her to lie back down. Instead, she forced herself to the edge of the bed, a nagging inner voice assuring her that Jacob would not approve of her waking at such a late hour. Where was Jacob?

His side of the bed looked as if it had not been slept in. Had he even come to bed? She did not recall. Yesterday's events were a blur. She struggled to clear her mind. A preacher, she was married. So they'd had sex? That must be why she was so sore. The pain ebbed slightly upon standing, as the rest of the day's events came flooding back. Yes, they had consummated the marriage. Several times. The first time she'd been willing but the next… He'd raped her! Is it called rape if you are married? She took a step, the pain was real. Why was she having trouble remembering? The pill! He'd given her something before making love to her a third time. Making love? How could she have consented to having sex with him after he'd forced her? She couldn't have consented. But she had. He'd given her something, knowing she would not be able to object. Still, the last time had been different. It was nice. He'd taken his time. He'd made sure she was satisfied. She swallowed. Her mouth felt like someone had swabbed it dry with a cotton ball. Water, yes, she needed a drink. Her eyes cut to the closed door. He was out there… somewhere. He said she had to follow the rules. What were the rules? Had she overslept? If she had, would he punish her for it? Punish her? What had she gotten herself into? She'd known Jacob all of her life. Why had she never seen this side of him before? She wondered if she should go in search of him, but decided to take a shower instead. If he was going to reprimand her for sleeping in, she was not in any hurry to succumb to her fate.

* * *

She found him brooding on the sun porch. Newspaper in hand, he didn't bother to look up when she took the chair next to him. She sat staring out the screen, wondering if her neighbor was sitting in the shadows of the large magnolia, lurking, watching them.

Jacob turned the page, scanning the print before acknowledging her presence. "What was the name of that crazy woman you spoke to?"

What on earth are you talking about? What crazy woman? She wondered if the drug was still messing with her mind. "Excuse me?"

He folded the paper in half.

"The woman that read your palm that day we went into town. The one that warned you that you were marrying an old man," he said as if talking to a simpleton.

Where was he going with this? "I don't remember. Eva something."

"Eva Radoux?"

"Yes, that sounds right," she said cautiously.

He handed her the paper, pointing to a picture of the woman. "It says here someone killed her yesterday. Walked right up to her and slit her throat and then cut her tongue out, right in broad daylight."

Involuntarily, Abby's hand went to her throat. "Cut her tongue out? Why would someone do that?"

Jacob gave a slight chuckle. "I guess someone took exception to what the crazy witch had to say."

Abby swallowed hard. "And you find it funny?"

"I find it gratifying, my dear. The woman gave unsolicited advice and someone didn't like what she had to say. People like her are too fast to tell people things that are none of their business. If everyone knew what the future held, they might make different decisions than they would normally make. Sometimes decisions must be made for us when we are incapable of making them on our own."

"You mean like whether or not to marry someone if you knew that person was abusive?" The words were out before she could stop them.

He gingerly sat the paper down on the table between them and glanced at his wristwatch. "Why, Abigail Buckley, it has barely been twenty-four hours since the wedding. You are not saying you regret your decision already, are you?" he said in an overemphasized southern accent.

"I'm not sure what to think. I guess I didn't expect to be raped or physically attacked on my wedding day." She watched the gold specks spring to life in his eyes. She was treading on dangerous water.

"I did not rape you, my dear. I merely took what was mine," he said dryly.

She felt the jab as if he'd physically punched her. The comment left her appalled. He didn't see anything wrong with what he had done? "I am not your property."

Another laugh. "Oh, but I assure you that is just what you are. I have the marriage license to prove it, dutifully signed by both the judge and witness."

"Our witness was not even there to verify we were legally wed," she said, seething.

He picked up the paper, tracing a finger over the photo on the page. A slow smile spread across his face. "I assure you he had other pressing matters to attend to, my dear."

She recalled the stain on Merrick's suit. It was dark and wet. Blood? She felt her stomach clench. Their witness was a killer? But why? She recalled the agitation in the woman's voice when she'd told her she was to marry an old man. But she had not actually said those words. Her words had been in French. Words that Jacob had interpreted for her. She struggled to remember the exact phrase the woman had used.

"Il est le fils du diable. L'homme a un coeur noir," she repeated, staring at him. "She did not say you were an old man, did she?"

He smiled, obviously impressed by her deduction. "Not quite. She said I was the son of the devil. That you were marrying a man with a black heart."

She somehow managed to find her voice. "So you killed her?"

With a shake of the head, he tossed the paper onto the table. "Of course not. I was with you."

"But you are responsible."

"No, my dear, you are responsible," he said.

She started to object, but he stopped her. "I told you to stay put, but you didn't listen. You broke the rules. You followed me into the alley, spoke to an innocent woman, and got her killed. The rules are in place for a reason. If you don't follow the rules, someone will get hurt. It may be you or it may be someone else, but either way, YOU are ultimately responsible."

She sprang to her feet. "You're crazy! I'll go to the cops."

He glared at her. "They won't believe you. Merrick was at our wedding at the time of the death. I have both the marriage certificate and the word of the good reverend to prove it. Hell, even the reverend's wife will testify to that."

Abby sank back into the chair. "Why did you marry me, Jacob?"

"Whatever do you mean?" To his credit, he looked truly puzzled by her question.

"It's apparent you don't love me, so why did you pursue me for all of these years?"

"Abigail, you are talking nonsense. Of course I love you. I've loved you your whole life."

"You have a funny way of showing it."

"You say that after all I've done for you? I saved your life on more than one occasion."

"You saved me from the fire," she corrected him.

"I saved you from yourself many times after that, Abigail."

"Meaning?" An icy feeling was tugging at the pit of her stomach.

"You were young. You made unsavory choices." The gold flecks were dancing at a dangerous pace.

"What unsavory choices?"

"Your choice to wed that boy, for one."

What did Brian have to do with this? "That 'boy' was older than I was."

"Well, he was not at all suited for you. But I had that situation remedied."

A chill traveled up her spine - a feat, considering the heat within the enclosed porch. "What do you mean, you had that situation remedied?"

"He was not good enough for you, Abigail. I warned you not to marry him, but you didn't listen, so the boy had to pay."

"No…Brian overdosed," she said carefully.

"Brian didn't know the end of a needle. He was a lightweight. But I assure you, he enjoyed the ride."

She closed her eyes against the image of Brian sitting in the chair, needle teetering in his vein, foam dripping from his mouth. Her stomach lurched at the memory. She batted a tear as it made its escape, trickling down her flushed cheek. All the pain and loathing she'd felt over the past few months hit her. He had not betrayed her.

"You killed him?" she hissed.

Jacob placed two fingers at the bridge of his nose and heaved a heavy sigh. "You are not listening to me, Abigail. You are the one who killed the boy. You didn't follow the rules and he got hurt."

She sprang to her feet, toppling the chair she'd been sitting in. "He's dead!"

Jacob remained unfazed. "Semantics, my dear. So now you know how the game is played. All you have to do is follow the rules and we can live our lives in wedded bliss. That is all I have ever wanted from the start."

A game? Her? Brian? They were all a game? She glanced at the door. "And if I don't?"

"Oh, but you don't have a choice Abigail. You are mine. You signed the paper!"

"The paper?"

Another sigh. "Do try to keep up, dear. The marriage license. Till death do us part, and all of that, remember?"

"Holy shit...You really are crazy," she said, backing away from him.

He closed the distance between them. "No, I'm a man who is patient enough to get what I want. I could have had you so many times over the years, Abigail. You were such a trusting young thing."

He closed his eyes briefly. "I should have been your first. I could have taught you so much."

She took a step back. Who was this monster she'd married? She turned away from him and saw movement within the shadow of the magnolia tree. Pain seared through her scalp as Jacob's fingers wrapped tightly around her hair. She cried out as he pulled her back toward him.

"You came to me, Abigail. You wanted me. You married me under your own free will. It was all your choice."

He released his grip, but remained close enough so that she could still feel the heat of his breath.

"I married you because you made me feel safe." If she'd not been so terrified, she would have laughed at the irony of that statement.

"I assure you, my dear. You are safe with me." He leaned even closer, the warning clear. "You are much safer with me than you are without me."

She watched his eyes flick to something behind her. His mouth came down on hers, hard, demanding. She tried to pull away from him, her effort fruitless. Thankfully, this time, her body did not betray her. It wanted nothing to do with him.

He pulled away from her, wiping her mouth with his thumb. "You have felt what can be between us, Abigail. I have needs."

She inched further away. He was not going to touch her.

He obviously took her move as a challenge as a slow smile played upon his lips. "You are my wife and I will have you whenever I wish. How I take you will be up to you. If you play nice, it will be pleasurable…for the both of us."

He leaned in and lowered his voice.

"If you don't, there will be consequences. What do you say, my dear? Do you want to be responsible for even more deaths? I assure you that Merrick loves a good chase. The man's a little warped that way. I think he's hoping you'll run. He'd really love to bring you back to me. Only something tells me I'd have to kill him afterwards." His eyes darted to the newspaper. "As you can see…he doesn't always play nice."

CHAPTER FOURTEEN

Abby stared at her reflection in the mirror. It'd been one week since she'd wed Jacob, and already she did not recognize the person staring back at her. Of course, the black eye she was sporting didn't help. She struggled to recall what she'd said to provoke him this time, but her memory was hazy. Did it even matter? He'd struck her. It wasn't the first time and she doubted it was going to be the last. She needed to figure a way out, but she had trouble putting her thoughts into action.

Her mouth was dry. She went in search of water, figuring she'd probably run into Jacob along the way, wondering in what kind of mood she'd find him.

She tiptoed down the hallway, hoping not to bring attention to herself. Gulliver followed her down the hall. Had she fed him? She swallowed in an attempt to relieve the dryness. It didn't help. What was it with her mouth these days? More so, what was it with her memory?

The door to his office was closed. Was he even in there? She made it to the kitchen unnoticed, reached for a glass, and turned on the tap. As the water rushed into the glass, she spied the keys on the hook near the door. She turned off the faucet, her mind slowly forming a plan. She downed the contents of her glass, all the while eyeing the keys. She was so close. The keys were so close. This was her chance; all she had to do was grab the keys and go. Where? It didn't matter, as long as she got away. Silently, she placed the glass on the counter, then walked to where the keys hung. Why did it feel like she was moving in slow motion? Noiselessly, she lifted the keys from the hook. She would be in the car and racing from the city in seconds. She wasn't sure where the police station was, but she'd find it. She would turn him in, him and his goon. Then she would be free.

"Going somewhere?" he said.

She froze. Why hadn't she heard him enter the room?

He crossed the room, took the keys from her hand, and returned them to the hook. Why? Why would he leave them there, knowing the temptation?

"You weren't thinking about running away, were you?" he said, taking a step closer.

"I was thinking of going to the grocery store." She tried to duck, but was too late. His hand met her cheek with a loud slap, sending her backwards.

"I loathe dishonesty, Abigail."

"I wanted to make you something special for dinner." She expected the remark to garner another slap, but it was not forthcoming.

"And you were going to pay for it how?"

"I guess I hadn't thought that far in advance. My mind does not seem to be working right this morning." At least that part wasn't a lie.

"Then I will drive you."

"No, I will be fine. It is not that far. If I could just get some money, or the credit card, I can get what I need."

"Nice try." His voice was almost humorous.

She shrugged. "Okay, your choice. I was going to fix a mouthwatering pot roast."

"Well, now, how could I resist something that tempting?"

Really? He'd bought it? She felt her heart quicken. She was really going to get away with a story that lame.

"How much do you think this roast will cost?" he asked, opening his wallet and producing a wad of cash.

She tried not to show her disappointment. She could get much further with a credit card. At least she could start with a full tank of gas before he canceled the card. She suddenly wished she had told him she was going shopping for the week. "Oh, forty dollars should do it."

"Pretty expensive roast," he said, plucking two twenties from the wad of cash.

"I have to get potatoes and carrots too," she said, squirreling the cash into her pocket. It was not a lot, but it would get her to the police station. After that, it would at least get her out of the city. She would be able to put some distance between them before running out of funds. What then? She didn't know, but she would figure that out after she left. She'd call a woman's shelter if she had to. She smiled. Jacob seemed to be in an agreeable mood. Maybe she could get him to give her a bit more.

She walked to the pantry, pretending to take stock of the contents. "We are running low on several things. Would you like me to pick up what we need, or would you like to go back out later?"

He pulled out a hundred-dollar bill and handed it to her. "You may as well pick them up while you are there."

She held onto the bill as if it was a life ring. He had fallen for it. She would be long gone before he even realized she'd been playing him.

"Are you sure you don't want me to drive you?" he said, his voice full of concern.

Hell no! she thought. "No, I'm fine. It will do me good to get out and shop for my husband," she said, her voice dripping with honey.

She smiled, surprised that she'd actually said the words without gagging.

"Don't forget your cell phone, Abigail."

She unplugged the phone from the charger. She'd take it, but she would turn it off the second she left city limits. "Got it."

She snatched up the keys and pulled on her sunglasses to hide the black eye he'd given her. "I'll be back in a jiffy."

She'd just reached the back door when his words pulled her back. "Aren't you forgetting something?"

She froze, almost afraid to look back. "I don't think so."

"You can't leave the house without a kiss."

She swallowed. He was right; she must act normal. She willed herself to turn around and managed a smile. He met her halfway, pulled her into his arms, and kissed her full on the mouth. Pulling off her sunglasses, he kissed the bruise around her eye. She fought a flinch as his fingers traced the tender flesh.

"This is much better, Abigail. This is how a wife should act."

Act was right; no way did she want to be in his arms or feel his mouth on hers. "I know, Jacob. I will try to follow the rules from now on. Thank you for trusting me."

His hands slid along her jaw, squeezing just a little too tight. "You have to earn my trust, Abigail. Don't let me down."

Oh, she wouldn't let him down. Deep down, she knew he expected her to run. She wouldn't disappoint him. She gave him a peck on the cheek. "See you in a few."

Her fingers had just grasped the doorknob when he spoke. "Abigail, just in case you are thinking about leaving, I think it only fair to warn you, you have enough drugs in your system to be arrested. I will tell the authorities that you are a junkie. I have some 'friends' at the precinct who could make sure you are put away for a very long time."

Drugs? Of course, the cotton mouth, the memory fog. She turned to face him and emitted a cry of alarm. Gulliver was on the kitchen counter, Jacob's right hand firmly planted around the cat's neck.

"Hurry back. You know how much I despise animals," he said coolly.

She blinked to fight back the tears. "You're not going to hurt him, are you?"

"That is entirely up to you, my dear. You are well aware of how the game is played." He hoisted the cat and left the room without another word.

***

Abby walked aimlessly through the aisles of the supermarket. She knew she should speed up, but the mini reprieve from Jacob's watchful eye felt too good to rush. She'd spent all her tears on the short drive over, which was why she was still wearing her sunglasses. That and the nice shiner that she knew would evoke curious glances from fellow shoppers. She didn't need their pity. She already had plenty of her own.

She placed cat food into the cart and thought of Gulliver. If it were not for him, and Ned, she'd be well on her way to the state line. Why had she insisted on bringing them with her to Louisiana? The same reason she would sacrifice her freedom, because they were the only friends she had left. They were her family: them and Jacob. But she would not count him amongst her friends, not anymore. Once again, her actions had placed those she cared about in danger. She picked up her pace. She didn't want to think about what Jacob would do to Gulliver and Ned if he thought she'd left. Common sense took hold. She was pretty sure they were safe, at least for now. He'd seen her face, heard the way her voice quivered. He would hold onto those bargaining tools for as long as he thought they were useful.

She rounded the corner and turned down the next aisle. As she lingered in the cereal aisle, she was approached by a frail woman with sun-baked skin. The woman brightened upon seeing her.

"Ah, I knew you'd come. The drems, they doont lie." Her bayou accent was thick, causing Abby to strain to understand her. The woman moved closer, invading Abby's space. The action unnerved her. She tried to steer the shopping cart around the woman, but the lady took hold of her buggy, proving she was stronger than she looked.

Abby resisted the urge to leave her basket and run the other direction. "Do I know you?"

"Muh nam is Pearl Duval. Muh sister, she come to me in muh drems. She done told me you need protection. She said I bring. She tell me come find you that you'd be herin today."

Abby looked around for help. How could it be they were the only two people in the cereal aisle when the parking lot was packed? "I'm afraid you have the wrong person."

This elicited a cackle from the woman. "Na! You spoken with muh sister Eva Radoux, did you not, child?"

Abby stared at the woman in disbelief. How had she known? "Yes... I'm sorry."

The woman clicked her tongue. "Na not your doing. Eva done told me who'd be to blame."

"You spoke to your sister? But I thought she was dead?" Abby's voice was hopeful; maybe Merrick had not killed the fortuneteller after all.

The woman sighed. "She dead, but we are same. We speak in drem world. She done told me about you and the devil man. She say to you that he is the son of the devil. The man has a black heart."

Dream world? Too bad... she doubted the authorities would investigate a murder on the word of a ghost. Abby ran a hand through her hair, wishing she'd understood the warning at the time. "But she said it in French. I don't understand French. I didn't even know what it meant until it was too late."

The woman's eyes grew wide. "That why you did not heed warning. Sister say she warn, but you no listen. She say she tell you man has black heart. She say tell you he son of the devil."

Abby swallowed her fear and the sudden urge to sink to the floor. "Yes that is why he had her killed, because she tried to warn me against marrying him."

The woman nodded in agreement. "Sister say he sent a man. Man told her she no should speak to people she not know."

Chills rose up Abby's spine. She knew the woman was right. She also knew the woman in front of her was now in danger. "I must go. It is not safe for me to speak to you."

The woman released the hold on Abby's cart and dug into her purse, producing a pouch. "You take. For protection."

Abby took the pouch and wondered at the lumpy confines. "What's in it?"

"Powerful magic. You hide. No tell Devil-man!"

Abby felt more than heard someone coming up behind her. The woman shot her a warning look before hurrying along her way.

"Looks like someone got a prize with their cereal this morning," a voice said mockingly.

Abby turned toward the familiar voice of her neighbor. "Are you following me?"

He rolled his eyes. "Don't flatter yourself, darling. I assure you, you are not my type."

He reached around her and plucked a red box from the shelf. "I was in the mood for Fruity Pebbles."

"Doesn't surprise me one bit, princess," she said on a giggle.

"Oh, isn't that just precious. You walk around here in your Hollywood glasses, acting like queen shit, and you call me a princess."

Ouch, she'd earned that one. "I'm sorry. I guess I had that one coming."

"Yes, you did. Are you always this mean?" He tossed the box in his cart. "I saw you and your husband having words the other morning. I guess it comes with being a redhead, always looking for a fight."

This stopped Abby cold. He had been spying on them; he'd seen her disgrace. She wondered if he'd heard anything. No, if he had, he would have called the police. She shoved the pouch into her pocket, snatched up a box of cereal, and tossed it into her own buggy. "If you'll excuse me, I need to be going."

"Oh, by all means, Queenie," he said, moving out of her way.

What the heck was this guy's problem? He had short shorts and was literally floating down the aisles. And yet he was calling *her* a queen. Without thinking, she ripped off her glasses and glared at him. "Really? You want to go there?"

She'd allowed him to push her buttons and had reacted in an effort to control at least some aspect of her life. She remembered too late, watching, as his eyes focused on the reason she'd left the glasses on in the first place.

"Oh my." His voice was contrite. "Did he..."

Abby returned her glasses to the perch atop her nose. "I have to go."

He stepped aside without further comment. She looked at her watch; she'd been gone way too long. She hurried to the meat case to pick out a roast. She'd just placed it into the cart when her cell rang. It was Jacob.

"Hello?" she said hesitantly.

"Just checking on you, my dear. You've been gone for a while."

Please don't hurt Gulliver. "I'm still at the market. It's pretty crowded today."

"Yes, Merrick told me the parking lot is full," he said.

Merrick? He'd followed her... Had he seen her talking to the woman? To her neighbor? "He's here?" she said, looking around.

"He's always near, my dear. That's his job. He's waiting for you outside." The phone went silent.

Abby's hands started shaking, then her body followed suit. She'd kidded herself into thinking she could get away from Jacob. Even if she had tried to leave, Merrick would have stopped her. She looked around once more. Merrick was nowhere to be seen. She paid for her purchases, holding the conversation with the clerk to a minimum. She could not risk being overly friendly to anyone now. She left the building and made a beeline for the car. As she approached, she saw him leaning against the trunk. He held out his hand and she gave him the keys. He loaded the trunk without speaking, handed her the keys and gestured towards the car. Her hand brushed against her pocket. Feeling the pouch that lay within gave her hope. Pearl had told her it would protect her and it

was increasingly apparent that she needed all the help she
could get.

CHAPTER FIFTEEN

Abby ran the dust cloth across the dustless table as she'd done yesterday and the day before that. Cook, clean, and service Jacob when the mood hit him, which was too often, since she no longer enjoyed coming in such close contact with the monster she'd married. She sighed, going through the motion of cleaning.

She was thinking clearly. Thinking thoughts that were dangerous, given her precarious situation. Her mind was scheming, something that could bode very badly for the rest of her. She had caught Jacob on an agreeable night and convinced him to stop drugging her. It had not been hard since she had told the truth. That she was too scared to leave. She was afraid he would kill her animals and she didn't want to think of the things Merrick would do to her if she left. He called her smart and had told her as long as she continued to obey the rules that he would stop giving her the drugs.

That had been just over a month ago, and while she enjoyed having her mental faculties back, it made it that much harder to bear his advances. He was taking his husbandly duties to heart and insisted on nightly satisfaction. It was all she could do not to cringe when he touched her. This morning he'd left her feeling so ill, she'd actually vomited afterwards when remembering his touch.

She moved to the sofa, fluffing the pillow, not that it needed it. Jacob insisted the house be perfect. She inspected the pillow closely, removing several feline hairs. She held the pillow up to the light; the last thing she needed were more bruises from not following the rules. She threw the pillow across the room in disgust. She was a grown woman, not a wayward child. She hurried across the room to pick up the pillow once again, fluffing and inspecting it before setting it delicately onto the couch. She gave thought to sinking onto the couch and taking a much-needed nap, but fear of not hearing Jacob return kept her on her feet.

The thought of a walk pulled at her; she did some of her best thinking when she walked. Crossing the room, she peeked out the front window. While Jacob had stopped drugging her, it was clear he didn't trust her to keep her end of the bargain to be the perfect wife and obey all the rules. Merrick was sitting in a car, two houses down, keeping vigilant watch over her, lest she decide to leave while Jacob was away. Where had he gone? She would have asked, but then she was only his wife. She had no need to know where he went, how long he would be gone, or what he did for a living. She needed – no, wanted – answers to all these questions.

She tiptoed down the hall and stood in front of his office door. Tiptoed? God, what had she been reduced to? He was nowhere in sight and yet she was terrified of the man. She reached for the doorknob and gingerly tested it, knowing the effort fruitless. He kept the door locked, even when at home. Sure enough, it refused to turn. She still had a hand on the knob when the doorbell rang, causing her to jump. *Don't be silly,* she chided, Jacob would not be ringing the bell. She wiped her fingerprints clear of the knob and hurried to see who was at the door. A solicitor no doubt; they had not had any visitors since her arrival.

Opening the door, she stared into the smiling face of her next-door neighbor. Dressed in khaki shorts and a hot pink polo, he stood holding a plate of chocolate chip cookies. They must have been fresh out of the oven, as her mouth watered the second the smell invaded her nostrils. Her stomach rumbled in anticipation as she glanced over his shoulder. Merrick was craning his neck in their direction; she would not be able to accept the gooey delights. At least not without consequences. She had to get rid of her neighbor before Merrick decided to do it for her. Only she was fairly certain his method would be far more permanent.

She smiled at the man in front of her, careful to insure her greeting did not appear overly friendly. She had no doubt Merrick would relay everything back to Jacob. The thought pissed her off. Seriously, what kind of man hires a murderer to stake out his wife? *Rein it in, Abby.* She made an attempt to appear normal as she redirected her attention to the person in front of her. "Can I help you?"

His feet remained firmly planted, while his whole body leaned to the side in an attempt to peer into the house. "Aren't you going to invite me in? It is the neighborly thing to do. Especially when one of the neighbors has fresh baked cookies."

She smiled inwardly; the guy was like a cartoon character. For all his femininity, he sure was a ballsy little thing. Part of her wanted to invite him in; even if he was obnoxious, she missed contact with the outside world. But she knew all too well that inviting him in would be signing his death certificate. "I'm afraid now is not a good time."

"Listen, Sunshine, I'm afraid we got off on the wrong foot. I wanted to say I was sorry." He hoisted the plate a bit higher, making sure to fan the air toward her. "Did I mention that I have fresh baked cookies?"

She nearly reconsidered inviting him in. It would give a whole new meaning to the term death by chocolate. No, she couldn't let her stomach get the better of her. Merrick had the phone to his ear, no doubt relaying information to Jacob. She thought about simply closing the door in the guy's face, but somehow felt it wouldn't be enough. Still, he had to go. He'd been standing there far too long. Jacob was going to wonder what they'd been discussing. She had to get rid of him, fast. She decided truth was the best option. "I really appreciate the effort, but really, my husband doesn't like company."

"I'm sure that's so, but I happen to know he's not home. I wasn't born yesterday; I waited until I saw his car leave. I'm pretty smart that way," he said, looking proud of himself.

She heaved a sigh. "Well, that was mighty nice of you, but, if you were as smart as you claim to be, you would have seen my babysitter parked down the street."

His face turned incredulous. He faked a sneeze into his armpit in an attempt at getting a better look.

She had to admit, the guy was a quick study. "Nicely done."

He returned her smile. "I have my moments."

"Now if you would be so kind as to leave, I would prefer not to be reprimanded for disobeying."

He opened his mouth to say something, but changed his mind. Instead, he clung to the cookies and turned to leave. When he'd reached the edge of the porch, he hesitated, pivoting back to face her. Then, speaking loudly enough to be heard several houses away, "Just because I'm gay doesn't give you the right to reject my cookies. I'll have you know they were my mother's recipe." He stuck his nose in the air and made an elaborate show of storming back to his house.

Abby closed the door. She had to give it to him: he-she realized she didn't even know his name, was a damn good actor. She peeked out the window. Merrick was off the phone, but had not left the confines of his car. She locked the door and leaned against it. She was a prisoner in her own home, a prison without bars. She laughed out loud. *Oh, there are bars all right, even if they are not visible to the naked eye.*

She heard a noise in the kitchen. Jacob? No, he never used the back door. She started after Gulliver, who was going to investigate. Cautiously, she followed, wishing not for the first time, that he was in fact a dog.

Gulliver raced ahead of her. She was almost surprised to hear her neighbor's voice exclaim, "Oh, what a pretty puttie cat. What's your name?"

Entering the room, she shook her head in disbelief.

Her neighbor was standing in the middle of her kitchen, a cookie plate teetered in one hand and two oversized coffee mugs in the other. "It would be a shame to make me eat all of these cookies by myself."

She glanced over her shoulder. The action was fruitless she couldn't see anything but the hallway.

"Don't worry. Lurch didn't see me." He waved the cups. "Tall bushes are the perfect camouflage and makes it impossible to see from the road, even if he was parked right in front of the house."

She moved forward, shooed the cat from the counter, and took the plate from him. "His name's Gulliver. Do you make it a habit of breaking into people's houses?"

"I didn't break in. The door was open. Well, unlocked, anyway."

"Are you always this pushy?"

"Only when I like someone."

"You like me? You sure have a funny way of showing it."

"I brought cookies; what more do you want from me?" When she didn't say anything, he added, "What can I say? I'm... complicated."

Complicated? Is that what he called it? She was pretty sure she had him figured out. Needy. Annoying. Her eyes traveled from his eyes, encased in eyeliner, to his bright pink shirt. She was just about to speak when he beat her to it.

"See, you're doing it again. I can see it in your eyes. You think you've got me pegged." He held out the coffee cups. "Which would you prefer?"

She read the writing on the cups. Sure, she'd misjudged him. She reached for the cup that read, "*I'm not having a bad day. I'm always a bitch*," leaving him

holding a cup that read, *"She who should be obeyed."*
"You were saying?"

Ignoring her, he moved to the coffee pot and poured
himself a cup. "So what's with surveillance team? Are
you married to the mob or something?"

She had asked herself the same question many times
of late. But wouldn't Jacob have told her if she were? She
watched *The Sopranos*. The TV wives were always in the
know.

She answered with a shrug. Her first thought was to
ask him what business it was of his. But a part of her
admired his boldness. The part that wished she'd asked
the same question before rushing to marry a man she
barely knew. "Before we start with the inquisitions, do
you think I could get your name?"

He'd been in the middle of dunking a cookie into his
coffee. "What, you don't like *She who should be
obeyed*?"

She poured coffee into her own cup. "Correct me if
I'm wrong, but aren't you the one who got offended when
I called you 'princess'?"

"Of course I did." He rolled his eyes. "If you are
going to be derogatory, you could have at least called me
a queen."

She laughed. The simple act caught her off guard. She
missed normal conversation. Okay, highly unorthodox,
but still semi normal compared to most she'd had of late.
"Would you prefer me to call you 'Queen'?"

"Not unless it has a 'The' in front of it."

She rolled her eyes.

"Okay, fine...my name is Kevin. Kevin Bishop."

She crossed behind him and pulled some crème from the fridge, offered him some, poured a touch into the cat's bowl, and returned the carton to the fridge. "What not Kev or Kevie?"

He tilted his head and took on a faraway smile. "Depends on who's doing the talking."

Her entire body shuddered. Okay, she really did not want to go there. "Forget I asked."

She picked up the cookies and he followed her to the table.

He finished the cookie he was eating and proceeded to lick the chocolate from his fingers. "So the mob, then?"

She sighed. "I wish I knew."

Kevin's hand stopped in midflight, hovering just above the cookie plate. "Correct me if I'm wrong, but you did say you are married to the man?"

Abby nodded her head in reply.

Kevin picked a cookie from the pile and pointed it at her. "I chose this cookie because it had the most chocolate chips. It said 'eat me.' So... tell me, why did you choose your husband?"

She feigned innocence. "What do you mean?"

He sighed, setting the cookie down without taking a bite. "You are obviously not in love with the man. He treats you like a punching bag and he leaves his henchmen to make sure you don't leave the house when he's away. I mean, I'm not trying to be the bearer of bad news here, but surely you know this is not what married life is supposed to be like."

He was right, of course, but what gave him the right to point out the obvious. They'd spoken only a couple of times and none of it very amicable. Just because the guy lived next door did not give him the right to interrogate her. She busied herself with clearing the cookie crumbs. "What are you, a detective or something?"

He nearly choked on the cookie he was eating. "No, but I'm available if you know one. I'm sure we could find something interesting to do with the handcuffs."

Oh God. Really? "I assure you, if I did know someone on the police force I wouldn't be in this mess."

He leaned in. "I can be a good friend to have, Abby."

She wanted to believe him. She wanted to tell him everything and have him help her out of this mess. She looked at his hot-pink shirt. No, he might be a nice guy, but he was no knight in shining armor, ready to whisk her safely away. She was pretty sure of that, even at his advanced age, Jacob could make short work of the guy without any help from Merrick. Kevin baked cookies. He did not save the day. It was best to keep him at arm's length.

"You called me a ginger," she reminded him.

"You have red hair. Besides, you called me a princess first," he countered.

"I'm sorry. I should have called you a queen." She tilted her head, biting her lip to keep from laughing.

He wagged a finger at her. "Play nice."

"I'm trying."

"Okay, so you don't want to talk about the mob, then tell me what was up with you and the voodoo priestess."

"The who?"

"Really? And people call me coy. You know the lady in the supermarket. What was in the pouch she gave you, anyway?" he asked casually, stroking the cat, which had climbed onto his lap.

Abby pulled the pouch from her pocket and untied the delicate string. Pulling apart the linen fabric, she held it up for him to peer inside. His wide-eyed expression matched her own the first time she'd seen the contents. He reached for it, but she shook her head, retied the string, and returned the pouch to her pocket.

He blew out a deep breath. "A chicken foot is supposed to be powerful magic. I can only imagine that one coming from a voodoo priestess is even more powerful. Must have cost a fortune?"

"She gave it to me."

"And you met her where?"

"In the supermarket."

He sat back in his chair. "So you're telling me that you are walking along in the grocery store, minding your own business, when out of the blue a voodoo priestess stops and says 'here take this'?"

Abby adjusted herself in the chair. "Yep."

"And you had never met her before?"

"No...but I did talk to her sister once right after I moved here." Abby thought about telling him what the old woman, Eva, had said, but she was beginning to like the guy. She could not risk telling him something that could get him hurt. Or worse.

His next question caught her off guard. "Did you know her sister, Eva Radoux, was killed about a month ago?"

She stood up. "How is it you know so much about this?"

His faced remained nonplussed. "Sunshine, it was all over the front page of the paper. Besides, this is New Orleans. When a voodoo high priestess is killed, it's big news. Whoever did it was sending a message. Did it in broad daylight. It was brutal. They still haven't found her tongue. Word gets around. Her sister moved up in ranks and now she is contacting you. Don't you think that's a bit coincidental?"

She rinsed out her cup and handed it to him. "You sound like a cop."

He let out a hardy laugh. "Do I look like a cop?"

"No." At least not any cop she'd ever seen. Then again, she'd seen some pretty strange things since moving to New Orleans.

"I'm just inquisitive. I recognized the woman from her picture and let my curiosity get the best of me."

As he flicked cat hair from his lap, disappointment washed over her. A part of her had wished he was a cop. Then just maybe she could have had a way out of this horrible mess in which she'd found herself.

A muffled car door caught her attention. She raced down the hall and peeked out the window. Jacob had returned. She ran back to the kitchen, determined to get Kevin out of the house before Jacob discovered him. As she entered the kitchen, relief washed over her. Kevin was gone, cookie plate and coffee cups nowhere to be seen.

CHAPTER SIXTEEN

Even though he'd not made a sound, she knew when he entered the room. Was it perhaps a change in the room's energy or had her sixth sense warned her? She turned from the sink, where she'd been rinsing out the coffee pot, and plastered a smile onto her face.

He was closer than she'd thought, catching her slightly off guard as he gathered her in his arms. "Miss me?"

Not even for a moment, she thought. "Every moment you were away."

His lips brushed against hers. "You are such a lousy liar, Abigail."

She pulled away from him. "Well, maybe I'd feel different if you didn't leave your hit man to babysit me."

"Would you prefer me to drug you?" The words came out light, but she did not miss the warning they held.

"No, of course not, but how can you ever trust me if you don't give me the opportunity to earn it?"

He must have found that amusing, as his eyes lit up with delight. "Abigail, I sleep with one eye open just to make sure you don't knife me in my sleep. Do you really think a mere six weeks of training has readied you to be a dutiful, loving housewife?"

She narrowed her eyes at him. "Training? You mean beating the shit out of me for the least little infraction?"

His hand shot up, smacking her hard across the face, its impact sending her backwards into the counter. She caught the edge with the small of her back. Gasping in pain, she ducked unsuccessfully as his fist rounded on her once more. She sank to the floor as he stood towering over her.

"Now look what you've gone and made me do. You bring these things on yourself, you know. " He looked pained as he extended a hand to help her up.

She took it and rose on a sob, flinching as he brushed the hair from her face. "As I was saying, Abigail, you are much too spirited to be left alone to your own devices."

She tried to turn her head away as he lowered his mouth to hers. His breath was coming quicker. How could he take such pleasure in her pain? Her back hurt with each breath. She had to distract him. The pouch harboring the chicken foot grew warm, as if reminding her of its presence. Her hand sought out the lumpy confines, fingering the fabric for inspiration. "I had a visitor today."

He pulled back a bit. "So I heard."

She brushed at the tears, trying to sound normal. "It was the gentleman from next door."

He laughed. "I think that is probably the first time he has ever been called that, my dear. So tell me, what did the little weasel want?"

She moved to dry the coffee pot. It felt tangible in her hands. She stifled an impulse to hit him alongside the head with it, knowing she was no match for him. She set the pot onto the frame on a shrug. "He was just trying to welcome me to the neighborhood. He brought cookies. I didn't take them," she added when his eyes went in search of them.

"Pity, I hear guys like him are pretty good cooks."

She feigned innocent. "Guys like him?"

He met her eyes. "Fags."

"Just because he dresses differently doesn't mean he's gay."

"And I'm Mother Theresa."

Not by a long shot. She unplugged the pot and moved to wipe the sink dry with a towel. Jacob did not like water spots; she'd once had a busted lip to drive home the point. "If you want cookies, I can make some."

He waved her off. "No, I think we need something much better than cookies since we're having company for dinner."

She whirled around. "Company?"

"A business acquaintance from out of state. I expect he'll be spending the night."

Spending the night? Her thoughts raced. What kind of person would Jacob be associated with? Did he know of Jacob's dark side? Would he even care? She tried to keep her thoughts from showing on her face. Shit, Ned was in the guest room. While Jacob was tolerating the cat, he'd never warmed up to the bird "Oh?"

"I promised him a home-cooked meal and a room for the night."

"I need to go to the store if I'm expected to fix something company worthy."

"Agreed," he said, reaching into his wallet and pulling out some bills.

Alarm bells were ringing in Abby's head. Something was not right. Jacob was being too agreeable. Her mind returned to the chicken foot. Maybe it was powerful magic after all. "Can I drive or do I need to ask Merrick for a ride?"

He glanced at the key rack. "I think you can drive. Make sure to pick up some cat food. I'm sure Gulliver will be hungry when you get home."

It was a veiled threat. He'd found her weakness and was not afraid to use it.

"I'm sure he will." She brushed past him on her way to the door.

He caught her by the arm. "Abigail, why wasn't there a coffee cup in the sink?"

She felt her body tense. Could he know she'd had a visitor? "What do you mean?"

"You were washing the pot when I came in, but there was not a cup."

"I washed it first," she lied. "I know how you like things to be in order."

He released her arm and she turned towards the door a second time.

"Abigail?"

She paused. "Yes, Jacob?"

"You wouldn't think of leaving without a goodbye kiss, would you?"

She took a deep breath before turning towards him. "No, Jacob, it would never cross my mind."

* * *

Abby was browsing the meat aisle when she saw her. The elderly woman jerked her head to the side and disappeared down a center aisle. Abby didn't know why she felt compelled to follow, but somehow knew it was what was expected of her. Sure enough, the woman was waiting midway down the aisle.

As Abby approached, she noticed the woman's red-brimmed eyes. Without speaking, Pearl placed her hand at the small of Abby's back, causing a chill to race the length of her spine. She couldn't tell if it was from the woman's touch or from the fact that she'd known about her injury.

"You are thinkin' bout leaving, but it no good. He the devil. He will fin' you. You mus' stay. It the only way. You are protected."

The pain was easing. She felt laughter bubbling up inside of her, yet did not know what she found amusing. "Yeah, I feel protected."

"He strong man child. You mus' listen to Pearl. You mus' wait for the sak of you and your *bebe*."

"Baby? I'm not pregnant!" It was an accusation, but Abby knew it was made out of fear. She felt like her legs were going to give out. The nausea, vomiting; she'd thought it was because Jacob revolted her, not because of pregnancy. There'd been a time when she'd have given anything to have a baby, but not now. She would not let a child suffer at the hands of her husband. Fear welled inside her until she thought she'd scream.

Pearl reached up and placed a hand along her face, calming her instantly. The woman produced a pouch and handed it to her. "You take this."

"Will it get rid of the baby?" she asked, her voice fearful. It was early enough in the pregnancy, but even still, the thought nearly broke her heart. She would never even consider such an option under other circumstances.

The woman shook her head. "No, child. It will help with the sickness. Make this into a tea each morn. It will keep you weel. He must not know about the *bebe*. It's too dangerous to the wee one."

Abby was not sure if she was relieved or disappointed. But her hair stood on end at what the woman said next. "I will tell ya when the time is right. I will show you the way out."

The lady took her hand and squeezed it hard in warning. "You no leave. No matter what happens. Tis the only way. You understood?"

No, she didn't understand. Not any of it. She shook her head in protest.

"I know tis hard, child, but you must endure this. It is the only way you will be safe. You need to know who you are. Find the key and you will find yourself," the woman insisted.

Abby searched the woman's eyes. "What key?"

"The key will unlock the past. So many things are not as they seem. You must know the past to protect your child's future."

Abby wrung her hands. While she really wanted a child, she was afraid. "But the child is his. It will be like him."

The woman's face softened. "No child. The baby will be yours. You must believe."

She did believe. She had to. But that didn't mean she wasn't still scared.

"You no leave till you find what you are looking for. You understood?"

Abby nodded her head yes, but in reality, she didn't. Not by a long shot. How did this woman know how to find her? Know she needed her? Kevin must be right. It was the only explanation. If he was right and Pearl was indeed a voodoo priestess, ignoring her could be more dangerous than anything Jacob could ever thrust upon her.

The woman smiled. "I no mind a hurt you, child."

More chills. The woman had read her mind.

"My sister, she deed because of your man. She no wish you the same fate."

Deed? Oh, dead. The thought tugged at Abby's conscience. "I'm sorry."

"No need. T'wasn't you."

"I go now. Remember, you must no tell about the *bebe*. It no safe. Stranger no safe." The woman turned, disappearing around the corner before Abby could ask what she meant.

"Hey, you'd better hurry before your babysitter decides to come looking for you."

Abby froze. Was everyone following her? No, this was no mere coincidence; was this the stranger Pearl had warned against? She whirled around and faced her neighbor, her words louder than intended. "Why are you following me?"

He put his hands up. "Whoa. Put a leash on the psycho, Sunshine."

She lowered her voice, but didn't let down her guard. "You can't tell me that this is just another chance meeting."

"Well, it is the closest store to the house."

"Well, maybe we'll just have to see about that," she said, reaching into her pocket and pulling the small pouch.

His eyes went wide with the knowledge of what she held. "Now, wait a minute. I was only trying to help. I thought maybe I could give you a ride somewhere. You know, take you away from all this."

She felt herself relax in spite of herself. "Kevin, I didn't think you were the type to ride a white horse."

He returned her smile. "Well, if I did, I'd want you to ride it with me, my queen."

She laughed. "I'm really not the queen type."

"No, I guess that is more my slate in life. Besides, I'm afraid your babysitter may take exception to your leaving with me."

Babysitter! Shit, she was taking entirely too long. "I have to hurry."

He followed her as she filled her cart. "You may want to get some witch hazel."

"For?"

He shook his head sadly. "The bruises. I hope they were not because of me."

"No, he was a bit suspicious, but I threw him off." She touched her face gingerly. "No, I'm afraid these are on me. I can't seem to keep my mouth shut."

He wagged a finger at her. "You are not to blame. That man is a monster." His eyes hardened. "He gets turned on by hurting others."

She dunked a package of pork chops in a clear plastic bag before setting it in the cart. "You seem to speak from experience?"

He waved her off. "Another lifetime, darling."

"But you got away?" The hope was evident in her voice.

He clutched her shoulders in determination. "As will you, my love. As will you."

CHAPTER SEVENTEEN

Clutching all the bags, Abby stomped up the stairs, hoisted the bags to the other hand, and fumbled with the doorknob. She felt Merrick's eyes drilling into her back and got angry. If he was going to be watching her every move, the least he could do was make himself useful and help her carry the damn bags. The thought made her laugh and she nearly dropped the bags she was wrestling with. She didn't want that monster anywhere near her. The door swung open. Jacob stood, eyeing her suspiciously.

"You seem in particularly good spirits," he accused.

"I was just chiding myself for not making two trips," she said, wielding the heavy bags.

He moved to allow her to enter, but did not offer to help relieve her of her load. Gulliver followed her down the hallway, mewing mournfully. The sound unsettled her. It was obvious he did not like it when she left him alone with Jacob. "Did you miss me, big guy?"

"As a matter of fact, I did," Jacob replied.

I was talking to the cat. "I think Gulliver did too," she said, shuffling the bags to ease the load.

A frown fleeted across Jacob's face.

"I don't think you'll be so happy to see him when you hear what he's done," he said, following her to the kitchen.

She heaved the bags onto the counter, her unease mounting. "Oh?"

"Yes, well there is no easy way to say this, Abigail, but I'm afraid he's killed your bird."

Ned was dead? She pushed past him, making it to the guest room in seconds. The bird lay unmoving on the play roof of his cage. She scooped him up, his head falling limp as she did. Tears rolled unbidden down her face as she lowered herself to the bed. Gulliver jumped onto the bed, meowing. He sniffed the bird. Purred up against her hand, then meowed. He nudged her hand a second time, as if waiting for the bird to spring to life.

"Would you look at that? The little bastard is back to finish the job," Jacob said, his voice full of disdain.

Abby jerked her head around. Jacob was leaning against the doorframe. His hands tucked into his pocket, as if he didn't have a care in the world. His hair was freshly combed and he had changed his shirt, this one being long sleeved. In this heat? Understanding washed over her. Gulliver had not killed Ned, Jacob had. But why now? Their visitor, they needed the guest room. She placed the bird inside his cage and turned toward Jacob.

"Gulliver would never hurt Ned. They've been friends since day one," she said on a sob.

He stood taller. "Are you calling me a liar, Abigail?"

She pushed away the tears with the back of her hand and swallowed another sob before she answered. "It's a bit warm for long sleeves, don't you think?"

He bristled, but then sank back against the doorframe. "While I would love nothing more than to see where this conversation may lead, I'm afraid we don't have time for

141

such… pleasantries. Our houseguest will be arriving soon. Don't you think he would feel much more at home in a room without a dead bird in it?"

She glared at him. "Are you going to bury him or am I?"

He laughed a hearty laugh. "Oh, I doubt you would care for the way I would dispose of the thing, Abigail."

"He's not a thing. His name is Ned!" she shouted.

"Was," he corrected.

"What?"

"His name was Ned," he said, pointing at the bird.

She balled a hand into a fist. She didn't care anymore; she would just run at him and claw his eyes out. Yes, that was what she'd do. She'd never really fought back. So what if he killed her? At least she'd be free of him.

He called to the cat, the action bringing her back to her senses. It was not just about her. She had Gulliver to think of and, even more, there was a strong possibility that she had another life to think of. The prospect stilled her. She could not afford to do anything rash.

"I will keep an eye on this guy while you say your goodbyes. I'm sure we agree you wouldn't want him to run out the door while neither of us were looking. He could get hit by a random car," Jacob said, meeting her eye. He hoisted the cat and left the room without further comment.

Numbly, she made her way to the bathroom to blow her nose. She glared at her reflection in the mirror. *This is all your fault, Abby,* she screamed silently to her reflection. *You allowed this to happen. It was your choice to come. You allowed this to happen. It is your fault Ned is dead!* Her lip quivered. It *was* her fault. She had been the one to insist on bringing her animals, even though Jacob had told her he did not want them. She didn't listen. She thought once he spent time with them, he would learn to love them as much as she did. If only she'd known. But how could she know the extent of his hatred? She had known him most of her life and yet she could never have guessed that the man was insane.

She had to find a way to escape. She remembered her encounter with Pearl. "You no can leave; he will find you," she had said.

Maybe she couldn't leave, but she had to find a way to get Gulliver to safety.

She looked at the lifeless body of the bird. It was only a matter of time before Gulliver met the same fate.

She splashed water onto her face. The cool water assaulted the newest bruises. Maybe she would be better off asking Jacob for more pills. At least when she was drugged, the reality of her situation didn't hurt as bad. Once again, her mind thought of her possible pregnancy. Instinctively, her hands traveled to her still flat stomach. No, if she were indeed pregnant, drugs were not an option. She would have to find a way, at least until Eva revealed her plan to Pearl.

She carefully patted her face dry, feeling as if she had just found her breaking point. "Your husband is psycho and he just killed your bird. It's only a matter of time until he kills your cat and maybe even you, and here you are waiting for a dead voodoo priestess to reveal her plan. Maybe you can get yourself committed; there's no need in waiting for the man down the hall to beat you to it," she whispered to her reflection.

Grabbing a hand towel, she left the bathroom on a wave of fresh tears. She carried Ned, cage and all, to the far recesses of the backyard. Setting him down, she walked to the garage in search of a shovel. Seeing her car, her anger bubbled. She hiked her leg and kicked the side panel repeatedly.

"Damn you for bringing me here!" she screamed at it as she continued to release her anger.

She saw the shovel hanging on the far wall, rounded the car and snatched it from the wall. Turning on the car once more, she slammed the shovel across the roof.

"What good are you? Without keys and gas, you are nothing! You just sit in here, day after day, taunting me. I hate you!" she said, slamming the blade across the windshield in one shattering motion.

She stood there, her chest heaving, staring at the damage she'd done. No doubt, she'd pay for that in the future. Pushing the hair out of her eyes, she wielded the shovel, and returned to the yard. She pushed the blade into the ground, stepping her foot onto the edge to push it further into the hardened ground. Heaping a shovel full, she tossed it to the side and repeated the process. She was already sweating from her tirade in the garage and the Louisiana heat was lending a hand to see that she was thoroughly soaked.

"Psst."

She stopped digging, peering into the shadows of the yard next door.

"Keep digging; he's looking out the window," Kevin said.

She pushed the shovel into the dirt and continued working on the hole.

"What happened? It sounded like an explosion in the garage."

"I smashed my car window," she said, scooping out more dirt.

"Any particular reason?" he said.

"Jacob... killed... my bird," The words came out on a sob.

"Oh, Sunshine, I'm so sorry!" he said on a gasp.

She sank the shovel deeper into the dirt, scooped out a shovel full, and tossed it onto the pile. "Kevin, I need help. I need to find a way to get Gulliver out of the house. It is only a matter of time before Jacob kills him too."

"What about you? Will you be leaving with him?" His voice was filled with hope.

She pressed the shovel into the freshly loosened ground. "Not yet."

"Why not?" He was clearly incensed.

"I had another visit from Pearl," she said as way of explanation.

His voice rose an octave, sounding like a teen going through puberty. "The Voodoo Priestess? When? Where?"

The shovel met with resistance. Reaching down, she removed a rock, which clanged off the back fence when she tossed it. "At the store. Didn't you see her?"

"No," he said, sounding hurt. "What? Are you two girlfriends now?"

Her tears were dwindling with her exertion. She wiped at the sweat-mingled tears, finding unexpected humor in the fact that Kevin was jealous. "No, Kevin, I assure you we are not girlfriends. The woman kind of freaks me out, to tell you the truth. How does she always know where to find me?"

That seemed to appease him. "What did she say?"

Abby reached for the hand towel, carefully wrapped it around the bird, and lowered him into the hole. "She told me not to trust strangers."

He choked out a cough. "It would have helped if she'd given you that bit of advice before you married the 'asshole,' don't you think?"

She looked up toward the sky, tears spilling anew. "Please forgive me for causing this and please watch over Ned."

Resisting the urge to turn in Kevin's direction, she bent to pick up the shovel. "Can I trust you, Kevin?"

Her words were met with silence.

She took a deep breath. "I guess not."

"You guess not, what?" Once again, Jacob had slipped up on her unnoticed.

She fought a sudden panic, wondering if he had heard her earlier question, but then knew he hadn't or he would not be standing there.

"I guess," she said, covering her tracks, "Ned is not going to fly away before I cover him with dirt."

His hand clasped the shovel, enclosing his fingers over hers. "I will finish here; you need to get cleaned up so you can start dinner."

She held firm to the shovel, fighting the urge to use it on him. "You'll be sure to pack the dirt in firm so nothing digs him up?"

"Of course, Abigail." He peeled her fingers from the shovel and nodded for her to go.

She hesitated.

A frown washed across his face. "What kind of monster do you take me for?"

She stared, unbelieving. How could he ask her that after what he'd done? Meeting his eyes, she saw the gold flecks dancing within the brown, a sure sign of the battle he hoped to wage. She declined to answer, grateful he could not read her mind, for it was screaming the words she wanted to say. That he was the worst kind of monster there could ever be. He was the son of the Devil. Instead of speaking the words aloud, she hurried to the house, leaving him to bury the latest of his sins.

CHAPTER EIGHTEEN

Numb. It was a single word, but the only one that could describe the way she felt. Freshly showered, she moved in slow motion, putting the finishing touches on dinner. The pork chops were in the oven along with a dish of roasted root vegetables. It was an attempt at a normal dinner on a not so normal day.

"It smells divine in here. I have to give the woman credit; Marsha sure did a great job training you to cook."

"You mean teaching me to cook?" She knew it was dangerous to back talk, but a part of her didn't care; his comment pissed her off. No, at this point, everything he said tended to piss her off.

"No, it was Marsha's job to train you," he repeated.

Opening the cabinet, she gathered the plates for the table. "It's a mother's job to love you and teach you."

"Yes, well, call it what you wish. The woman who raised you did a fine job," he said, plucking a tomato from the salad bowl and tossing it into his mouth.

She let it go. It was clear Jacob was bucking for a fight and she was just too mentally drained to accommodate him. "What time should your friend be here?"

"My friend?" He chuckled softly. "Abigail, in my business, there are no friends."

No friends? Then why was he allowing a stranger to spend the night? A stranger! Pearl's' words floated back to her, causing the hair on the back of her neck to stand on end. *It no safe. Stranger no safe.* "Jacob, just what kind of business is it that you're in?"

He made a move to speak, but the doorbell caught his attention. He winked at her. "Alas, saved by the bell."

She checked on dinner before following him down hallway. Just before opening the door, Jacob turned to her, voice lowered. "Remember, my dear, we must be on our best behavior. No more breaking things."

Jacob had seen what she'd done to her car. He opened the door before she could respond.

Their guest bowed extravagantly upon seeing them. "Greetings, Earthlings!"

Abby giggled at his exuberance. She didn't know what she'd expected, but the man that greeted them was not it at all. Their guest appeared to be in his mid-thirties, had the body of an athlete, and a confident air that warned of danger. Sandy blonde hair floated just above his shoulders in loose springy curls. A well-defined jawline was etched with a slightly darker beard, a full tuft of hair resting just below his bottom lip. His blue eyes twinkled with mischief as they locked on hers. Feeling Jacob stiffen beside her, she lowered her eyes and waited for introductions.

"Nathan, always one for an entrance. Did you have any trouble finding the place?" Jacob greeted the man warmly, but Abigail noticed that the warmth did not reflect in his eyes.

"No, no trouble at all," the man replied.

Turning his attention to Abby, he smiled a perfect white smile. "And you must be Abigail. Jacob speaks so highly of you. I can see why."

His comment surprised her. If Jacob spoke so highly of her, then why did he elect to treat her like a punching bag? Her mind went to her bruises, which she hoped she'd successfully hidden under mounds of makeup.

"Yes, Nathan Riggs, this is my wife, Abigail." Jacob draped a possessive arm around her, placing emphasis on the word "wife."

Moving to allow for entrance, Jacob beckoned the man inside. "Where are my manners? Come in, Nathan."

Once inside, Abby was able to get a better look at the stranger. If it weren't for Pearl's warning echoing in her head, she would have found the man most attractive. His looks, confidence, and his charming smile, were all things she found utterly appealing. Especially the smile. She missed laughing just for the sake of laughing.

Gulliver jumped onto the sofa and meowed his greeting. Nathan greeted the cat before turning his attention to Abby. "Go figure. I never had Jacob pegged for an animal lover."

His comment gave Abby a great sense of foreboding. There was no way Jacob was going to be pleased with all this attention the guy was lavishing on her.

"Well, yes, the cat belongs to me," she said, casting a glance towards Jacob, who smiled a tight smile.

"A package deal, if one must know." Jacob interjected. "Abigail is quite the animal lover."

Directing his comment to her, Jacob continued, "Although I don't know why she bothers, the things don't live nearly long enough. She had to bury one of them just this afternoon. Met a tragic death at the jaws of that wicked beast there, truth be told."

Her head jerked up. How could he be so callous? Truth be told...what a crock! Truth be told, he was a murderer. Eva was right; he was an evil man with a black heart. She found herself wondering what had happened to him to render him so cruel. His hand sought out hers. She lowered her eyes and, for the first time, saw several fresh wounds on his hand. Ned must have put up a fight. Her stomach clenched; nausea suddenly overtook her. She wrenched her hand free from his.

"Excuse me. I need to go check on dinner," she said, jumping up.

Abby hurried down the hall, making it to the bathroom just in time to lose the contents of her stomach. Heaving a final time, she stood, mildly surprised to find Jacob standing in the doorway. Could the man be any quieter?

He looked from her, to the toilet, and back to her. "Is there something I should know?"

"Only that being reminded of what you did to Ned makes me sick." Not the best answer, but knowing her houseguest was within earshot of her screams left her feeling a bit bold.

"Clean yourself up and see to dinner like a good wife, would you, dear," he said, leaving the room without further comment.

I'd rather spit in your food! she screamed after him, at least from the recesses of her mind. Emboldened or not, she was not brave enough to voice that thought out loud.

Instead, she rinsed her mouth and brushed her teeth before making her way to the kitchen under the veil of being a good wife.

* * *

Abby heard them talking as she walked down the hallway. She wondered if they'd heard her coming, as the voices dropped off just as she neared. She made sure to focus on her husband when she entered. "Jacob, dinner is on the table, if you and Mr. Riggs are hungry."

Nathan stood, drawing her attention.

"Mr. Riggs? Coming from you, it makes me sound so...old. You make me sound like the cradle robber here." He gestured toward Jacob, who was wearing a thin smile. No doubt he was mentally deciding how to dispose of the man's remains after having Merrick kill him.

Nathan brushed past Jacob, patting him on the shoulder as he did. "Easy, old man. Looks like your blood pressure may be up a bit."

He placed Abby's arm in the crook of his and ushered her towards the kitchen. "Please call me Nate; all my friends do."

She considered telling him she preferred Abby, but her sixth sense was in overdrive. She was not sure of the game unfolding, but she was fairly certain she would not be the winner by the time it was finished.

Approaching the table, Nate released her arm and pulled out her chair for her. While a noble gesture, Abby was furious. Why didn't the guy just kiss her and get it over with. The results would be the same in the end. She took her seat, mumbling her thanks. It's hard to be appreciative when you know the consequences. She wondered about her bruises. While she made a valiant attempt to cover them, she knew they were still visible if one looked closely enough, and Nate had barely taken his eyes off of her.

Jacob was standing at the center island. He cleared his throat and held up a wine bottle. "Nathan? What is your preference? White or red?"

"Red." His eyes came to rest on Abby's hair. "It has always been a preference of mine."

Unsettled, Abby jumped up and knocked into the table, rattling the glasses.

"I forgot to take the rolls out of the oven," she said, busying herself at the range long enough for Jacob to take his seat. Returning to the table, she tried to steer the conversation away from her.

"So, Nathan," she said, using the more formal name her husband had used, "Jacob tells me you are a business associate of his."

Nathan's eyebrows rose slightly. "Did he now?"

Jacob's fork hit the table with a clang. Shit, what had she done now?

Jacob padded his mouth with his napkin. "Yes, I said we were associates, but didn't go into any details. I hate mixing business with pleasure. I don't like to bring my work home with me, you know."

This comment evoked a hearty chortle from the man at the end of the table. "No, I wouldn't advise doing that more than once."

Jacob took a sip of his wine. "Careful there, lad."

The two men glared at each other for several seconds before Nathan broke the trance. This brought a genuine smile to Jacob's lips. "Merrick tells me there was an issue with your acquisition."

Merrick? Nathan knew Jacob's hired assassin. Pearl was right. No way would she trust this man.

Nathan set down his fork. His spiral hair bobbed as he turned his head towards Jacob. "I assure you, it's nothing I can't handle."

Jacob pushed his food around on his plate. "I always worry about acquiring the merchandise so close to home."

Abby listened in rapt fascination. She had no clue what they were speaking of, but it was obvious something had not gone as planned. She could tell that by the gold flecks dancing within her husband's eyes that he was displeased. She tried to eat with as little movement as possible, not wishing to remind them of her presence, hoping she'd learn more about her husband's mysterious line of work.

"This was the best time to fill this particular order," Nathan said, his tone even.

Jacob shook his head. "Then what went wrong?"

The younger man shrugged, his ringlets danced seductively above his shoulders. "There were... complications."

Jacob sat back in his chair. "Complications are not acceptable in our line of work."

Nathan tilted his wine glass, draining its contents before returning it to the table. "Neither is bringing your work home with you."

Both men turned in her direction, as if suddenly remembering she was there. Abby picked up the dish sitting in front of her and smiled sheepishly. "More potatoes, anyone?"

Both men declined, but the conversation had run its course. She was resigned to the fact that she'd learned nothing new about her husband or what he did for a living. She swiped butter across a roll, replaying the conversation in her head. What was the merchandise they were acquiring and why was it bad to fulfill orders close to home? Wasn't it more cost effective to do so? And what did it have to do with her? That part of the conversation had been clear enough. Nathan had said something about bringing your work home and they'd both looked at her. Drugs! Abby recalled the pills Jacob had given her on more than one occasion. She'd never seen a prescription bottle. That had to be it. If they were drug runners, they would want to keep them far away from where they lived in order to remain anonymous. She cast a sideways glance at Jacob. He was handsome and distinguished, and impeccably dressed, as was his routine. His was not the face she would have given to a drug lord. Then again, she would not have taken him for a murderer either.

CHAPTER NINETEEN

The remainder of dinner passed without incident, both men having eased into casual conversation, until finally finishing and excusing themselves to Jacob's office. While Abby was happy for a brief reprieve, she was slightly incensed that Nathan was welcomed into Jacobs's office when clearly she was not. She finished cleaning up the kitchen before silently slipping out the back door. The illusion of freedom pulled at her. It was dark, Jacob was busy, Merrick's car was not out front. It would be so simple just to keep walking, disappearing into the night, never to be heard from again. Pearl's words echoed in her ears. *"You are thinkin' bout leaving, but it no good. He the Devil. He will fin' you. You must stay; it the only way. You are protected."* The woman had said she would show her the way out. She pinched the bridge of her nose, amazed at how crazy her life had become. She was staking her life on the musings of a crazy lady and her dead sister. No, not crazy. While the knowledge Pearl possessed might seem crazy, there had to be more to it than that. Kevin called it voodoo, which kind of made her uneasy. Wasn't that witchcraft? And wasn't witchcraft bad? Obviously, the ones who practiced voodoo must not have thought so. If they did, they would not have tried to warn her against marrying Jacob. Surely if Eva and Pearl

156

were bad people, they would want her to marry "the son of the devil." That thought eased her mind slightly.

She lightly traced the tender flesh around her eyes with her fingertips and sighed. She had to believe that everything would be all right, that Pearl would show her the way out before things escalated any further. It was the only thing that was keeping her sane, the only thing that kept her from asking Jacob for more pills. It would be so easy just to say yes the next time he offered her the bottle. She shivered against an unknown chill.

Easing soundlessly off the porch, she walked toward the back of the yard. She couldn't see him, but had no doubt he was there.

"Kevin?" she whispered.

"I'm here, Sunshine. How was dinner? Your houseguest looked good enough to eat." He said keeping his voice low.

She bit her lip to keep from laughing. Somehow, Nathan did not seem like Kevin's type. "He's cute, but Pearl warned me not to trust him," she said.

"Really? Such a pity. Did he do anything to merit her warning?"

She swatted at a mosquito. "Yes. No. Maybe."

"Well, which is it?" he pressed.

"It was just the whole dinner conversation. I felt as if they were talking in code," she said, sighing.

"What did they say?"

She glanced at the house before speaking. "Nothing that made any sense. There was some kind of acquisition that went wrong and Jacob was pissed that Nathan, our guest, had tried to pick up the merchandise locally. Then they kind of argued about bringing their work home and I got the distinct impression they were talking about me."

A twig snapped in the darkness. "Do you have any idea what any of it means?"

"Not a clue," she said, shrugging her shoulders.

"Where are they now?"

"In Jacob's office."

"So wait until your husband leaves and have a look see in his office," Kevin said helpfully.

As if it was that simple. Jacob would likely kill her if he found her there. Then again, there was no reason to believe it would not come to that at some point, even if he didn't. "He keeps the office locked."

"And you've never seen the key?"

"I have, but he keeps it with him. It is not even attached to his car keys, which he hangs in the kitchen," she said, sounding frustrated.

"Think about it, Sunshine. Every door comes with two sets of keys. Every lock set, car, house; they all come with at least two keys. He's not going to keep the spare key in his office because it would not do him any good if he keeps the door locked. There has to be a spare key somewhere; you just need to find it."

She hadn't thought of that. But where? She did a mental sweep of the house. She'd been in every room but the office. Still, she hadn't actually searched the rooms. Where did Jacob spend time? The office, of course, but where else?

"Yes," Kevin said firmly.

The word brought her back to the conversation. "Yes, what?"

"Earlier, when you were out here, you asked me if you could trust me. I assure you that you can, Abby," he said.

She felt the sincerity within his words and it reminded her of what she'd intended to ask him before. "I need your help. I know Jacob killed Ned. I've got to get Gulliver out of here before he kills him too."

"Somehow, I felt there was more to the question earlier." The words were low in the dark.

"Yes, I suppose there was, but I need to see to Gulliver's safety first. I'm sorry for bringing you into this, but I don't know what else to do. Please, Kevin," she said, her voice cracking.

She heard a heavy sigh from under the magnolia tree. "Okay, let me work on it."

The porch light came on, illuminating the backyard. Turning, she saw Jacob standing on the screened porch, peering out at her.

"Got to go," she whispered before hurrying toward the house.

She steadied herself before opening the door and joining him on the enclosed porch.

"It's a bit late for a stroll, don't you think?" His words came out more in the form of a question than an accusation.

She rubbed her arms to collect herself. "I just wanted to say goodnight to Ned."

"Well, that is done, so come make some coffee for our guest, now, won't you?" he said, turning back toward the door.

Fighting the impulse to tell him to fix it himself, she followed him inside.

* * *

She carried a tray with the coffee and warm cookies, just out of the oven, to the living room. Short on time, she'd opted for prepared heat and eat cookie dough she'd found in the refrigerator section of the supermarket.

Nathan stood as she entered the room, relieving her of the tray. "Here, let me help you with that."

She resisted momentarily before relinquishing the tray. "I'll be down the hall if you need anything else."

Jacob smiled and waved her over. "Nonsense, my dear, join us, lest our houseguest think you rude."

Oh, well, we can't have that now, can we? She took a seat beside her husband, wondering at his jovial mood. They must have worked out their differences in the office.

Nathan plucked a cookie from the tray, took a bite, eyes closed, obviously savoring the flavor. "And she bakes too! What I wouldn't give for a taste of what you have, Jacob."

She felt herself blush. Surely he meant he wished for a wife, not to actually taste her.

"Well, yes, you need to find a nice woman and settle down," Jacob interjected.

"Well, that too," the man said with a wink.

"There are many fine specimens out there, just ripe for the plucking. Some may take longer to come around, but if you're willing to wait a bit…you can see the results are worth it, " Jacob replied.

She had no doubt he was talking about how long it took him to win her over. She bit her lip to keep from screaming at him. You lie to someone for long enough and they believe the lies. Specimen? Ripe for the plucking? What was this caveman talk? She reached for a cookie, chomping it forcefully. How could she have misjudged her husband so? He thought women were here to be molded and trained. Specimens, to be plucked when ripe for the taking. What kind of backwards Neanderthal had she married? *The kind that will beat you senseless if you voice the words aloud,* she reminded herself. She finished her cookie in silence, watching for an opening where she could leave the room. She found it when the coffee carafe ran dry. She reached for the pot, gawking in surprise when Jacob took it from her.

"Here now, let me get that," he said, rising.

Nathan watched him leave the room before turning his attention to her. "I can't help but notice the tension between the two of you."

Pearl's words screamed at her. *No trust the stranger.* She pulled back slightly. "I have no idea what you are talking about."

He scooted closer, his voice low. "Jacob is old enough to be your father. Surely he can't satisfy you the way a husband should."

She stiffened. "I assure you that neither my marriage nor my sex life is any of your concern."

"I could take you far away from here and treat you the way a woman should be treated," he said smoothly.

Her heart leaped at the thought. She'd seen the discontent between him and Jacob firsthand. He didn't appear to be afraid of Jacob. Maybe he could withstand the likes of her husband, at least help to get her out of her current situation. Of course she'd leave as soon as she got safely away. He seemed so nice. She doubted he would keep her under constant surveillance. She could just slip away unnoticed just as soon as she was free. *No trust the stranger. No leave.* Pearl's words hovered above her in warning until regrettably, she shook her head. "No, thank you."

He brushed the hair out of her face, his fingers tenderly grazing the bruises that were not quite camouflaged under her makeup. The soft digits continued to roam along her cheek, and into her hairline, lingering with casual intimacy. "You enjoy his kind of attention, do you? I promise you, I play so much nicer."

Her breathing quickened at his touch. "Please take your hands off of me."

Not taking no for an answer, he brushed his mouth across her ear. "We could be so very good together, Abigail."

"I told you to remove your hands," she said with more force.

A seductive smile played on his lips. "And if I don't?"

"If you don't, then I will scream for my husband and have him remove them for you," she said through clenched teeth.

"Bravo!" called a voice from the hallway. She turned and, for the first time, saw Jacob leaning against the doorframe. He'd returned to the room unnoticed, at least by her.

Jacob clapped his hands together as he crossed the room. "Well played, my dear! I told young Nathan here that you were the loyal type."

Nodding his approval, their houseguest returned to his original place on the couch. "That you did, old man. Not even an ounce of hesitation; she's as loyal as you said."

Jacob took his place next to her, beaming his approval. "You passed the test, my dear."

Test? His advances had been some kind of test. What would have happened to her if she'd taken him up on his offer? She thought back to Pearl's warning; the one she'd nearly ignored only moments before. *No trust the stranger.* She glared at the men. "You can both go screw yourselves!"

Jacob caught her red mane as she attempted to rise. "You'll have to excuse my wife's manners, Nathan. She's quite the firecracker."

She pulled her hair free and stormed from the room. Once inside the bedroom, she waited. She may have passed the original test, but she'd still have to pay for her outburst. She didn't have to wait long. She hadn't expected to. He entered the room, silently closing the door behind him. A mere formality, as the screams that followed could not be fully muted behind a hollow bedroom door.

CHAPTER TWENTY

Abby moved through the house, wiping the dustless tables, fluffing already fluffy pillows, and cleaning things not in need of cleaning. There were multiple motives for her obsessive need to clean. First and foremost, it seemed to appease her husband. Seeing her in the thralls of her wifely duty apparently gave him the sense that his heavy-handed rule had indeed paid off. She didn't like that assumption, but if she toed the line, the beatings, while still frequent, were less intense.

A second motive was for the exercise it offered. Now, certain she was pregnant, she was determined not to gain weight too quickly. She needed time to plan her escape, or wait for Pearl to tell her of a plan, whichever happened to come first. Her stomach was getting rounder, but if Jacob suspected, he had not made mention of it. Her only suspicion to him possibly knowing was that he was keeping his fist away from her stomach of late.

She moved through the room, searching for the hiding place of the backup key she was sure existed. Thus far, she had not found it and she'd been searching since Kevin had given her the idea.

Gulliver sidled up to her, startling her. She stopped dusting, swooped up the cat, murmuring her affection. He'd been increasingly clingy in the month since Ned's death, not letting her out of his sight for more than a few moments, seeking her with vocal distress if she left the house for more than a few moments.

Jacob was not handling the added distraction well, scolding the cat at every opportunity. She wanted to tell him he'd brought it on himself, but knew that would only start a fight and they had enough of those without her egging him on. For some reason, unbeknownst to her, Jacob had not left the house without her in the month since Nathan had visited. Nor had she been allowed to go to the store on her own. She wasn't sure the reason, but his close proximity had not allowed her to speak with Kevin, to see if he'd formed a plan to get Gulliver to safety.

The cat grumbled his displeasure as she sat him down. She was on a mission. The key had to be in the house somewhere. She'd just finished checking the top edges of the windowsill for the umpteenth time when Jacob entered the room.

"I need to go out for a bit."

"Oh." She tried to sound indifferent, even though inside, she was jumping for joy. With Jacob finally leaving the house, this could be her chance to speak with Kevin.

"Yes, we need to run to the post office." He waved a large manila envelope for her to see.

Shit, so much for the reprieve. "We?"

He gave her a stern look. "You have a problem riding along with me?"

She tried to hide her disappointment as she followed him to the car. "Of course not. It will be nice to get out for a bit."

Buckling her seatbelt, she reached for the envelope. "Want me to hold that for you?"

He pulled it from her reach, placing it on his lap. He backed out of the driveway and drove slowly down the tree-lined street. It occurred to her that only a few short months ago, she thought this was the prettiest street she'd ever seen. A picturesque setting that offered safety and security. She couldn't have been more wrong. The Norman Rockwell view hid a sinister evil, not fit for the weak of heart. How many similar scenes had she seen in her lifetime? She wondered now if the settings were as perfect as they had seemed or if every neighborhood hid cracks within its foundation. Her eyes searched each window they passed, wondering at the truth that lay hidden inside. Did other houses hoard secrets more sinister than her own, or was hers the darkest of them all? She had seen victims of domestic violence on TV shows, but she had never imagined herself in the role. Watching the shows, she had felt anger toward the women. No way would she allow herself to be treated in such a way. She was a strong, opinionated woman with dignity and self-respect. Yet, here she sat, a statistic. She felt a sudden kinship for the women she'd once loathed. It was true, domestic violence could happen to anyone.

"You seem rather melancholy today," he said, pulling her from her pity party.

"I was just thinking how different my life is from what I imagined it would be."

"How so?"

She searched his face, wondering how he could have asked that without laughing. "I guess I just didn't expect to wind up anyone's punching bag."

He was silent so long, she didn't think he was going to answer. "Is that all you think you are to me?"

Wow, he still was in denial. "What would you call our relationship, Jacob?"

"One of honor and respect," he said without taking his eyes from the road.

She turned toward him, noticing his face remained perfectly sincere. "How do you figure?"

He took a breath. When he spoke, it was as if he were speaking to a child. "Abigail, you know what I expect in a wife. I want respect and honor. I want you to abide by my wishes and follow the rules of the house. When you do, we get along splendidly. When you don't, then you need to be... reminded."

"I am not a child, Jacob. I am your wife."

"You promised to love, honor, and obey," he repeated.

"But what gives you the right to beat me senseless?"

"I am your husband."

"That still does not give you the right." It was the first time they'd discussed it so openly since their wedding day. Maybe it was the fact they were in public; maybe she felt he could not do much harm within the confines of the car.

He smiled suddenly. "There!" She flinched at his outburst. "When you set your chin like that, you remind me so much of your mother."

He'd said that before, but she'd never seen it. With her red hair and green eyes, she didn't look like either of her parents. Thinking of her parents left a hollow feeling in her stomach. Their recent deaths still weighed heavy on her heart. She sighed. If they were still alive, they would offer her sanctuary. No way would they put up with the way Jacob was treating her, especially her mom. While her mother was a bit mousy, she had stood up to her father on numerous occasions when she'd felt his punishment too severe. Abby pulled down the visor, turning her head back and forth. "I don't see it."

He took on a faraway look, his smile expanding. "Oh, but you do, Abigail. Someday, you will see it."

They drove the rest of the way to the post office in silence, the envelope resting on Jacob's lap, writing side down. He might wish for her company, but it was clear he did not wish for her to see the nature of his business. She decided to use this knowledge when they arrived at the post office.

"Would you like me to mail that for you, Jacob?"

He clutched the envelope. "No, I can manage."

"Okay, if you want, I can fill out the proof of delivery form. I'm sure you will want one with a parcel that large."

He seemed to consider this. "No, I am quite capable of doing it myself."

Unlatching the seatbelt, she reached for the door.

His hand rested on her shoulder. "You can wait in the car, Abigail."

Yes! It worked. Her jubilation was short lived as he rolled down the windows, turned off the car, and took the keys, leaving her in the sweltering heat.

She watched as he entered the building; the frustration of her situation was weighing heavy. She bit at a fingernail, contemplating her next move. The parking lot was full; maybe she could approach the next person that came her way, explain her situation, and ask for help. A woman, in the late stages of pregnancy, walked towards her. She had a child that looked to be nearly two toddling along beside her. Abby opened her mouth to call out to her when a withered hand clamped against her mouth. Her eyes widened as Pearl's face came within the confines of the car.

"It no good, child. I told you he will fin' you." She turned her head toward the woman as she waddled past. "She be but an innocent woman, but she would be dead and her *bebes* too if you go with her." Pearl closed her eyes as if in pain. "I saw what he did to them."

Abby looked in the mirror. "What he did?"

"If you were to go like you were just tinking."

Tinking? Oh, thinking. She turned her eyes to the older woman. "But how did you know I would be here?"

The woman smiled. "Pearl knows all, child. I come to give you what you are looking for."

Abby's head jerked up. "You have the key? Where? How?"

"No me." Pearl pointed toward the center console. "What you seek is in there."

Abby was confused. "How could you possibly know that?"

The woman waved her off. "No time to dawdle. He returns soon. The answers you seek are at hand. You must hurry."

Abby sighed. "Even if I find the key, he won't leave me alone long enough to use it."

Abby resisted a flinch as Pearl reached in the window, cupping her chin with a well-aged hand. She relished in the warmth of the woman's touch. The hand felt warm, yet not uncomfortable, even in the heat of the day. It was as if the contact calmed her instantly. The hand was lowered, but the heat of it remained, giving her a sense of intense serenity.

"Write his name on a piece of paper. Place that paper in an ice tray in the freezer. This will help."

Abby blinked. "Help?"

Pearl clicked her tongue in response. "It will help him to chill out."

Abby suppressed the urge to laugh; somehow, she felt voodoo magic would be more complex than putting a name in the freezer.

Abby watched as the woman left without further comment. She followed Pearl's movements as she pulled a pouch from her pocket, emptying the contents into a cup she'd not previously noticed. Pulling herself up to her full height, Pearl walked with determined steps towards the stately brick building. Once she disappeared from view, Abby opened the compartment and searched through the contents. The search was futile, producing nothing of importance. Obviously, Pearl had been mistaken. She lowered the lid, keeping a close eye on the door, as she moved on to the glove compartment. Once again, a quick search produced nothing more than the usual registration and insurance papers. Still, Pearl had seemed so certain. Reopening the center console, she rummaged through the contents once more. She'd just about given up when she noticed the compartment had a false bottom. She raised it and nearly screamed. There, hidden in the recesses of the console, was the key she'd been searching for. At least she was fairly certain it was the one, as it looked identical to the one on Jacobs's key ring. Holding her breath, she removed the key, replaced the lining along with the remaining contents of the compartment. She placed the key within the same pouch that held the chicken's foot, praying the act would somehow protect her from discovery. Her exertion was evident. She was sweating profusely by the time Jacob returned to the car.

His mood was less jovial when he returned. His mouth twitched as he took in her sweat-soaked shirt.

She wiped the moisture from her brow in mock disgust. "I guess next time I should go in with you. The car windows are no match for the Louisiana heat. Now I know what a dog feels like when left in the car."

She tilted her head and for the first time noticed a pungent odor. "What on earth is that smell?"

He bristled, sticking the keys in the ignition. "Some crazy old bat bumped into me and spilled the contents of whatever she'd been drinking all over me."

Abby's eyes were beginning to water from the smell. "Someone was drinking something that smelled like that?"

Frowning, he raised his arm to sniff at the shirt. "Hard to believe, isn't it?"

She rolled her eyes. "What did you do?"

He shrugged his shoulders. "Nothing much I could do. The damage was done. I told her she needed to be more careful and she told me I needed to chill out."

An image of Pearl emptying unknown contents into a cup flashed before her eyes. "Chill out?"

He started the car and fastened his seatbelt, an uneasy smile plastered on his face. "Sounds more like something you'd hear from a teenager, not a woman old enough to be my grandmother."

Keeping her face turned away from him, Abby fought a giggle.

Idling at a red light, Jacob spoke for the first time since leaving the parking lot. "Did you see an old woman enter the building?"

"No, I was not really paying attention to who was coming and going," she lied.

"I feel as if I should know her," he said, sounding distracted.

She wanted to say something to divert him, something that would take his mind off of Pearl, but thought better of it. At least if he was concentrating on where he knew his assailant from, his mind would not consider what had warranted her own silly grin of triumph. Besides, she was pretty certain that Pearl could take care of herself. She eased her hand along the fabric of her shorts, resting her hand atop the pouch hidden within her pocket. She felt a small surge of hope swell within her. For the first time in months, she felt as if just maybe she would survive this terrible ordeal. Her fingers traced the lining of the key and the promise it held. The promise of unlocking Jacob's secrets, once and for all.

CHAPTER TWENTY-ONE

Abby dropped the trash in the can and lowered the lid. It had been two days since she found the key, but finding it and being able to use it were two different things. Jacob had not left the house, leaving no chance for her to test the key, much less snoop in the office. She walked to the rear of the house, then ventured further into the backyard. She pulled some weeds around Ned's grave and noticed a small rock she hadn't noticed before. She picked up the stone, intending to toss it aside, when she noticed writing on the underside. It was a phone number. Kevin. It was the only explanation, although the act could have backfired had she not been the one to find it. She peered into the shadows of the magnolia tree and saw nothing.

"Are you there?" Her words were met with silence. Carefully, she slipped the stone into her pocket alongside the pouch containing the ever-present chicken foot.

She returned to the house and busied herself with her morning chores, cleaning, cooking, and cleaning some more. Surely life was supposed to hold more than that. Then again, she'd chosen her own fate when she'd married Jacob. It wasn't the first time she had questioned her own motives. She'd felt betrayed by the man she had loved. Her mind went to Brian, who she now knew had not betrayed her. What would her life have been like if he'd lived? She stared at the bruises on her arms. She was certain he would never have struck her in anger.

An image of Jacob flashed in her mind. He'd told her he killed Brian to protect her. Protect her from what? Love? Was Jacob so deranged that he thought living like this was better for her? She filled the mop bucket, watching the foam form in the bucket. Brian's image formed in the suds. As the water filled, it was replaced by the last image she'd had of him. He was sitting in the recliner, the needle still in the crook of his arm, foam edging from the sides of his mouth. She slammed her hand into the slurry of bubbles. The suds splashed along the edges of the bucket, parting the bubbles briefly before coming together once more. This time, they merely looked like suds in a bucket, nothing more.

She reached for the mop, smiling as Gulliver raced after the flowing ends. "Yeah, you won't like it so much in a minute."

Picking up the pail, she dipped the mop into the sudsy water. The mop slid across the floor with ease. Gulliver lost interest the second he felt the moisture on the floor, scurrying out of the room and disappearing down the hall. She thought about the number on the rock. Did that mean that Kevin had formed a plan? She wanted to call him to find out, but it was too risky. Jacob might be behind the closed door of his office; the man didn't miss much. Besides, he was too adept at sneaking up on her unaware. No, she'd have to bide her time.

"The house will keep. I'm famished," Jacob said, entering the room.

She jumped at the sound of his voice. She looked at the clock. Eleven o'clock, a tad early for lunch. "I'm almost finished with the floor. I'll make you lunch as soon as it dries."

"No, I'd prefer to go out today." He took the mop from her hand. "Get cleaned up."

She relinquished the mop without objection, wondering at his sudden thoughtfulness. While she relished the thought of getting out of the house, she knew better than to question his motives.

"Any particular dress code?"

He gave her a sour look. "Such a silly question, Abigail. One should always strive to look their best."

She took a deep breath. *It would be easier to look my best if my body were not covered with bruises.* She bit her tongue, not wishing to voice those words aloud. Instead, she left the room without further comment. Hurrying to her room, she showered and made a valiant effort to cover the bruises with heavy makeup. In the end, she opted for a lightweight sweater, which would cover her arms, but do nothing to abort the heat.

* * *

He'd surprised her by taking her to Muriel's, where he'd snagged prime seating on the second floor balcony overlooking Jackson Square. They dined on Eggs Benedict and grilled asparagus while watching the horse-drawn carriages carrying brightly clad tourists through the square. Abby relaxed against the back of her chair, lulled by the sounds of jazz, which floated up from the street below. Working on his second glass of wine, Jacob was tranquil, jovial even. Regaling her with stories, and hoarded secrets from his past. He filled her with antics of his childhood, even making mention of a brother, which she never knew he had, and speaking of his parents for the first time since she'd known him. This side of him was the man she had once cared for. Fun, kind, caring. This was the man she could have easily fallen in love with. She pulled at the sweater, sweltering in the heat. She caught a hint of purple, a sudden reminder of reality. This was merely a mirage, and she could not afford to let her guard down.

Seizing advantage of the public venue, she ventured a question, making sure to keep her voice just within the range of their table. "Were your parents cruel?"

His eyes flew open. "My parents? No. Why would you ask such a thing?"

She lowered her eyes. "I've just heard that abuse is hereditary."

"Abuse?" He seemed to contemplate the word as he took another sip of wine. "You consider me abusive?"

She fought not to laugh. "It has crossed my mind, yes."

He sat back in his chair as if this stunned him. "I'm afraid I do not share your assessment of the situation, Abigail."

She pulled at her sleeves just until the bruising showed. "No? Then what would you call it?"

He sighed as if the subject bored him. "Must we go through this again?"

She knew she was treading a fine line and decided to take another approach. "Okay, you call it discipline, right?"

He narrowed his eyes. "That is correct."

She let out her breath. "Okay, so where did you learn this form of discipline?"

"Learn it?"

The man was quite exasperating. "What made you say 'someday, when I get a wife, I must control every aspect of her life'?"

He took another sip of wine. He rolled the contents of his glass, staring into the liquid as if remembering something from long ago.

She remembered a brief conversation about the one that got away. It was worth a shot. "Was it her?"

His head jerked up as if she'd caught him in a memory. "Yes, I suppose it was."

She felt a sudden pang of sadness. If only the girl had not jilted him, then maybe she'd have had a chance at happiness. Maybe they both would. "So, in essence, you are punishing me for her mistake. Why couldn't you have given me the chance to love you?"

He set down the glass and pushed his plate to the side. "You are too much like her, Abigail. I couldn't take the chance."

Her eyes burned as she fought to remain in control. "So instead, you'd rather me hate you?"

He looked as if he'd been slapped. "You mustn't say things like that."

She'd gone too far. Oh, the words were true all right, but if he knew how she really felt, it would only make him trust her less. "I'm sorry, Jacob."

"I told you from the beginning, Abigail, you will grow to love me as soon as you learn to follow the rules." He smiled unexpectedly. "You've come so far already. You are turning into such a fine wife. The house is spotless and your cooking is phenomenal."

What was she a wife or an employee? She smiled sweetly. She had to bide her time, at least for now. "I'm glad you approve."

He reached for her hand. "I do."

The feel of his hand on hers made her skin crawl. She let him linger until she couldn't take it any longer, then pulled her hand away, standing abruptly. "If you'll excuse me, I have to use the ladies' room."

He looked as if he would protest, then relaxed. "By all means, my dear."

She made her way into the building and to the facilities. Once inside the stall, she withdrew her cell phone and punched in Kevin's number.

"Hello?"

"Kevin, it's me, Abby."

"Abby! I hoped you got my message." He sounded relieved.

"Yes, that was risky, but it worked. I can't talk long; Jacob will be looking for me."

"Where are you? I hear an echo."

"In the bathroom at Muriel's."

"Ooooh. Fancy, smancy. What's the occasion?"

"I haven't figured that out yet. So why the phone number?"

"I've been waiting for him to leave, but it seems he's quite the homebody lately," Kevin said.

"Yeah, tell me about it. I found the key, but haven't been able to use it."

"You found it? Really? Where'd you find it?"

Abby lowered her voice as someone entered the room. "In the console of his car."

There was complete silence.

"Kevin? Are you still there?"

"Yes, but I don't like this, it's too…"

"I know," she agreed, cutting him off. "But I have to find out what he's hiding. If it's drugs, then I can go to the authorities. Surely he can't have every agency in his pocket."

"Drugs?" he breathed into the phone.

"It's the only thing I can think of."

The sound of a toilet flushing reminded her she was not alone. "I've got to go before he comes looking for me."

"Abby, wait; I'm worried about you. You've got to get that key back before he notices it is gone."

She sighed. "I know, but I need the key and it is not like I can get away long enough to have a copy made."

"No, but I can." The excitement in Kevin's voice was palatable. "Leave the key by the grave as soon as you get home. I will take it and have a copy made, then you can put the original back before he notices it's gone."

She thought about it for a moment. "I think that could work. I just need to figure out how to get him to let me in the car without him. Don't worry; I'll figure out something."

"Okay, I will put another rock on the grave. Just put the key under it as soon as you get home, if you can. I will watch for you and then get it made today. I will turn on my porch light after I put the key back, but I am going to hang on to the key until you can use it."

She started to object, but knew it was too dangerous for Jacob to find her with the key. Besides, she would feel much better having a lookout when she ventured into the room.

Kevin drew her back to the conversation. "Hey, before you go, I've got a plan for your cat. No need to get into the details now. Call me when The Dick leaves the house and make sure the goon is watching."

She snickered. "The Dick?"

"Oh yes, that man is a DICK and I assure you I know a dick when I see one!"

Good ole Kevin; he knew how to make her smile. She was just about to answer when a knock on the bathroom door startled her.

"Got to go," she whispered into the phone. Shoving the cell into her pocket, she flushed the toilet.

She opened the door and stood face to face with a waitress. "I'm sorry to bother you, ma'am, but your husband was worried and asked me to come check on you. I'll let him know you were just on the phone."

Abby panicked, grabbing the lady's arm as she turned to leave. "Please don't!"

The lady started to pull away from her grip, but stopped when she caught sight of the bruises that peeked from under the sleeve of Abby's sweater. She relaxed, sympathy showing in her eyes. "You take all the time you need, honey. I'll tell him you are just finishing up."

Abby breathed a sigh of relief. "Thank you."

The waitress reached for the door and hesitated, turning her attention back to Abby.

"I don't mean to talk out of turn, but if I was you, I'd clear your call log," she said, nodding towards her pocket.

The woman's words nearly sent Abby into a panic. She had not even thought of that. She reached for her phone, fingers trembling as she deleted Kevin's number.

"I had a boyfriend who was a control freak. He was a crazy asshole, but he never laid a hand on me." Her eyes narrowed. "I'd of cut his dick off if he had."

Abby smiled a weak smile. She'd once had pretty much the same thought. It struck her that it is easy to be brave and give advice when the situation does not affect you personally. She remembered yelling at the television screen while she was watching a talk show, asking the woman how she could allow herself to be abused like that. Her face must have shown her frustration as the waitress shrugged, leaving the room without further comment.

Abby looked at her reflection in the mirror. She was not a weak person. She just needed to have a plan. She took a deep breath. Kevin had a plan. She felt like beating her head against the mirror, but refrained. Desperate times meant trusting unlikely heroes. Even though she didn't know what Kevin's plan was, she felt hopeful. Gulliver would soon be safe. Feeling optimistic for the first time in months, Abby washed her hands and pulled open the heavy door.

Jacob was leaning against the wall, waiting for her in the hallway. A frown pulled at his face. "I was getting worried."

"I got that when the waitress came looking for me. Didn't she tell you I would be right out?"

"She did."

"I had my cell phone with me. You should have called."

He shrugged his shoulders. "I didn't wish to disturb you."

"So you decided to send in a search party instead."

He took her by the arm, gently leading her through the dimly lit building. "It seemed more… personal."

No not personal, more like a stalker. She corrected, silently. "'Things' just took a bit longer than expected."

She followed him outside into the gleaming sunshine. Jazz music melded with a throng of people bustling freely down the street. The urge to follow was intoxicating. For a moment, she thought about joining the procession. Jacob must have sensed her indecision as he took her firmly by the arm and led her in the opposite direction.

CHAPTER TWENTY- TWO

Jacob eased the car into the driveway and shut off the ignition. As he got out of the car, Abby toyed with the strap of her sandal. Keeping a close eye on him, she silently slid her cell phone into the space between her seat and the center console.

Jacob appeared beside her door just as she was opening it. "Problem?"

She shifted her legs out of the car. "No, just adjusting the strap on my shoe."

His eyes grazed across her feet. "If they don't fit right, we can go shopping."

She loved shopping. She used to love it anyway, but now she was pretty sure Jacob would want to tag along, or worse, insist Merrick accompany her. Somehow, shopping did not have the appeal it once did. Besides there was nothing wrong with her shoes; she was just using them as a stall tactic. "These are fine. I just had to adjust the strap a bit."

He reached his hand to help her out of the car. "Still, we have not been shopping since your arrival. Your clothes seem to be fitting a bit snug. I think we need to get you a few new things, that…or a membership to the gym."

She stiffened. So he had noticed.

He opened his mouth as if to continue, then hesitated. Instead, he tilted his head as if to ask what she thought.

She huffed, pretending to be hurt. Better for him to think she was getting fat than to guess that she was pregnant. She kicked up her right foot and took off her sandal, then followed suit with the left. "I think I will take a walk through the backyard so I can work off all that wonderful food I just ate."

"The yard is not that big," he called after her.

"Not helping," she retorted over her shoulder.

She did three circles around the yard while he stood there watching. She had just started on a fourth when at last he turned and went inside. She decided to complete the lap, just in case he was still looking. Turning a final time, she eased the key out of her pocket, slowly making her way to Ned's grave. Lowering into a squat with her back to the house, she quickly placed the key under the rock. She did two more squats for good measure before heading back to the house.

Sweating profusely, she stopped at the sink for a drink of water. Gulliver jumped onto the counter next to her. Arching his back, he meowed his relief at seeing her. She shooed him off the counter just as Jacob entered the room.

"That cat is getting on my last nerve with all his bellowing," he growled.

Abby wondered at his sudden mood change and decided to tread with caution. "He is just a bit insecure of late."

"He is a pain in the ass. Maybe he would be happier outside."

She felt the start of a panic attack and struggled not to let it show. "We can't let him outside. He wouldn't survive."

A smile floated across his face as if that comment appealed to him. "Animals lived outside long before it became cool to allow them inside."

"Yes, but that was before cars and declawing. Now they are domesticated and all they know is the safety of being inside." She knew he was baiting her, but her defensive instincts had been engaged.

"Yes, well maybe we should send him out and see how he fares," Jacob said, eyeing the cat.

"He goes, I go," she threatened.

He chuckled. "Such an idle threat, my dear."

No, as soon as I make sure he is safe, I will plan my escape. "We are a package deal, remember?"

Another chuckle. "Oh, yes, lest I forget. Now why don't you get a shower? All of this foreplay has made me hungry."

She was incredulous. How could someone get turned on by arguing? "Are you friggin' kidding me?"

He moved closer, cupping her chin firmly in his hand. She attempted to pull free, but his grip was unrelenting. "I never kid about sex. Now hurry along. I'm starving."

He eased his hold and she pulled free, breathing deeply to quell the nausea that threatened. It was getting harder and harder not to recoil when he touched her. How much longer would she have to endure his wrath?

Gulliver sidled up to her. She screamed as Jacob's foot made contact with the cat's belly, sending him spiraling across the floor. Arching his back, Gulliver scurried out of the room, hissing his discontent.

Tears sprang from her eyes. She pulled herself up to her full height, ready for battle. "You asshole!"

He slapped her solid across the face. Her hand flew to the point of contact. He came in for a punch this time, which she deflected with her forearm. The impact caused her to cry out. He drew back again. This time, she was not as lucky; his fist clipped her in the left shoulder, sending her backwards. His breathing was coming in heavy breaths. Her eyes traced the length of him. His pants showed his erection. He was enjoying her pain. The realization left her cold and took the fight out of her. She let loose a stream of tears.

Jacob reached for her hand, helping her to her feet. She felt like she was moving in slow motion, could see what was happening, knew she was a part of it, but not able to connect her mind with her brain in order to stop it. It was as if her body had suddenly become detached from her. If only she could detach herself from the pain. Tears streamed down her face as he led her into the dark recesses of the bedroom.

* * *

Abby winced as she put away the last supper dish. The purple knot on her forearm caused her alarm. Glancing out the window, her heart leapt. Kevin had finally turned on his porch light. She moved around the kitchen, wiping the counters and drying the water from the sink. She swiveled in place, her eyes trailing each surface to insure she had not missed anything. The cabinets were void of any fingerprints; dishes were washed, dried, and put away. The counters had been washed and wiped dry, as had the table and center island. The floor was freshly swept, rugs shaken and placed precisely in line with the square edge of the fourth tile from the counter, just as Jacob preferred. She removed her apron, draping it on the hook. She took her time to make sure it was hanging properly with each tie perfectly in line before turning on the porch light and easing soundlessly out the back door.

She stood on the porch for several seconds, peering in the window, half expecting to see Jacob rushing down the hall to see what she was up to. When he did not appear, she hurried across the yard towards Ned's grave. The back light did not reach the far recesses of the yard. Reaching the grave, she groped around in the dark until she felt the rock. Lifting it, she let out a breath of relief. Her fingers trembled as she hastily tucked the key into the folds of her left pocket. She had a sudden feeling of being watched. Acting on instinct, she rose and walked the edge of the lawn. When she neared the porch, her suspicions were confirmed. Jacob was at the door, peering out at her.

He moved to the side to allow her to enter. "Odd time to take a walk."

She wanted to lash out at him, telling him she was trying to work off her dinner, but she didn't have it in her. She was still sore from their last go round. Instead, she stuck to the truth. At least the truth she'd invented. "I was looking for my cell phone. I seem to have lost it. I thought it might have fallen out of my pocket when I was walking earlier."

His eyes lowered to her pocket, causing her to inhale in alarm. If he chose to call her on her lie, he would discover not only the key, but the chicken's foot as well. He would demand to know where she'd gotten it. His own cell phone rang just as he took a step forward. Looking at the caller ID, he grimaced. "I have to take this."

Abby seized the opportunity, keeping her face set in a worried frown. "Okay, take your time. I think I will check to see if my phone is in the car."

She reached an expectant hand out for the keys. As he answered the phone, his eyes traced over her. Obviously deciding she would not get very far without shoes or wallet, he handed her the keys.

It was all she could do not to smile as she took them. She turned and walked calmly to the door. Once outside, she hurried to the car. Her hands shook as she unlocked the passenger door. Cursing the dome light, she used her body as a shield and opened the center compartment. She reached for the hidden section, hastily replacing the coveted key. She had no sooner closed the lid and wedged her hand between the seats when a shadow loomed over the car. Pretending not to notice, she brought her cell phone up in a show of victory.

"Ha, I found you!" she called out for good measure.

"So you did."

She jumped as if his voice had startled her.

"Holy crap! You scared the blazes out of me."

He rounded the car, opened the driver's side door, and lowered himself onto the seat. Not taking his eyes from her, he opened the center console, removed the top, thus exposing the hidden compartment. His fingers opened the partition and, for the first time, his eyes left hers. Seeing the key lying where he'd left it, a startled look crossed his face.

She swallowed hard. Had he seen her replace it?

The lines of his face relaxed as he shut the lower lid, replaced the contents, and closed the center console. So he hadn't known. He must have thought she'd come out to snoop. Slowly, she released the breath she'd been holding.

He reached out his hand. "Let me see the phone."

She relinquished the phone to him, watching as he scrolled through the call list. Relief washed over her as she silently thanked the waitress who'd had the forethought to have her clear her call log. Once again, she thought about calling him on the trust issue, but decided to leave well enough alone. Not finding anything to berate her about, he handed her the newfound phone.

She reached the back of the house, feeling like a weight had been lifted from her shoulders. Thank God, Kevin had insisted on making a copy so she could return the key. She mouthed the words thank you to the dark, somehow feeling he was watching.

Once inside, Jacob took up residence against the counter. His presence left her feeling uneasy. It was as if he was looking for something with which to rebuke her. She busied herself with filling Gulliver's water bowl. Gulliver seemed unharmed by Jacob's earlier rant; however, he remained wary of the man's presence, giving him a wide berth whenever he neared. Abby decided to distance herself from the cat for the time being, not coddling him in Jacob's presence for his own protection. It was obvious that Jacob was jealous of the attention she lavished on her animal friend. Her thoughts went to the child that she carried within her womb. She met Jacob's eyes, his stare so intent that she worried he was reading her mind. If Jacob was this jealous over attention spent on her animals, what would happen when her attention was spread even thinner? Chills raced along her spine as the seriousness of her situation hit her. It was no longer about her or even Gulliver. She had to protect the child. Her child. She swallowed hard against the fear.

Menacing gold flecks danced within her husband's narrowed eyes. He would never allow a child to come between them. She would have to find what she was looking for quickly, for she was running out of time.

CHAPTER TWENTY-THREE

Abby gripped the edge of the curtain with the tips of her fingers - the fabric pulled only a fraction away from the window. Once Jacob's car disappeared from sight, she dialed the number now committed to memory.

"Hello? Tell me The Dick has finally left the house." The voice sounded significantly irritated.

Abby hesitated. It was not the response she'd expected. "Yes, he just left, but I don't know for how long."

"Good. I'll be over as soon as I put Satan back in his cage."

"Satan?"

"Just unlock the door and keep an eye out for The Dick." The phone clicked off.

She hurried to unlock the back door, then retraced her steps. Seeing Merrick sitting at the wheel of his car, she breathed a sigh of relief. If Merrick had been brought in, Jacob would not be returning anytime soon. An angry growl from the back of the house drew her attention. She was not sure what was going on, but the ruckus chilled her to the bone. She had never heard that sound from Gulliver. Had Jacob returned after all? She ran down the hall, determined to save her four-legged friend.

Entering the kitchen, she stopped. Kevin stood in the center of the room; beside him sat two cat carriers. One empty, the other held an incredibly pissed off cat, which held a strong resemblance to Gulliver, who was investigating the crate, making throaty feline sounds of his own.

"What on earth?" she said on a giggle.

"Abby meet Satan. Satan, Abby."

Abby looked from Kevin to the cat. "I thought the plan was to get Gulliver out of here, not bring in a psycho cat."

He tilted his head. "Oh, Satan won't be staying."

She wrinkled her brows. "So tell me the plan. You do have a plan, don't you?"

"Of course I have a plan. I haven't lived with this evil little pussy for the past two weeks for nothing."

She peered at the cat. Black paws dug wildly at the metal bars; deep-throated growls emanating from within the plastic carrier echoed throughout the room.

"Two weeks?"

He rolled his eyes. "I assure you, it was not by choice. I was waiting for your call."

She smiled a weak smile. "Sorry. This is the first time he's left the house."

He waved off her apology. "Don't apologize for The Dick, Sunshine. Let's just get this plan into action before he gets home, or we are going to have to come up with something new? No way is this piranha setting foot back into my house."

She giggled. "Okay, so what do we do?"

Kevin didn't hesitate. He picked up the empty carrier and placed it on the center island. "Okay, first, put your little man into this crate."

She hesitated. "Where are you going to take him?"

He patted her hand. "We have to get him out of here. He can stay with me."

A lump formed in her throat. "You'll... you'll take care of him?"

"No, I'm going to toss him in the bayou and let the alligators feed on him. Of course I'll take care of him. What kind of question is that?"

"I'm sorry. I'm just not sure how he will behave if he doesn't have me around. He's been a bit...unsettled with Ned gone."

He wiggled his fingers near the other carrier. The act was met with a hiss; an angry claw snaked out of the front grate. "Anything has to be better than this saber tooth. Now can we please hurry?"

Abby swooped down, picked up Gulliver, who growled a warning to the other cat. She held him close, as if it were to be the last time she saw him. Tears welled in her eyes by the time she coaxed him into the empty carrier. Wiping them away, she faced Kevin. "Now what?"

Kevin picked up Gulliver's carrier and headed for the door. "First things first; let me get him out of here in case The Dick comes back."

Deciding a check was in order, she hurried to the bedroom, peeked out the side window, relaxing only after verifying the driveway was empty. A quick check of the front window ensured that Merrick was still in place. She arrived in the kitchen just as Kevin was returning.

"I opened the carrier so he can settle down and get used to his surroundings." Seeing her face, he added, "Don't worry; you will have him back in no time."

She smiled, then turned her attention to the hissing cat. "Don't you think Jacob will notice the change?"

"Oh, he's not going to stay." He picked up the carrier. "Do you have a water jug?"

"Yes."

"Good. Get it and fill it up with water," he instructed before heading toward the front of the house.

Hoping he knew what he was doing, she did as she was told, then joined him in the front room. He had set the carrier on the floor, the opening facing the front door.

"Okay, so here is the plan. You will go out and check the flowers on the porch. Take your time. You want to make sure your babysitter sees you."

"Merrick."

"What?"

"His name is Merrick."

He shrugged. "Okay, make sure Merrick sees you. Make a show of it, and then come in to get the water container. Go out and water the flowers. Just make sure he is watching. When you open the door to come back inside, I will release the beast."

Her eyes flew open. "And Merrick will think that it's Gulliver that runs away!"

A smile spread across Kevin's face. "That's the plan."

"It's brilliant!"

His smile broadened. "I have my moments."

She wrapped her arms around him. "Oh, Kevin, how can I ever repay you?"

He pulled back, holding her at arm's length, his face serious. "You can follow me to my house and let me get you out of this mess."

She ran a hand through the length of her hair. "I can't, Kevin. Not yet."

His mouth quivered. "Your life is more precious than that of your cat, you know."

She blinked to ward off the tears that threatened. "If I thought I could get away, I would, but Pearl insists I have to stay until the timing is right."

His eyes narrowed. "Does Pearl know the man is beating you black and blue?"

She swallowed. "She knows."

"And that is okay with her?" His voice was incredulous.

"It's complicated."

"So un-complicate it."

"I will tell you everything, but let's finish this first, okay?" She nodded toward the cat, who was trying desperately to escape from its enclosure.

He let out a sigh. "Fine."

She kissed him on the cheek. "Why didn't I marry you instead?"

His mood lightened. "Sunshine, you know I love you, but I'm afraid you're not my type."

"And what type is that?"

"Tall, dark, and swinging, and if I have to tell you what part is swinging, then we have more troubles than a pissed off pussy." He wagged his eyebrows for emphasis.

She threw her hands up in response. "Forget I asked!"

He ushered her out the door, making sure to stay out of view.

Abby fluttered about the porch, peeking into the flowerpots, pulling out dried flowers, and plucking at imaginary weeds. She kept her head lowered, turning her eyes sideways to see if Merrick was watching. When she was sure he was, she pulled down one of the heavy hanging baskets, setting it on the railing before returning to the house.

"Is he still watching?" she asked Kevin, who was peering out of the window.

"Girl, he didn't take his eyes off you once. That man gives me the willies, and not in a good way."

She rubbed at her arms. "Me too." She lifted the water jug. "Ready?"

"Sunshine, I was born ready." He gave her a quick peck on the cheek. "Make it a good show."

She nodded and returned to the porch. She emptied the contents of the water jug and turned toward the door. "It's show time," she said only loud enough to be heard from inside.

She closed her eyes briefly before opening the door. *Please let this work.* She opened the latch and squelched a scream as a streak of black and white fur scrambled past her and hustled down the street. She turned, amazed at the speed at which the cat had run away. *Make it real, Abby,* she cautioned.

"Gulliver!" she screamed. Tossing aside the water jug, she raced down the sidewalk after the fleeing feline.

"Gulliver, come back! What's gotten into you?"

She was completely out of breath by the time Merrick caught up with her. He was faring no better, wheezing, the cell phone plastered to his ear. "Boss man says you are to go home."

She looked about wildly. "No, I have to find Gulliver."

His pitted face remained impassive. "I have my orders."

She placed her hands on her hips, struggling to recover her breath. "Not without my cat."

His mouth twitched. "I was told to take you home."

She tucked her hair behind her ear, wiped the sweat from her face with the back of her hand, and glared at him. "Just as soon as I find my cat."

Merrick's eyes roved across her heaving breast. "I was hoping you'd say that."

He moved towards her.

She took a step back. "What are you going to do?"

He flexed his massive arms. "I aim to carry you if need be."

Okay, this was not going as planned. "You wouldn't."

He returned the phone to his pocket. "Nothing would please me more."

She ducked out of the way just as he reached for her.

"Keep your filthy hands off of me," she hissed.

His eyes twinkled. "Jacob told me you have spunk. Told me to use whatever means necessary to get you back to the house."

"I'll scream," she warned.

His mouth turned up. "I'm counting on it."

She stiffened; her charade had gone on long enough. The cat was nowhere in sight; it was safe to return home. "Then I expect you to go find him for me."

She stepped around him with the thought of heading home. He took her by the arm, roughly leading her up the sidewalk.

"Get your hands off of me," she said through clinched teeth.

He tightened his hold on her. "Not until you get what's coming to you."

Her mouth went dry. Surely he wouldn't do anything to anger his boss. But what if Jacob had indeed given his permission? No, he wouldn't. She was almost certain of it. "You wouldn't dare."

His grip lessened. She pulled away from him as she reached the bottom stair of the porch. He made a move to follow her up.

Playing her hunch, she turned toward him.

"My husband uses you to do his dirty work, but I assure you, you can be replaced. If you step one foot in my house, I will tell him you raped me." She prayed he couldn't see her trembling, prayed even harder that she had not just given him an idea.

He stopped in place as if debating. "You are playing a very dangerous game, Mrs. Buckley."

She glared at him. "I was only trying to find my cat."

He turned, heading back to his car without further comment.

Her heart was still pounding as she entered the house. Shutting the door, she stifled a giggle. Kevin stood behind the door with a large hardbound book poised sinisterly above his head.

"Um, watcha doing, Kev?" she asked.

"I was going to protect you." Blinking, he lowered the book.

"Thinking of reading him to death, were you?"

He returned the book to the table. "It was the closest thing I had."

She nodded towards the same table. "I think next time, you would fare better with the lamp."

Ignoring her teasing, he moved to the window and peered out. "That man is S.C.A.R.Y.!"

She could still feel where Merrick's hand had gripped her arm. Bringing her fingers up, she rubbed at the area in question.

"What on earth is that?" Kevin asked in a horrified tone.

She followed his gaze to her forearm. Self-consciously, she lowered her arm. "I deflected a punch."

He raised her arm, inspecting it. "Is it broken?"

She shrugged. "Don't know."

"Does it hurt?" His voice was nearly a whisper.

"Not as bad as it did at first."

"That's it; you are coming with me this instant," he asserted.

She sank onto a cushion near the window where she could see out, yet not be seen from outside. As much as she wanted to investigate the office, she knew it was only a matter of time before Jacob returned. Pulling her knees to her chest, she motioned for Kevin to sit.

He joined her on the couch, turning his body to face her. Kicking off his shoes, he pulled his legs up to mimic hers. Leaning his chin on his knees, he looked at her expectantly.

"Where to start?" she mused.

"How about the beginning?"

"I'm not sure if we have that much time. Merrick called him." From her vantage point, she could see Merrick sitting behind the wheel of his car.

"Do you love him? Is that why you refuse to leave? I've heard about women who enjoy this sort of thing, but somehow, you don't strike me as the type."

Her eyes returned to Kevin. "No, I've never loved him. There was a time when I thought I could learn to, but then he showed me who he really was."

"When was that?"

She bit her lip remembering. "On our wedding day."

"He beat you?"

She gripped her legs tighter. "Among other things."

Kevin lifted his eyes. "Such as?"

Another peek out the window. "He raped me."

"And yet you stayed."

"It's complicated."

"So you've said."

"I have no family. There was no place else to go. No way to get there."

"How about the car you drove up in."

"I wanted to. Threatened to even, but I had no purse. No money. Not even a driver's license. Even if I had all those things, I didn't have any keys."

Seeing his questioning look, she continued. "Shortly after I got here, Jacob took me sightseeing. While we were out, someone stole my purse with everything in it."

He sat back a little. "Seems a little convenient."

"I didn't think so at the time, but now I know Jacob was involved. It was his way of controlling me."

"I agree. But still it doesn't add up. You've been out by yourself several times. You could have left. Gone to the police or a woman's shelter even…"

She caught movement outside, watched as a car eased past the house. "Jacob was drugging me at the time. He told me if I went to the police, he would tell them I was a drug addict and have me arrested. He told me he had the police in his pocket."

"And you believed him?"

"I had every reason to." She placed her feet on top of his, needing the connection. "The day my purse got taken, I met an elderly lady on the street. She spoke very thick Cajun and some French. She told me that Jacob was the son of the Devil."

Kevin blew out a low whistle. "Shit."

"Yeah."

"And yet you married him anyway."

"She said it in French and, at the time, I didn't know what it meant. I asked Jacob and he told me it meant I was marrying a very old man."

"That was nice of him."

"Wasn't it, though?"

He wiggled his feet under hers. "Okay, so I'm assuming he asked you where you heard it?"

When she spoke, her voice cracked. "He did and I...I told him."

He raised his head with sudden awareness. "Eva Radoux?"

She nodded.

"You're not saying that the Dick killed her?"

"Not him; Merrick," she said through a stream of tears.

"Oh, sweetie!" He grasped her hands. "No wonder you're scared. But you can't stay here out of fear."

"I'm not. Well, not totally," she corrected. "Remember when I said it was complicated? Well, now Pearl is telling me that I need to know the truth first. She said if I leave now... Jacob will find me."

She reached into her pocket and produced the pouch. "She, Pearl, gave me this chicken foot to protect me."

His hand rested delicately upon the knot. "Some protection."

She shoved the pouch back in her pocket on a sob. "He hasn't killed me yet."

A reflection caught her eye. Jumping up, she pulled him from the couch. "He's here."

Kevin was halfway down the hall when she called to him, "Kevin, your shoes!"

She tossed them to him and sank back onto the couch. Reaching a hand to brush away the tears, she stopped. Letting the tears flow, she waited for Jacob, knowing he would expect her to be distraught over losing her beloved cat.

CHAPTER TWENTY-FOUR

Abby was still sobbing when Jacob entered the house. Dropping his briefcase at the door, he crossed the room in four quick steps, sank to the couch beside her, and scooped her into his arms. It was all she could do not to recoil from his embrace, although she did flinch when at last Jacob extended a hand, tenderly wiping the tears from her face. She wondered at his sudden sensitivity.

"He's gone." The words came out on a sob, as if her heart were breaking. She wasn't acting. While she didn't doubt Kevin would take care of him, she already missed her cat. He had a knack for climbing onto her lap, helping to take her mind off of whatever was troubling her.

"I know, Merrick told me." His voice was unnaturally compassionate.

"Merrick." The name rolled off her tongue like acid. "He wouldn't let me look for him."

"That's my fault. I thought it would be best if Merrick looks; he's searching now."

She stiffened. What if Merrick did find the cat? Then Jacob would know it wasn't Gulliver. No, she would simply tell him he'd found the wrong black and white cat.

Her hesitation had not been lost on Jacob. "You're not happy he's looking for the cat?"

Another sob. "I'd rather not have him anywhere near that animal."

"I doubt he's worried about a cat."

"I was talking about Merrick. He's the animal. He manhandled me today. "

"He didn't hurt you?" His voice was tight.

Again, she wondered at his sudden compassion. "No."

"So tell me what happened to make him run off like that."

"I don't know. He hasn't seemed himself since... Then today, he seemed like a whole different cat all together." That was putting it lightly. She remembered the pissed off imposter clawing at the grate with fierce determination. "I was feeling claustrophobic, so I decided to water the flowers."

She sniffed for good measure. "I'd just finished and was coming back in, when he bolted out the door, like someone had shot him with a rubber band, and took off running down the sidewalk. He never even looked back. He's gone... my Gulliver is gone!" She let loose with a newfound flood of tears.

He rocked her back and forth in his arms. "That's why I've never had any use for animals. You love them, take care of them, and they leave you the first opportunity they get." His voice sounded pained.

Stifling her tears, she turned to him. "You sound as though you speak from experience."

He sat back against the cushion. "I had a dog once. An old brown and black mutt, beagle something, I think. He and I would go everywhere together. We'd play in the creek. Take long walks in the woods. One time, we stumbled into a hornets' nest. We both got stung repeatedly. I made it home, even though to this day, I don't see as to how I made it. My eyes were swollen shut. I couldn't even see by the time I arrived. Rex, that was the dog's name, didn't make it home for three days, but he did finally come home. I doctored him, took care of him, even stayed up with him, then one day, he up and left. Never did even find a trace of him."

Listening to him, she felt her sadness ebb. Why couldn't Jacob be like this all the time? "Maybe whatever happened was beyond his control," she offered.

His mouth tightened. "He made his choice. Everyone makes a choice."

"You're talking about her again. What was her name?"

He answered without hesitation, proving her right. "Clarice."

Abby felt as if she truly hated the woman, feeling it was somehow because of her that Jacob treated her so badly. She had wounded his soul, hardened his heart, and, in the process, ruined Abby's life. She wondered, not for the first time, what life would have been like if Jacob were normal. The thought passed as quickly as it had occurred, because she knew if Jacob had been normal, she would never have married him. She would instead be living with the man she had loved. Brian. The thought brought on a whole new round of tears. Reminding her once more that the man who was being so compassionate about her missing cat had admitted to killing the man she loved. Jacob, thinking she was still grieving over the loss of her cat, pulled her close, murmuring softly into her hair. She gritted her teeth against his touch, his closeness repulsing her. When at last her sobbing subsided, he released her.

"I'm starving," he said, his voice once again light. "I think a pizza is just the thing to cheer you up."

She started to protest, then realized just how hungry she actually was. "Should I order something?"

"No, we will go out. You said yourself you were feeling claustrophobic."

She hesitated, not wanting to seem overly eager. "What if Gulliver comes back?"

"I'll have Merrick come back and watch the house. If the cat comes back, he will let us know." He cast a look towards the door. "Don't worry; I'll make him promise to be on his best behavior."

* * *

They walked through the mall, hand in hand. Dinner had been just what she needed to rejuvenate her. While still tired, she felt as if a weight had been lifted from her shoulders. She might not be safe yet, but Gulliver was. If it wasn't for Pearl's warning, she might be tempted just to slip away into the crowd, never to return. While the thought had some merit, she now worried about not only her safety, but that of her unborn child. If Pearl was right, she had to stay, at least long enough to get her answers. Did she need them? Answers? Pearl seemed to think so. But what if Pearl had been wrong? Doubtful. The woman knew where she was going to be at any given time, knew where she was hurting, and even had told her she was pregnant. No, not likely that Pearl was mistaken about the importance of staying.

Jacob stopped in front of a store, bringing her out of her musing. She glanced at the sign, suddenly feeling dizzy. Only Jacob's grip on her elbow kept her from teetering backwards while reading the words "maternity apparel."

"You know?" she whispered.

He chuckled. "Abby, you are getting quite the gut. And unless you've been sneaking a six pack every night, then I think it fairly obvious you are pregnant."

"You're not mad?"

"When an opportunity presents itself, you run with it."

She quirked her head at him. "What the hell does that mean?"

"It means, my dear Abigail, that we will deal with things as they come our way. While your pregnancy is not optimal, it does present a golden opportunity."

"Such as?"

"For the time being, it means the opportunity to buy you some new clothes," he said, ushering her into the store.

They were greeted by a large woman with smiling eyes. "Welcome! We were expecting you," she said with ease.

Abby felt herself tense. They'd been expecting her? Just how long had Jacob known? Her unease was short lived as the woman greeted the next customer in the very same way. Of course, it was a maternity shop. She smiled inwardly at the play on words.

Jacob stood near the dressing room door, playing the attentive father-to-be, giving the thumbs up or eye roll for each outfit she tried on. She felt slightly guilty about enjoying the sudden onset of attention. She left the store with seven new outfits, which Jacob insisted on carrying. He was good at playing the doting husband. Maybe she should have let him in on the news before.

They strolled through the mall with the appearance of a couple in love. Smiling, laughing on occasion, and making pleasant small talk. She followed without question as Jacob led her into a high-end jewelry store. He stopped in front of a ring case, lowered the bags to the floor, and beckoned a salesperson who was all too happy to oblige.

A stocky gentleman, not much taller than Abby, adjusted his perfectly tailored black suit before hurrying in their direction. His pupils were dilated in anticipation of a sale. Abby, feeling like a lamb who'd suddenly found itself in the middle of a pride of lions, eased closer to her husband, suddenly grateful for Jacob's presence.

The salesman ran a quick pass over his balding scalp, as if to insure the placement of his comb over. He greeted them with enthusiasm, flashing a cigarette-stained smile. "Good evening sir, madam. Robert Kerns at your service."

Producing a rather large ring of keys, Kerns waved an open palm over the glass case. "Are you looking for something in particular or can I get you one of everything?"

Abby looked to Jacob to gaze his reaction of the greedy little man. Jacob's face remained nonplussed, his eyes searching the contents of the display case. Abby followed his gaze, her eyes resting on a rather large, glimmering stone. She caught her breath when Jacob gestured at the same stunning two-carat diamond, which rested atop a thin, white gold band.

"Excellent choice, sir, simply splendid." The sparkle in the man's eyes matched the stone as he removed the ring and handed it to Abby. Jacob smiled his approval as she slid the monstrosity onto the ring finger of her right hand.

Kerns exhaled heavily as the ring passed over the knuckle with ease. "It's as if it were made just for you, my dear."

She met his gaze, half expecting to see dollar signs instead of the green irises that were beaming back at her.

"I'm afraid it's a bit large," she replied in return.

He reached for her hand, roughly examining the fit. He smiled triumphantly. "Nonsense, the fit is perfect."

She pulled her hand from his clammy grasp. "I was talking about the size of the stone."

Jacob reached for her hand, judiciously inspecting the ring for himself. "I agree with Mr. Kerns here; the fit is perfect."

The remark evoked a giddy chuckle from the man behind the counter.

Kissing the ring atop her finger, Jacob met her eyes. "We'll take it."

"But…" Didn't she have any say in the matter?

Apparently not, as Kerns pulled himself to his full pint-sized height, turning his full attention to Jacob. "Would you like to put this on your account, sir?"

Jacob shook his head. "No, I'll pay cash."

Kerns nearly choked. "But, sir, the ring is eleven thousand dollars." The words came out on a squeak.

Abby's mouth went dry as she blinked at the stone upon her hand. Eleven thousand dollars.

Jacob tilted his head at Kerns. "You do take cash, do you not?"

Kerns struggled to regain his composure. "Why yes, most assuredly. Cash is splendid."

"Good." Jacob reached into the lapel of his jacket, pulled out a wad of cash and began counting off hundred-dollar bills.

Abby wasn't sure who was more stunned, her or Kerns, who was now holding onto the counter with whitened knuckles. She'd never seen such a large pile of cash. Apparently, poor Kerns was caught off guard as well, as his face now matched his whitened knuckles. At this point, she was not sure if the poor man was even breathing. The amount of cash Jacob had placed on the counter, and the remaining stack that was stuffed back into his coat reinforced what she'd suspected. Only the drug cartel would carry around that kind of cash. The bold ring suddenly felt heavier than before.

Kerns scooped up the bills, motioned for what appeared to be the manager to follow, and hurried to the rear of the store, presumably before Jacob could change his mind and declare it all a nasty joke.

Lowering her hand for the first time, Abby finally found her voice. "Do you always carry that kind of cash?"

He laughed. "No, my love, only when I procure a most delectable business deal. Today was rather productive, even if I was called away from the negotiations early."

Knowing he was referring to her losing Gulliver, she allowed her lip to quiver.

It worked. Jacob reached for her hand, moving it back and forth to allow the light to catch in the stone. "There, there, Abigail, if this diamond ring doesn't do the trick, Papa will find you something else to make you smile."

A chill raced up her spine. Papa? He was treating her like a child, trying to buy her love. Next, he'd be comforting her with ice cream.

Kerns returned, beaming at Jacob as if he'd just met his new best friend. He carried a receipt for the purchase, a black velvet ring box, and letter of authenticity for the diamond. He briefly explained the letter of authenticity, stressing the importance of keeping it safe in case Jacob ever decided to trade up for a larger stone.

Jacob listened intently, but didn't comment when the man paused for effect.

On a sigh, Kerns placed everything into a small black plastic bag, and slid it in Jacob's direction. "Here you go Mr...."

Jacob took the bag, tucking it into the pocket where he'd stored the money before stooping to pick up the clothing bags that rested on the floor. Without giving the man the information he'd been fishing for, Jacob turned toward Abby. "Come along, my dear, I have a sudden desire for ice cream."

CHAPTER TWENTY-FIVE

Much to Abby's surprise, she didn't have to wait long for her next reprieve. Two days had passed since Gulliver had been moved to safety. Disappointment washed over her as she opened the door to allow Kevin entry.

Picking up on her disappointment, he gave her the once over. "What's with the Debbie Downer?"

"I guess a part of me thought you were going to bring Gulliver with you," she said, closing and locking the door behind him.

He shook his head. "Too dangerous. Besides, he's fine. When I left, he was munching on a jelly doughnut."

"Surely you're joking?"

The question was met with a shrug.

"So did Dicky buy it?" Kevin asked, changing the subject.

"Yes, he's been rather nice since then."

He looked her over. "How nice?"

Abby lifted her hand for inspection.

His brows shot up as he blew out a low whistle. "And just what did you have to do for that?"

She pulled her hand back. "I didn't DO anything."

His glance moved to her belly, which protruded slightly under a new flowing top.

"Well, somebody did something."

His lips formed a pout as he turned his head away. "I'm hurt. I thought best friends were supposed to be the first to know."

His statement took her by surprise. It was true; Kevin was her best friend. Actually, he was her only friend, but that was beside the point. "I wanted to tell you, but Pearl told me not to."

"She actually said that? The Voodoo Priestess actually mentioned me by name?" he questioned, his voice rising.

"No, she didn't mention you by name." She reached out a hand to calm him, rubbing the fabric of his sleeves. His sleeves? It was August in New Orleans.

She took a step back, her eyes roving over his attire. He was dressed completely in black. Black snug-fitting jogging pants, a matching long-sleeved warm-up jacket, and black sneakers. A black camera and sunglasses completed the look. He looked like a bad eighties joke. She fought to maintain control of her voice. "Kevin, what the hell are you wearing?"

He pulled at the snug fabric. "I'm channeling my inner Tom. Do you like it?"

A giggle escaped her. "Your inner Tom?"

His chin rose a notch. "Tom Cruise, *Mission Impossible*. I can't possibly do any breaking and entering if I don't channel my inner Tom."

Another giggle. "We're not breaking and entering. You have the key and this is my house, remember? You did bring the key, right?"

He became indignant. "Of course I have the key. And if I want to channel Tom, I can channel Tom."

Pushing past her, he started down the hall.

If it had not been for the seriousness of the situation, Abby was certain she would have been rolling on the floor, giving in to the fits of laughter the situation warranted. Somehow, she could not picture Tom Cruise tiptoeing along the corridor in an ill-fitting jogging suit. She bit her lip as she followed Kevin down the hallway, humming the theme song to *Mission Impossible*.

They peeked out the front window before retracing their steps, stopping just in front of the closed door that led to Jacob's office.

Kevin produced a shiny silver key, from where she didn't care to know. "Are you ready to do this?"

Taking the key, she eased it into the hole with trembling fingers. Turning it to the side, she pushed open the door. They were met with a warm, brightly lit room. The curtains had been pulled open. The effect was a pleasant, sun-filled room. They both stood, mouths gaping, as if they'd anticipated Satan's lair.

Kevin was the first to speak. "Not quite what I was expecting."

Abby entered the room, careful to stay out of view of the window.

"Seems rather ordinary," she admitted.

Kevin went to the desk, opened the laptop, and waited for it to spring to life. He nearly leapt for joy when it came awake. "Oh, sugar, we are in luck. Dick didn't password protect his secrets."

While Kevin engrossed himself with the contents of the computer, Abby pulled open drawers, looking through the contents, careful to leave things exactly as she found them. Not finding anything of significant importance, she searched the bookshelves before moving to a cabinet that adorned the rear wall. She'd just opened the cabinet when Kevin called to her.

"I think I found something."

Closing the door, she joined him at the desk.

He pointed to the screen. "A locked file."

"And that means what precisely?"

"I'm not sure, but I think it needs a closer look. The laptop is not password protected and so far as I can tell, neither is anything else, except this file."

She nodded her head. "So if that one is locked, then there must be something in there he thinks needs protecting."

"Ding ding, give the lady a prize."

Kevin sent the file to his flash drive and closed the laptop. "Just in case he comes home anytime soon."

At his words, she peered out the window before turning to him in question. Seeing her face, he elaborated. "If he comes home and the laptop is warm, he will know it's been running."

She smiled impressed with Kevin's sleuthing skills. "Impressive."

"Girlfriend, you ain't seen nothin' yet."

She walked to the closet, surprised to find that the door was locked. "Huh."

He came up beside her. "Problem?"

She shrugged. "Not sure why he'd need a locked door inside of a locked room."

He quirked an arched brow. "And a closet door at that."

"Yes...No! It's not a closet; it leads to the attic!"

He tested the handle once more. "Are you sure? Our houses are pretty much the same. My access is in the hallway."

She hurried to the desk in search of a key. "No, it's not in the hall. I think things got moved around with the remodel. It has to be in there, I heard Jacob in the attic the first night I arrived, and yet I've never seen the stairs."

She found the keys she'd seen during her earlier search and handed them to him. He dropped to his knees, testing each one.

"None of these," he said, handing the set back to her. "You didn't find any single keys?"

"No, I don't think so. Why?"

"I just get the feeling that he'd keep this key separate."

"Unless it is on the key ring with the key to the office."

"I'm sure he has one on his key ring, but there has to be a spare." He was still on his knees, wiggling a thin metal tool into the keyhole.

"Is that what I think it is?" she asked, moving in closer to see.

"Sure is."

"Kevin, should I ask where you got a lock-picking kit?"

He looked up at her, incredulous. "Why, from my underwear, of course. You don't see any pockets hiding in this jogging suit, do you?"

Her eyes grew wide. "Oh my God! I didn't want to know where you kept it. I asked where you found it."

"Oh, at the spy store, of course." He had returned to work, trying to jimmy the lock.

She threw her hands up. "Of course."

A faint click penetrated the air. "Eureka!"

They each leaned inside the darkened closet, both vying to be the first to see some great mystery. What they saw were stairs to nowhere, braced along the back wall. A sleek silver handrail stood out on either side of the stairs. Seconds later, Abby was surprised to see a flashlight beam shining on the closet ceiling, revealing what appeared to be a flush opening.

"Kevin, where did you get...never mind," she added when she saw his gaze shift to his crotch.

She tried unsuccessfully to stifle a giggle.

"What?"

"Nothing." She snorted.

"What?" he repeated shining the light in her face, a move that was unnecessary in the outer room.

"I was just thinking." More laughter.

"Out with it already!"

She burst into hysterics. "I was just... just thinking that there seems to be a lot of unused room in your underwear."

He switched off the light and crossed the room in a huff.

She stopped laughing and ran after him. "I'm sorry, Kevin. Honest I am. I didn't mean to insult your private parts."

"I guess I'm the only one who is taking your situation seriously."

"I'm taking this seriously. I promise. I just giggle when I get nervous. Please come back in the room. I need you to channel your inner Tom some more so I can find what I'm supposed to be looking for," she pleaded.

He picked up her hand, tilting his head at the ring. "You sure you still want to leave the man that buys you a rock this size? The interest payments alone will cost him a small fortune."

She pulled her hand away, did a quick check outside, and returned to the closet. "I did not marry him for his money. I sure as hell do not intend on staying with him for his money."

Kevin eased up beside her. "So why then?"

"Why what?"

"Why'd you marry the guy?"

She laughed, but this time nothing was funny. "He made me feel safe. Protected."

He flipped on the flashlight and shined it around the darkened closet. "Yeah, so how's that working out for you?"

"Not so good at the moment," she admitted.

The flashlight glinted off something in the roof above them. Kevin turned to her, his voice serious. "So why would a person choose to lock the attic that is behind the locked closet, which is in his locked office?"

He shined the light so she could see the silver padlock.

"Maybe that's where he keeps the drugs," she whispered.

"You've said that before. What makes you so sure he is into drugs?"

"It was only a hunch before. After the other night, I'm fairly certain of it. It's the only thing that makes sense."

"How so?"

She held up her hand. "He paid cash for the ring."

Kevin's eyes flew open in response. "That is at least a ten thousand-dollar ring."

"Eleven and some change."

He blew out a long whistle.

"Yep."

"That's a lot of dough."

"Sure was."

"Who carries around that kind of cash?"

"A drug lord?"

"Oh, sugar, what on earth have you gotten yourself into? No wonder the Voodoo Priestess says you cannot leave without finding the truth. Someone with that kind of money has to have power. He could find you and..." He stopped without completing his sentence.

She must have looked as worried as she felt because he wrapped his arms around her.

"It's going to be fine, little dove. We will find out all his dirty little secrets and you can fly away from here." He kissed the top of her head before releasing her.

She blinked away the tears that threatened and pulled the chicken's foot from her bosom. "I know. How can it not be okay when I have you and Pearl looking after me?"

He laughed unexpectedly. "Why is it okay for you to keep a dead animal carcass in your bra but not for me to keep a flashlight in my underwear?"

She caressed the rough edges of the foot. "Did you get your flashlight from a voodoo priestess?"

His eyes lit on the yellowed foot. "Well, if I did, I don't think I'd want it anywhere near my fountain of love."

Fountain of love? *Ewww!*

She continued to worry the ends of the talons. "I rather like the feel of it against my skin."

"Really? Next time you see Miss Pearl, could you maybe put in a good word for me?"

She stuffed the foot back where she'd found it. "Can we please just focus on getting what we need and getting out of here?"

He held the flashlight out to her in response. She shook her head, refusing to touch it.

He let out an exaggerated sigh. "Listen, Sunshine, one of us has to climb the ladder and unless you know how to pick a lock, then it's going to have to be me."

She took the light, holding it gingerly between her fingers. The effect was the flashlight drooping downward, the beam shining unproductively across the floor. His brow furrowed as he closed his eyes.

"You need to hold it a bit tighter, Sunshine. The big end needs to point up."

She recoiled in horror. "Do you know where that thing's been? I'm not touching it."

He took two fingers and placed them momentarily against the bridge of his nose. "Why does it feel as if we've just recreated the story of my life over the last four minutes?"

Without waiting for her to answer, he took the flashlight, placed it firmly in her hand, and wrapped her fingers solidly around the base. "When you are holding something of that size, it should know its being held."

He shook his head at her. "It's not going to bite you. And for the record, it wasn't where your dirty little mind thinks it was. Now shine the light at the lock."

She giggled and he glared at her. "I said lock, Abby, not cock."

Turning, he grabbed hold of the rail, carefully climbing the steps. Reaching the top, he ran his fingers along the edge of the opening.

"What are you doing?" she asked, following his fingers with the light.

"Looking for a key."

"I thought you were going to pick it?"

"I am," he replied after the search turned up empty. "But it would be easier with the key."

She held the light steady as he fiddled with the lock. "So how is it you are so good at picking locks?"

He paused for a second. "My father was a cop. Turns out, he didn't much like having a son like me, so every so often, he'd lock me in the closet."

He resumed his work with the lock. "Every now and then, he'd forget he left me there. After two or three times, I decided to get creative and started finding things that would fit in the lock so I could open it."

"Oh, Kevin, how awful."

"I got so good at picking the locks that he stopped putting me in the closet. I guess he figured it was time I came out. I never understood why I needed that skill until now."

He peered down at her and winked. "If my dad hadn't been such a homophobe, then I wouldn't be any use at all to you."

She heard a grunt, followed by an exclamation of victory. "One small step for gay men everywhere!"

He pushed open the hatch, the lock dropping to the floor with a thud. "What the hell?"

She craned her neck upward. "What is it? What do you see?"

A reflection flittered across the closet door. She turned just in time to see Jacob pulling into the driveway.

"KEVIN! He's back!" She tossed up the lock. "Hurry!"

Lock in place, Kevin slid down the rails without the aid of the stairs and locked the closet.

"Kevin," Abby whispered, "the window."

He crouched low to avoid detection and met her at the door. Abby locked the office as Kevin hurried to the back of the house. "Call me when the coast is clear," he called in a hushed voice.

Abby struggled to control her breathing, wondering what it was Kevin had seen in the attic.

CHAPTER TWENTY-SIX

Abby pushed the heavy water-laden cart down the aisle. At Jacob's insistence, she was stocking up on water. Hurricane Katrina was crossing Florida and projected to enter the Gulf of Mexico. Knowing people would be making a run for supplies, he'd sent Abby out ahead of the crowd, telling her to take her time.

She glanced at the ring that sparkled with each movement. Jacob had been so amicable since finding out about the baby. She knew the reprieve was temporary at best, but it gave her hope that she would be able to find a way out before things got worse. She knew not to let her guard down, not after everything he'd done, everything he'd put her through. He was, after all, a man, who, by his own admission, was capable of great evil. Her resolve strengthened as she continued through the aisle.

She stopped at the batteries, stooping to remove five packages of D cells from the lower rack. An arm swept past her, causing her to duck.

"Sorry, didn't mean to startle you. I hope we don't need them," the woman said. She leaned down, snatched up several of the packages, and grunted as she stood. It was then Abby saw that the woman was extremely pregnant.

"So you're not leaving either?" Abby asked, somewhat surprised.

The woman tossed the batteries into her cart. "Lord, no, it'd be a nightmare trying to get out of the city."

She circled her enormous stomach with her hands. "My luck, I'd go into labor in the car."

Abby felt her eyes grow wide as she took in the lady's massive size, then looked to her own early pregnancy pooch.

Seeing where Abby's gaze fell, the woman laughed and shook her head. "Twins. I wasn't nearly as big with the first two."

"Twins?" Abby hadn't even considered the possibility.

"Yep, hadn't even planned on one; now we're getting two." She rubbed at a spot on her stomach. "Both boys; going to be a handful too. I can tell. They've really been duking it out in there. My husband is already calling them his little gladiators."

Abby watched in amazement as the woman's shirt moved, reshaping her stomach before her eyes.

The woman readjusted her tight-fitting top. "See what I mean?"

"Wow, I've never seen anything like it," Abby said, finally finding her voice.

"Consider yourself lucky you're only having one. You are only having one, aren't you?"

"Yes," Abby confirmed, praying it was true.

Latching onto her cart, the woman smiled her approval. "Good, always good to start out with one until you figure out what you're doing."

Abby shook her head. "Yes, this will be a learning experience, that's for sure."

"Ah, babies are not that bad. Feed them and make sure you teach your husband how to change the diapers. Get him involved from the beginning or it will all be on you. Remember, he helped get you into this mess. Make him help with changing the mess." Having apparently given Abby all the parenting advice she needed, the woman waddled away without further comment.

Abby's thoughts turned inward. No way was Jacob going to touch this baby. She had to find out what Jacob was keeping from her soon. According to Pearl, she could not leave until she did. Her thoughts were interrupted by a firm hand coming to rest on her shoulder. Jumping, she turned to see Pearl peering down at her.

"It's you," Abby said, startled to see the woman she'd just been thinking about.

"Tis almost time. There's a storm coming," the woman warned.

Abby looked toward her cart filled with water. "Yes, I'm stocking up on water before the storm gets here."

Pearl shook her head. "That no the storm I be tellin' about. You have a storm coming. A vera bad one."

Abby felt chills. The hair on her arms stood erect at the woman's words. "You're not talking about the hurricane?"

Another shake of the head.

"What then?"

"He knows about the *bebe*." It was a statement, not a question.

"Yes, but I didn't tell him." She sounded defensive.

"It no matter, he knows. Now the wee *bebe* is in danger. You canna leave."

Abby started to back away. Of course she had to leave. "But I found the key. I'm close to knowing his secret. You said I can go after I know. "

The woman gripped her cart. "That was before. Now you must wait. Not long now. The storm is coming."

"What storm?" Abby questioned.

"The hurricane," the woman replied, maintaining her grip on the cart.

Abby took in a breath. The woman was talking in circles. "You just said you weren't talking about that storm."

Pearl's eyes grew intense. "You listen me, child."

Abby stood her ground, afraid of moving. The last thing she wanted to do was anger this woman.

"There be two storms. One is wit' your man. The other tis a hurricane. People will tell you go, but you must stay. You must stay!" she repeated.

The woman leaned closer. "It the only way you live. The only way your *bebe* is safe."

Abby was confused. "But you said if I find out what he's hiding, I'd be safe."

Pearl's hands gripped the basket tighter. "You no hearing what I say. That before he fin' out about the *bebe*. Now you must stay."

Abby felt her lip quiver. Tears were piling in her eyes. "Forever?"

Pearl's eyes softened. "No, tis almost over. You must remember my words. Very important."

Abby ran a finger along the bottom of her eyes. "I'm listening."

The woman smiled. "You stay and wait till the time is right. Then remember this, the way up is the way out. Only one must go up. It the only way."

Abby felt her mouth go dry. "I don't understand."

"You will," the woman promised. Easing her grip on the cart, she met Abby's eyes. "Now, tell me what I say."

"I must stay. The way up is the way out. Only one must go up. It's the only way."

Unfortunately, even repeating the words did not help Abby to understand them.

"You will know when the time is right. I go now. There's a storm coming."

That statement took Abby by surprise. "Wait! So you get to leave and I don't?"

Pearl closed her eyes briefly before speaking. When she opened them, they were etched with pain. "You must stay. It de only way."

Fear nagged at Abby, but she nodded in response. "I will stay."

"And remember?" the woman said.

"Yes, I will remember." She might not understand, but she'd remember.

Pearl placed her palm alongside Abby's face. "Tis okay to be scart. Fear will help to keep you safe."

Releasing the cart, she turned to go. Three steps into her retreat, she swiveled and returned to where Abby was standing, and placed her hands against the swell in Abby's abdomen. The woman's touch radiated heat, evoking a sudden calm within Abby.

Pearl muttered a few unintelligible words before removing her hands. "The *bebe* will be born with protection. You will see it's true."

Abby stood in stunned silence as Pearl turned once more.

"Remember, tis the only way," she called as she rounded the corner.

Pearl had been gone several moments before Abby resumed her shopping. She went over the conversation multiple times feeling somehow it had all been a dream. More like a friggin' nightmare. How was it that the woman always knew where to find her? A little unsettling perhaps, but was having a woman like Pearl as a guardian angel so bad? Could a voodoo priestess be considered a guardian angel? So many questions, so few answers...

***

They sat watching continued coverage of now tropical storm Katrina.

The weatherman's face was intense. "Katrina is currently making its way across Florida, towards the Gulf of Mexico. While the storm's intensity has lessened, we do expect the storm to strengthen back into a major hurricane once it gets back over the warm waters of the gulf. Have no doubt, no matter where the storm comes on shore, this will be a major storm."

"Such hype," Jacob lambasted as he turned off the TV.

Abby pulled her feet up on the couch, rubbing at them. "You don't think the storm is going to be that bad?"

He looked doubtful. "It's never as bad as they say it's going to be."

This would be her first hurricane. "Have you been through many?"

His brow screwed up in concentration. "I've lived in New Orleans twenty-seven years, so I'd say I've been through my share of them. I've never had to leave my home yet," he offered as an afterthought.

"You've lived here nearly all my life. Where did you live before?"

He appeared startled by her question, but answered without hesitation. "California."

She took advantage of his willingness to talk about himself. "What part?"

He paused, as if deciding how much to tell. "San Diego. I grew up there."

"I hear it is beautiful. What made you leave?"

"I just felt it was time for a change." His voice was abrupt.

She searched his face. "It was because of 'her,' wasn't it?"

His mouth twitched. "Let's just say there was nothing there for me anymore."

A sad smile fleeted across his lips.

Abby changed the subject. "So you think this house can withstand a direct hit?"

He pulled her feet into his lap and began massaging them. "The house will be fine. We have enough food and water to last over a week. I've seen videos of how people act after a hurricane. Looting and stealing everything in sight. "

"Stuff can be replaced," she offered.

He glanced at the ceiling. "Not everything."

"Like?"

"Like you," he said, pressing firmly on her feet.

"Yet, you'd have me remain in harm's way."

"I'd have you remain with me," he corrected. Bringing her foot to his face, he kissed the bottom lightly.

She cringed, knowing what was forthcoming. She wanted to push him away, but knew that doing so would be futile. In the end, he would have his way and she'd have the bruises to show for it. At least this way, he'd be gentle about it and neither she nor the baby would be harmed in the process.

His hands caressed her feet, traveling up the lengths of her calves. Firmly caressing her with strong yet tender hands, she felt her body respond to his touch. How could a monster evoke such a yearning? The thought pulled at her heartstrings. Why couldn't he have been like this from the beginning? Maybe he could change; he'd been different since learning she was pregnant. So caring. So attentive. What was she thinking? He's so attentive, he leaves his murdering henchman to watch over you. The thought hardened her heart. She would not allow him to seduce her.

His hands roamed higher, massaging her thighs, firmly kneading, pressing, warming her in places that ached to be next. This was how it should be. This is what she'd longed for. Not the sex, but the feeling of being wanted, needed.

Brian needed you, she reminded herself. She swallowed to keep from throwing up. His hands traveled between her legs, slowly caressing back and forth, yet never fully touching what ached to be touched. Damn her body for responding. Damn him for knowing how to make it respond. He teased her relentlessly. Without warning, he paused, rose from the couch, holding out his hand to her. She took it without hesitation and followed him down the hall to the bedroom. As she was following him down the hallway, she carefully removed the pouch she'd placed in her bra, quickly hiding it behind a photo on the dresser as she passed.

He stopped at the foot of the bed. "Allow me, my dear."

She stood in compliance as he lifted the maternity top over her head, exposing the blossoming breast of pregnancy. He smiled his approval, gently fondling her erect nipples before taking each in turn into his mouth, sucking and flicking the tips with his tongue.

Feeling a pull deep within, she moaned her approval. He continued lavishing attention on her breast for several moments before moving on to the rest of her body. His hands, soft against her skin, roved across her flesh as if he couldn't get enough of her. Jacob's breathing increased as his fingers caressed her torso. Looping the edge of her shorts, he lowered them, placing his hand under her elbow to steady her as she stepped out of the elastic waistband. Her body quivered as warm fingers dipped into the waistband of her panties, stripping her of her last defenses.

He eased her back onto the bed before removing his clothes and joining her. Moving alongside her, he picked up where he left off, tracing her flesh with determined hands. She flinched as his hand neared her face, only relaxing after he cupped her cheek tenderly. She felt as if he were testing her, making it perfectly clear that he had the power to inflict pain or pleasure. Tonight, it appeared pain was not his intention. He traced her body as if it were a roadmap, stopping each time just before reaching the final destination.

Guilt washed over her as she gave in to the need that his hands had evoked, arching to his touch. He eased on top of her, spreading her legs, slowly pressing himself into her. She closed her legs around him, pulling him in further. With slow, deliberate strokes, he took her higher, until at last she called out her release. He joined her before collapsing on the bed beside her.

Tears trickled down her cheek, salty trails of shame, for allowing herself to enjoy pleasure at the hands of evil.

CHAPTER TWENTY-SEVEN

"Are you sure you don't want to come with me?" Jacob asked for the seventh time. "I'm going to be gone most of the day."

"No, I'm feeling rather queasy." Now that Jacob knew about her condition, Abby didn't see anything wrong with playing the pregnancy card to her advantage.

A frown creased his face. "Maybe I should cancel."

Abby was having difficulty dealing with this new compassionate side of the monster she'd come to know. The old Jacob would not have left the decision up to her. "No, that's not necessary. I'm going to eat some crackers and take a hot bath."

He checked his watch. "Okay, I need to be going so I can take care of things and get back at a decent hour this evening. Traffic is going to be rough with people heading out of town. Regardless, the storm is still at least a day and a half out."

That caught her up short. Even though Pearl had told her to stay, the weather reports were scaring her. "Are you sure we won't need to evacuate?"

He smiled at her. "It's only a little hurricane, Abigail. I've been through them before. This house is over a hundred years old. I assure you, it has seen its share of storms. We have all the supplies we need to weather it out, so don't worry."

Yes, she'd been the one to purchase the supplies and Pearl had assured her she should stay. Remembering Pearl's words calmed her. Besides, she was so close to discovering the truth.

Putting on a brave face, she smiled at Jacob. "Then go do what you have to do and hurry home before it gets bad out. I've heard the wind and rain will arrive way before the storm."

He stared at her as if deciding before snatching his keys from atop his briefcase. If only there was a way to get the key to the lock off before he left. The thought was lost as Abby watched him tuck them into his pocket.

She followed him to the front, stepping onto the porch to check the skies, blue, mingled with fluffy gray clouds. "Doesn't look very menacing, does it?"

He followed her gaze. "Nothing we can't handle. Just the same, you should bring in the planters after your stomach settles."

"Will do," she promised, looking past her to the car that had just driven up. Merrick had arrived, taking up his usual position, across the street two houses down.

Seeing him, Jacob gave her a quick peck on the lips and hurried to his car. Abby watched his taillights disappear before glaring at Merrick, stepping back inside, and bolting the door against his hard stare. She resisted the sudden urge to take a shower. The man gave her the creeps.

She pulled out her phone dialed the number, but canceled the call before she hit send. Instead, she took one last look out the front window and headed to the rear of the house.

* * *

She felt giddy as she rapped on the back porch of Kevin's house. It had been over a week since she'd seen Gulliver. She had to let him know she hadn't abandoned him. The curtains parted and Kevin's shock-filled face appeared in the window.

"Abby?" Her name came out on a squeak as he opened the door. "Is everything okay?"

"Yes, Jacob just left. He's going to be gone most of the day," she assured him. "I just had to see Gulliver before we got started."

He stepped back to allow her inside the kitchen. Abby took in the dated room, which seemed to be caught up in a time warp of laminate counters and white appliances. For the first time, she fully appreciated the work that Jacob had put into their home.

Gulliver raced down the hall, coiling blissfully around her legs.

"Someone is happy to see his mama," Kevin said, smiling at the duo.

She scooped the cat into her arms, struggling to control her tears. "And his mama is happy to see him too."

"Well, I'll give you two some privacy while I go change into my detecting clothes."

Abby giggled. "Channeling Tom again?"

"Laugh all you want, missy," he called from the other room.

She stroked the cat, needing the attention just as much as the cat did. "Hey, what the heck have you been feeding him? He weighs a ton."

"I told you he likes doughnuts," Kevin called from the other room.

Abby groaned. "I thought you were kidding."

"I never kid about jelly doughnuts," Kevin stated, returning to the room. He was wearing a pink Hawaiian shirt, a blue ball cap sporting the letter D, and khaki shorts that were entirely too short. For a second, she wondered if this were truly a costume or if Kevin too was caught up in some horrid eighties time warp.

Abby buried her face in the cat's fur. "What the heck are you wearing?"

He puffed his chest out. "Why, I'm channeling my inner Tom, of course."

Of course, they'd been through this before. "Yeah, but I can honestly say I've never seen a picture of Tom Cruise wearing anything remotely like that."

He rolled his eyes at her. "Don't be silly. You know there is more than one Tom. I'm channeling Tom Selleck. You know, *Magnum PI?*"

He took off the hat and studied it. "Got to love the big D."

She laughed in spite of herself. "I really don't want to hear your thoughts on Tom's big D."

Another eye roll. "I've heard about pregnant women and their hormones, but seriously, is sex all you think about?"

"Really? You're asking me that when you are making comments like that?"

He placed the hat back on his head and pointed at the lettering. "I was talking about this big D. You know, Detroit. Thomas Magnum always wore a hat like this."

"I take it you have a thing for the name Tom?"

"Sunshine, if I could change my name, I'd pick Tom in an instant," he said on a sigh.

"All righty then, Tom, shall we go see what is lurking in the attic?" She hugged the cat closely before releasing him. Only then did she notice the cat carrier sitting next to two suitcases and several boxes.

She glanced at Kevin. "Going somewhere?"

"Yes, we are," he said, looking at her pointedly. Nearing the sink, he turned on the faucet so that a light stream of water dribbled out. She watched in amazement as Gulliver jumped on the counter, ducked his head, and lapped from the stream.

"What are you doing to my cat?"

"Possession is nine-tenths of the law," he pointed out.

"It's temporary possession," she reminded him.

"I know. Besides, you're coming with me tonight and then he will be yours again. Although I must admit, I will miss the big guy."

She led the way out the door. "There's something I have to tell you."

"Let me guess, now that you've got the ring, you've fallen madly in love with your husband and now you've decided to stay."

Abby felt hurt. "You seriously think I'm that shallow?"

They entered the house in hushed tones, only continuing the conversation after making sure the house was empty.

"Tell me you're not staying?"

"I can't," she said lamely.

238

"Then you are," he accused.

"Yes, I'm staying, but it has nothing to do with the ring. I'm pawning it as soon as I'm free of him. I'm going to use the money for a fresh start for me and the baby."

"I can give you that. A fresh start, that is."

"I thought I wasn't your type," she replied, seeing the sincerity in his face.

"You're my best friend, Abby. You like me for who I am."

She bit her lip. "I'd like you more if those shorts weren't so short."

"They are a bit snug," he admitted, tugging at the edges. "Any shorter and I'll be singing soprano.

She giggled. "Something tells me you already do."

He tilted his head in response. "Play nice."

He handed her the key to the office, which she used to open the door. When she went to hand it back, he stopped her. "You keep it. I'm heading out this evening."

She felt a tinge of jealousy. "I do wish I could go with you."

"Why can't you?"

"Pearl." She told him about her latest encounter with the woman and how she made Abby promise to stay, even when people told her she must go.

"And you're going to listen to her?"

"Wouldn't you?" she said, unlocking the door.

"Yes," he admitted reluctantly.

She looked toward the closet door.

"An office," he said, as if reading her mind.

"What?"

"In the attic. There is a full office complete with computer, phone, the works."

"Kind of bizarre, don't you think?"

"This whole situation is bizarre if you ask me." He sat at the desk and opened the laptop. Waiting for it to come alive, he turned to her. "So what exactly do you know about your husband?"

She thought for a moment. "His name is Jacob Buckley, he's fifty-two years old. He works from home mostly, but has an office somewhere here in town that he sometimes goes to. He is a sadist, a murderer, and gets turned on by hurting women. He thinks marriage gives the man the right to control his wife and, for that reason, he sees nothing wrong with beating me into submission."

"Oh, what I wouldn't give to be a macho man so I could kick the shit out of the prick."

She smiled at him. "Kevin, you've treated me with more respect than that macho man ever has. Please don't ever change."

His lip quivered as he turned his attention to the computer. He pulled up the locked file, entered the password, and waited.

"How'd you get the password?" she asked, surprised.

He winked at her. "It's what I do."

"Passwords?"

"Computers," he said, tapping the keys.

"Let me guess; it was something simple," she pressed.

He let out a sigh. "Your name spelled backwards."

"So what did you find?" she asked, peeking over his shoulder.

"Nothing really. Just a copy of your birth certificate, baby pictures, and a picture of you and your mom in the hospital when you were born."

Disappointment traveled through her. "It must be someone else's; none of that stuff exists. We had a house fire when I was little. There are no pictures of me below the age of four."

His brows knitted together. He pulled up the file with the birth certificate. "Here it is. Abriella Clarissa Rodgers, born in San Diego, California, October 13th 1974."

Abby could feel her mouth going dry. "It's the right birthday, but everything else is wrong. Maybe I have a twin out there somewhere that was put up for adoption without me knowing it."

"Call your parents and ask," Kevin said, being practical.

"I can't. They passed away last fall."

"They?"

"Yes, carbon monoxide poisoning, happened in their sleep," she said, feeling the pang from their death.

"I don't know what to say."

"Nothing to say," she said, still reading over his shoulder, stopping at the name of the birth mother. "What the hell?"

"What?"

"The parents' names. Todd and Clarice Rodgers."

"You know them?" he said, staring at the screen.

"No, but I've heard that name enough. Clarice was the bitch that broke his heart," she breathed over his shoulder.

He looked up at her in earnest. "Sunshine, I don't know how to tell you this, but I think that bitch was your mother."

She laughed at the absurdity. "My mother's name was Marsha Turner."

"Describe her."

Picturing her mom, she smiled. "She has... had mousy brown hair, brown eyes, round face, loved to cook."

He sat back in the chair. "And your dad?"

"Tall, very thin, too thin, actually. Dark hair, brown eyes. Just normal-looking, I guess."

"And the red hair. Where'd you get it from?"

She smiled. "My mom said I got it from my aunt, but dad always joked I got it from the pizza delivery guy."

Kevin got up and motioned for her to sit in his chair. After she'd done so, he clicked the mouse. Abby caught her breath when a photo came up, showing her lying in a hospital bed holding a tiny infant. Only it wasn't her.

Grateful to be sitting, she sat staring at the picture. "She looks just like me."

"Pretty coincidental," he said softly.

Kevin clicked through all the other photos, each showing the mother and child at various stages of growth. One thing that was abundantly apparent in each photo was that the child had brilliant red hair. Just like her mother.

"I'm adopted?"

"I don't think so."

She was confused. It was clear she was the child in the picture. "Why not?"

"Look at the woman's face. Does that look like the face of a mother about to give her child up for adoption?" he implored.

Kevin was right. It was clear the woman in the picture adored the child. "Is there anything else?"

He shook his head. "Not in here."

She pushed the chair back. "Then I guess we will have to keep looking. Did you bring your lock kit?"

"I did."

"Then start picking while I have a go at the cabinet over here," she said, determined to get to the truth.

She searched several compartments to no avail. Opening the door on the last one, she hesitated. "That's odd."

Kevin came over to see what had caught her attention. "Find something?"

"This cabinet is empty, but it looks different than the others."

He opened the other door to see what she meant. "I wonder?"

She watched as he pushed and tugged at the back of the cupboard. Suddenly, the back of the cabinet swiveled, exposing a hidden compartment.

Abby stared at the contents, two rather large photo albums, a stack of shoe boxes, a key ring sporting several keys, and Abby's oversized purse. Abby let out a large sigh. It was here all along. If only she'd known.

"I take it that is your missing purse," Kevin said, watching her carefully.

She nodded. "Yes, and it doesn't take a rocket scientist to guess what the keys go to."

Kevin reached around her, scooped up the keys, and cast his eyes upward. "What do you say? Want to join me in the lair?"

CHAPTER TWENTY-EIGHT

Abby stood at the attic window, staring down at the car below. Merrick appeared to be taking a nap as his seat was fully reclined with him in it. "Hmm, wonder what his boss would think of that?"

Kevin looked up from the computer he was behind. "Think of what?"

"My babysitter is taking a nap," she said, crossing the room.

"I'm surprised none of the neighbors have called the police on him, sitting there nearly every day," he said, rolling his neck.

"You didn't," she reminded him.

He shrugged. "I guess I never noticed him until you pointed him out to me."

She placed her hands on Kevin's shoulders, rubbing out the tension. He let his head fall forward on a groan. "Mmm, that feels nice."

Abby couldn't stop thinking about the creep in the car. "He's a goon. How can people not notice a goon?"

Kevin typed on the keyboard. "Damn,"

"Still nothing?"

"Na, I'm not ready to give up yet, though. See if you can get one of those keys to fit that trunk over there," he said, trying another combination, to no avail.

A noise outside startled them, causing Abby to jump and run to the window. "Just a branch. The wind is really picking up out there. It looks like the skies are going to open any moment."

"It's just the rain bands ahead of the hurricane. Don't worry; the storm won't be here until tomorrow morning. And I for one plan on being away from the coast when it gets here."

"I'm glad you are going to take Gulliver away," she said, trying to hide her disappointment.

"I'd take you too if you'd let me," he reminded her.

"I know."

He went back to work on the computer.

"Where are you going anyway? That was a lot of stuff for a short evacuation."

"I'm going to visit my dad in Virginia. The storm will be headed north, so once I cut east, I should be fine."

"The cop? I thought he didn't approve of you?"

He kept his face tucked, concentrating on what he was doing. "Retired cop. We get along okay. He's gotten better over the years. At least he doesn't call me his daughter anymore."

She giggled. "Well, that's a plus."

"Yeah, I just try to tone down the eyeliner when I'm around him."

"That would help. Is he okay with Gulliver coming?"

"He would be okay if you come too." He took a piece of paper and jotted something on it. "Here is the address and dad's phone number if you change your mind."

She walked over, took it from him, and glanced at the computer. "Still nothing?"

"No, and we're eating up precious time. Let's try looking elsewhere and I will come back to it if there's time."

They moved to the large trunk, checking the keys they'd found in the cabinet below, none of which fit. Abby sat cross-legged on the floor while Kevin went to work with the lock kit he'd brought.

"Do you have any brothers and sisters?" Abby asked, watching him fiddle with the lock.

"Nope, just me and my pop."

"Your mom?"

"Died years ago, pneumonia," he said, turning the lock to get a better view.

"I take it you weren't close?"

"Not really, I mean she was my mom and all, but I never really felt as if I fit in at home. How about you?" he asked changing the subject.

"My family was okay..." She swallowed. "If they were my family. We wouldn't get an award for Family of the Year or anything, but they never locked me in the closet or anything. There was always something I couldn't understand though..."

"What was that?" Kevin asked when she didn't continue.

"Neither of them worked, yet we always had plenty of money." Their eyes met. "It didn't bother me... until now."

"And now you think?"

She bit at her bottom lip. "I don't know what to think. Maybe Dad was a drug dealer."

247

He eased the metal pick back and tried the lock again. "You don't seem to think highly of your dad."

"He was different. And he thought Jacob was the greatest person on earth. He'd have been ecstatic if I had married him when I was sixteen."

"And your mom, how did she take your marrying someone old enough to be your father?"

"They died before I married Jacob. But they knew him. She never said so, but I don't think she liked Jacob very well. She was thrilled when I eloped with Brian."

Kevin, sat back on his hills and rolled his neck. "Who is Brian?"

Abby let out a deep breath and told him about Brian, and Jacob's admission to killing him.

"Jesus, Abby, and you stayed with the man after he told you?"

"I was afraid. If he could do that to Brian without anyone knowing, what could he do to me?"

"Another reason for you to come away with me," he said, returning to work on the lock.

"Not yet. I promised Pearl. She told me it wouldn't be safe, if I left too soon."

"My dad's an ex-cop. He can protect you."

Abby wanted to say yes. She wanted to leave right now and never return, but she had the baby to think of. Pearl had been adamant. "She told me I must stay even when people were saying I must go." She could tell he was irritated, but it was only because he worried about her safety, as did she.

"I have the address, Kevin. I will be joining you by the end of the week." She took the paper he'd handed her and placed it into the pouch with the chicken foot for safekeeping.

She rested a hand on his shoulder to help push herself up. "I'm going to go back down and check out what is in the hidden compartment. Let me know if you get into this thing."

Abby checked the window before heading back to the office. Returning to the cabinet, she pulled out her purse. She opened it and found everything as she had left it, keys, cell phone, and wallet, complete with several hundred dollars in cash. She thought about taking the purse, but decided to leave it until she was ready for her escape. No sense taking it now and chance Jacob learning she'd been snooping.

She returned the bag to the cabinet, pushed it back in place, and peeked into one of the shoeboxes, a startled gasp escaping her. The box was filled to the brim with cash, one-hundred-dollar bills all neatly wrapped in even stacks. Blinking, she lowered the lid and slid out another box, then another. Each box was stacked to the brim with cash. A shiver ran through her as she replaced the last lid. She pulled out one of the photo albums and took a seat at the desk. The first page held a wedding announcement, an after the fact acknowledgement of the wedding between Clarice Brown and Todd Rodgers. Abby turned the page to find several photos of the woman whom she bore an amazing likeness to. The photos showed the woman in various stages of pregnancy, all outdoors or at public venues. The next page showed pictures such as those on the computer with the woman and the child, again all taken outside.

"He was stalking her," Abby whispered, turning the page. She swallowed hard, seeing a yellowed newspaper clipping that read 'Couple Dies in House Fire. Child's Body Not Found.' The article confirmed her suspicion that Clarice and Todd Rodgers had been the couple in question. She skimmed the rest of the article before moving to a follow-up piece below, which was dated several days later. 'Child Remains Missing after Suspicious Fire. Local Dominoes Offering Reward for Any Information on Child's Whereabouts.' Abby felt her body start to tremble as she read the article. Todd Rodgers had been a manager at Dominoes at the time of the fire. Her father's words came back to haunt her. *Your daddy was a pizza delivery guy.* Abby called out in surprise when Kevin came up behind her.

"Easy there, Sunshine. It's just me. What's got you so uptight?"

"He killed my parents and then kidnapped me…"

"Who?"

"Jacob."

Kevin sat on the edge of the desk, waiting for her to explain.

"When I was four, we had a house fire. I remember Jacob pulling me from the fire and telling me everything was going to be okay. He took me to my parents and I remember being really scared of them at first." She turned the album toward him so he could see the article.

Kevin's face was white. "That explains what I found upstairs."

She started to rise, but he placed a hand on her shoulder. "I got the chest unlocked. It is filled with photos."

She eased back into the chair. "Of?"

"Children. Lots of children, all young, with names, locations all over the United States and dates the orders were filled." His voice held an edge.

"So Jacob is not selling drugs?"

Kevin looked as if he were going to be sick. "No, he's selling children."

"People do that?"

"Apparently." He placed his fingers to the bridge of his nose.

"That would explain why he was so upset when he found out that Nathan was filling an order locally."

Abby looked out the window. The wind had increased substantially. "I don't get it. Pearl said now that Jacob knew about the baby, that the baby is in danger. So if the baby is in danger, why have me stay?"

He closed his eyes. "I don't know, but as much as I hate to say it, I think you need to listen to her. She has been right so far."

"Seriously, how could she have known about all of this?" He waved his hands around and stomped back toward the stairs. "I'm going back upstairs and figure out the password."

"Maybe I should come up and see the photos," she said, pushing back the chair.

"NO! No," he repeated more softly. "I don't want you near the chest."

His eyes pleaded with her not to push the issue. She nodded her assent. She could trust Kevin, this much she knew. He closed his eyes and took a deep breath before returning to the attic. Abby quelled the fear within and turned the page of the album. The pages that followed showed Abby in her new home with no further detail of events. Closing the album, she rose and traded it out for the other one, bringing it back to the desk. This one was much the same, only Abby was older. On next to the last page was a newspaper clipping of Brian's obituary and on the last page was a clipping of her parents'- fake parents'- death by carbon monoxide.

"Hey," she called up the stairs. "Why do you suppose Jacob would have a copy of the newspaper article from my parents' accidental death?" She sat back in the chair. "You don't think?"

"Why not?" he yelled down from above. "He got rid of everyone else in your life. Don't you see, Abby, he planned this from the start. He took you from your mother, and sold you to someone else, who raised you. He inserted himself into your life so that you would trust him, and then he killed them."

"Not bad," surmised a low voice.

Abby jumped at Merrick's voice. He was standing in the doorway, pointing a gun at her. "You're wrong in your deductions, though. Jacob paid them to take you in. He figured if he couldn't have your mother, he'd have you instead. So he found someone to raise you and keep you pure for him." He gave a snort. "I guess the keeping you pure part got past them."

He waved the gun towards the attic.

"Why don't you call down your little boyfriend for me?" Merrick said, keeping his voice low.

"He's my neighbor, not my boyfriend," she said a bit louder than necessary.

"I don't care what he is. Call him down."

She sent out a silent prayer, that he'd listen carefully to her words. "Oh, Kevie, can you come down here a moment?"

"Give me just a minute, Sunshine. I think I found something."

Dang, he hadn't taken the hint. She needed to find a way to stall Merrick.

"My parents were in on it?" Abby asked, turning her attention back to Merrick, who obviously did not consider her a threat as he was now casually leaning against the doorframe, waiting for Kevin to come down from the attic.

"Of course they were in on it. Your father was a bum. He never worked a day in his life."

Okay, her dad she could see, but not her mom. "But my mom, she didn't even like Jacob?"

"Na, your mom only agreed to the arrangement so she could have a child. She'd been born with something wrong with her." He waved off the comment. "I don't know what it was, but she couldn't get pregnant."

Abby was suddenly reminded of Jacob's remark when he'd told her that her mom cared too much. It was true. She had tried to protect her. She had been thrilled when she'd eloped with Brian.

Abby was trying to keep him talking, praying that Kevin would hear. "How do you know so much?"

Merrick smiled and it occurred to her this was one of the few times she'd seen him do so. "I'm his only true friend. I helped him come up with the plan right after he found out that bitch Clarice was pregnant. At first, he was just going to take you to teach the bitch a lesson, but then I came up with the idea of killing her and her lousy husband."

A thud in the front of the house drew Merrick's attention.

"A tree limb," Abby ventured. "They've been falling all day."

He scratched his head with the end of the gun, apparently satisfied with her answer.

"But why kill them?" she asked, feeling hollow.

"Jacob was head over heels in love with Clarice and she him, until Mr. Wonderful came along and fucked it all up."

Abby remained quiet, allowing Merrick to verify what she'd already deduced from the evidence at hand.

"The deal was your new parents would raise you and make sure you fell in love with Jacob and then when you came of age, you were to marry him."

She was fighting tears now. Jacob had planned this since before her birth. Then why wait? Why allow her to marry Brian in the first place? If not for his waiting, Brian would still be alive, even if she'd never been allowed to marry him. Jacob could have prevented his death in more ways than one.

"So if he was going to treat me like a prisoner anyway, why go to all the trouble? Why not just force me to marry him?"

He looked to the open closet before answering.

"Because the jerk was too proud. He said it had to be your decision. He didn't think you would love him if he forced you to marry him."

"Love him?" she repeated, appalled by the fact that she'd once thought that an option.

"Yeah, he had loved your mother and when the bitch betrayed him, he said he'd get her back by making her daughter love him."

"He's crazy," she murmured.

Apparently, Merrick didn't like her assessment of his boss. He waved the gun at her. "Tell pretty boy to get down here."

"He'll be down in a moment," she said, glancing at the ceiling. "One more thing, what is with all the pictures in the attic? How did all those kids get pulled into this?"

Her question evoked a chuckle. "Because taking you was so easy. One kid brings in tens of thousands of dollars. Sometimes more…depending."

Abby felt a sudden unease engulf her. "Then why is he so happy about our baby?"

"Because, Sunshine," he said, opting for the name Kevin had called her, "this baby is going to be the biggest payout of all. The child of the head of the largest child racketeering ring in the country will bring a small fortune. Best of all no-one will even care if it disappears."

"I'LL CARE!" Kevin's scream filled the air.

Startled, Merrick turned his head, but his reaction was not quick enough. The living room lamp slammed against the side of his head. He teetered momentarily before his legs crumbled, sending him crashing to the floor.

Kevin kicked the gun away.

He turned to her, his voice trembling. "You're right. Lamps do work better than books."

Tears streamed down her face as she ran to where Kevin stood. Trembling, she looked up at him. "How'd you get out of the attic?"

He wrapped his arms around her, his breath hot against her hair. She couldn't tell who was shaking more him or her.

"I climbed out the window, onto the porch, and shimmied down the column," he said, still trying to catch his breath. He took on a serious tone. "Please don't tell my dad that I shimmied."

She giggled. "Something tells me your dad will be very proud of your shimmying. "

She tapped a foot at Merrick. "Is he... dead?"

Kevin shook his head. "Not yet."

CHAPTER TWENTY-NINE

Abby was relieved to see Kevin cutting through the bushes, avoiding branches that were being stripped from trees by the heavy winds. He ran straight to her house, bursting through the door as if being chased.

"We're good to go. I parked his car in the driveway one street over. No one was home, probably already headed out of town. I broke the back window, and rummaged through some drawers to make it look as if he'd broken in."

Wow, he was really taking this seriously. "You broke into someone's house? Really?"

His brows went up. "Sunshine, I just killed a man with my bare hands and you have a problem with my breaking a window?"

This caught her up short. "Is he really dead?"

He brushed the hair out of her face. "There was no other choice."

She took a deep breath. "I know. How?"

"Do you really want to know?"

She took another breath. "Not really."

He looked at the skies, which were growing more ominous by the second. "Are you sure you don't want to come with me?"

"Of course I want to, but you know I can't. If what Merrick said was true, and I'm pretty sure it was, then

Pearl is right; the baby is in danger. She's been spot on so far, so I have to trust her on this."

Kevin checked his watch, obviously anxious to leave. "I just wish she'd given you more information. You don't even know what she meant."

"I know, but she told me I'd know when the time was right." She nudged him towards the back door. Now go. Get my cat out of here before the storm hits."

He gave her a quick hug and kissed the top of her head. When he spoke, he had tears in his eyes. "You take care of yourself, Sunshine."

"I'll be okay," she promised, blinking back tears of her own.

It was all she could do to keep from running after him. She was not a brave person, not really, but if Pearl told her she had to stay to save herself and her baby, then she'd stay. She ran to the front window and watched as his Mini Cooper drove out of his driveway and kept standing there long after he'd disappeared from sight, leaving her all alone.

* * *

Abby was sitting on the front porch when Jacob returned. His face looked haggard. Gold speckles mingled with the brown in his eyes, warning her of his mood. She watched as he glanced over his shoulder in the direction where his henchman normally parked. "What time did Merrick leave?"

She fought to keep her face neutral, when what she really wanted to do was to claw his eyes out. Just the sight of him revolted her. "I'm not sure. I've been out here about twenty minutes. His car was gone when I came out."

His eyes met hers. "You've not spoken with him today?"

"Why would I?" she asked as calmly as she could.

"Not at all like the man," Jacob replied, looking back to the empty curb.

"I guess he figured I wouldn't be stupid enough to leave the house with a storm coming. That is why you leave him here, to make sure I don't leave the house, right?"

"I keep him here to look after you," Jacob corrected. "What's for dinner?"

"I have a tuna casserole in the oven." She looked toward the late afternoon sky. The rain bands were increasing, even though the storm wasn't due to come ashore until morning. "I've never seen clouds swirl like that."

"They'll be swirling a lot more before this thing is over," he said, following her gaze.

The wind shifted, sending drops of water cascading over her.

"Come on in; you're getting wet. Worrying about the weather can't be good for the baby." His voice had an edge to it.

She closed her eyes, briefly praying for strength. Just his mentioning the baby sickened her.

"Still not feeling well?" he asked when she opened her eyes.

"It's been a difficult day," she said, rising from the bench and following him in.

He stopped as soon as he entered the room. "Where's the lamp?"

"It smashed on...on the floor, when I opened the window to try to allow some fresh air in," she lied.

"Why would you want to open the window when we have air conditioning?" he inquired.

"I was feeling queasy, and the wind has been blowing all day, so I thought a bit of fresh air would help."

He studied her for a moment before accepting her answer. "Have you watched the news today?"

"Nope, I just read a bit." She wanted to add that she'd been reading about all the evil things he'd done, but decided to let things play out as intended.

"They're saying this storm could be worse than originally intended. They've opened up the Superdome."

"The Superdome? Do you want to go?" What if he did? What would she say?

"Do you?" he questioned in return.

She remembered Pearl's words. *You must stay when they tell you to go.* "No, you said yourself that we will be fine."

He peered out the side window towards Kevin's house. "What about the neighbors? Are they staying?"

She felt a lump in her throat. "How should I know? It's not as if I talk to any of them."

He whirled, backhanding her hard against the face. "You lying slut!"

Her hand flew to her cheek. He raised his a second time. She ducked out of the way as he swung, backing across the room, out of his reach. His nostrils flared, but he remained rooted in place.

"Where's Merrick?" he repeated.

"How should I know?" She eased toward the hallway, wanting to keep as much distance between them as possible.

"I know about your affair with the neighbor," he said, taking a step forward.

She leaned against the wall for support. "I assure you I'm not having an affair with Kevin."

"I have the phone bill. Every time I leave the house, you call him." He seemed to consider this for a moment. "Was he here today?"

She didn't answer.

"Have you been fucking him in my house?" His voice was seething.

She took a deep breath. "No, Jacob, I assure you, you are the only person who is fucking me."

He moved a step closer. She groped along the wall, hoping she could reach the hallway before him. What then? No, she'd better reason with him now. "Jacob, you know Kevin is gay. We are just friends."

"Gay?" His head came up, as if remembering.

"Yes, I know I should have told you I was talking to him, but I didn't think you'd understand. Things haven't always been easy around here, so I just needed someone to talk to. We're just friends, Jacob."

"Where is he now?"

"He left a few hours ago. He asked me to go with him, but I told him no. I told him I had to stay here with you, my husband." The truth of her statement must have shown on her face because his shoulders relaxed slightly.

"And the two of you have never had sex?"

She smiled to reassure him. "No, Jacob, I swear Kevin and I have never so much as kissed."

"Good, then I won't have to kill him." The tension had left his voice.

Running a hand through his hair, he flashed a smile. "How long before dinner is ready? I'm famished."

Abby trembled as he walked past, relaxed, as if they'd just had a normal chat. While on the outside the man seemed in total control, she had no doubt that on the inside was a glass teetering precariously on the edge of a counter.

* * *

Abby yawned, then wiped the moisture from her eyes. She'd spent a long, sleepless night listening to the wind roar and rain hammer against the side of the house. The power had flickered several times during the night, but thus far was still working. She walked to the window, staring as the tree tops danced in circles. While they'd lost several branches, the tall trees were still rooted firmly in the ground. She stared at the bushes that separated the yards, knowing Merrick lay unmoving on the other side.

"What exactly did you do to Merrick?" Jacob, who'd been working in his office, had approached without her hearing. He was leaning against her, his words slipping warmly past her ear.

Her body grew stiff at his close proximity. "I told you, I haven't seen Merrick."

He eased her hair back, breathing fire along her neck. "So you said. I just thought maybe your memory may have gotten better since then."

She swallowed, wondering what had brought on this new round of questioning. She got her answer when he pressed something hard against the palm of her hand. His tongue flicked the lobe of her right ear.

"I found this little tidbit on the floor in my office." He hoisted himself up so he was sitting on the countertop.

She opened her hand, surprised to find a section of the lamp. He laughed as her eyes darted to the knife drawer.

"You don't have the upper body strength." He nodded towards her hands. "No, you don't have it in you. It had to be your boyfriend. Not bad for a fag. Too bad, though. Merrick was such a loyal friend."

"Your loyal friend sang like a canary before he…left." A limb bounced off the roof, causing her to jump.

His eyes appraised her. "He left, did he?"

Oh, he was gone all right. "He did."

Jacob tilted his head in response. "Walked right out of here on his own two legs?"

"Not exactly."

"Well, I don't see you dragging a two-hundred-pound man, at least not in your current condition, so I guess I will have to kill your boyfriend after all." He pushed himself off the counter and wandered down the hall.

She followed at a slower pace, nearly stumbling as she neared his office and found the door had been left open. Seeing her face, he smiled. "Don't see any reason to lock the door since you know all of my secrets."

"You're not afraid I'll call the police?"

"You haven't yet." His gaze shifted to the window. "Besides, I assure you the police will have more important matters to deal with for the next few days."

Jacob was right. The storm was in full force, the rain coming down in sheets. The wind roaring around the house sounded like planes circling overhead. It occurred to her she was more afraid of her husband than she was of the massive hurricane. She eased her way into the office, sitting in a chair well out of his reach.

"Why, Jacob?"

"I thought you said Merrick told you everything?"

She wrung her hands. "He did. At least I think he did. But I still would like some answers."

He leaned back in his chair. "Ask your questions, Abigail."

"Why did you let me marry Brian?"

"Let you?" he said, his voice seething.

"You knew how I felt. You knew everything else; you had to know. So why not force me to stop seeing him?"

"Don't you think I tried? Your parents…Brad and Marsha were supposed to keep me apprised of the situation." His face grew red. "I should have known the bitch would sell me out."

The bitch? He must have been talking about her mother, who had encouraged her relationship with Brian. "Mom liked Brian."

"It was not her place to like anyone. I paid her to care for you. To get you ready for me."

"But instead, she fell in love with me and cared for me as her own," Abby said finishing his sentence.

He merely nodded.

"So you killed her," she said, blinking back tears.

"No, Merrick killed her and your father."

"On your orders," she shot back.

"They were liabilities. Your mother grew suspicious over Brian. She was threatening to go to the cops."

"What now, Jacob?"

"What do you mean?" He sounded befuddled.

"I mean what happens now… with us?"

"Us? I don't understand the question."

Surely he couldn't think they could go on like nothing had happened. She shifted in her chair.

"Jacob, you kidnapped me when I was a child. You've killed everyone I've ever cared about and now, according to Merrick, you plan on selling our child." She wondered if she sounded as hysterical as she felt.

He waved her off. "We've no need for a child."

"You're not selling my baby." Her voice was incredulous.

"Sold," he corrected. "Brought a mighty good price too."

She couldn't breathe. "You've already taken money for my baby."

He pointed at her hand. "You're wearing some of the down payment."

Ice shot through her veins. Rising from the chair, she left the room, went into the bedroom, and opened the draw to her nightstand. Pushing the papers away, she pulled out the revolver. Merrick's gun, which Kevin had insisted she keep.

He was standing in the doorway when she turned, a wary look upon his face.

"My child is not for sale. Call the person and tell them the deal's off."

He put his hands up. "Nice sentiment, Abigail. Now give me the gun before someone gets hurt."

She fired a round into the doorframe. "I said make the call."

He brought out his cell phone and placed a call. Shaking his head, he put it on speaker so she could hear. "The phone lines are down due to the storm."

She waved the gun, motioning for him to move back. He started towards the back of the house.

"In the living room," she directed. Her voice sounded so calm, it frightened her.

She followed him into the room, motioning him to sit. She eased onto a chair on the opposite side of the room, keeping the pistol pointed in his direction. Her body started to shake as her adrenaline ebbed.

Jacob crossed his legs. "Do you mind pointing that thing in another direction? "I'd hate for you to shoot me by accident."

"If I shoot you, it won't be an accident," she assured him.

He uncrossed his legs, leaning forward as if to rush her at any given second. She aimed the gun at his head, daring him to move.

"You shoot that gun again and someone will call the cops."

"The wind is howling so loudly, no one will hear it. Besides, you said it yourself: the cops have more important things to tend to."

Laughing, he sat back in his chair. "*Touché, my dear, touché.*"

The house shook briefly. The lights flickered and were gone.

"Tree took down the wires," Jacob said to her unasked question.

* * *

As the storm lessened, Abby's rage grew. Jacob sat silently staring in her direction as if waiting to make his move. She yawned. The night was catching up with her. Jacob smiled when a second yawn followed suit. She must stay awake. Getting up, she paced the floor, keeping a close eye on Jacob, who was watching her every move.

When she met his stare, he smiled at her, white teeth gleaming even in the dim room. He was an attractive man. He could have had his share of women. Why had he chosen her? Okay, she already knew the answer to that question. It was because he couldn't have her mother. The image of the woman in the photo came to mind. The woman who'd given birth to her, loved her, if the pictures were to be believed. She wasn't sure when the tears began, wasn't even aware of them until they rolled down her face. She was so tired. She returned to her chair, sighing as she sank onto the cushion.

"You need to rest." His voice was gentle. "You look as though you're ready to keel over, Abigail. Just close your eyes for a bit. I promise I will stay right where I am."

His offer was tempting. Her eyelids felt heavy. If only she could trust him. Trust him. The thought rejuvenated her. She glared at him, sitting there gloating as if he were still in control, the smug face of a monster who'd accepted money for their child. Her child, she amended. She raised her arm and pointed the gun at his head.

CHAPTER THIRTY

The pistol was growing heavy in her grip. She'd squeezed the trigger multiple times in her mind, but her fingers had yet to cooperate. She was not sure how long she'd been standing there, willing her body to comply. Just pull the trigger and be done with it. Jacob had made it sound so easy to kill a person, just a means to an end. Clearly, it was not as simple as he made it sound. She moved her finger away from the trigger, lowering the pistol. Jacob let out a breath, but remained seated.

She wiggled her toes in the water at her feet. Water? She looked down, noticing for the first time the water that had penetrated the house. Ankle deep, it was rising rapidly.

"I guess they were right." Jacob's voice had a nervous edge to it.

"Right?" Her mind was numb with fatigue.

"I saw it on the news this morning. Some feared the levees would not withstand the storm. His brows rose dramatically. "At this rate, you won't have to kill me; we will both drown before the end of the hour."

"Drown?" she repeated, still not comprehending the severity of the situation.

"We have to move to higher ground," he said anxiously. "We need to get to the attic."

As soon as he said the words, she remembered what Pearl had said.

"The way up is the way out," she said, repeating the words Pearl had told her. Then to herself she added, *Only one must go up. Tis the only way.*

She pointed the gun at Jacob. "Toss me your keys."

"What keys?" he said, feigning innocence.

"The keys to your office, Jacob," she said evenly.

He smiled. "Are you forgetting the office is unlocked?"

She narrowed her eyes at him. "Yes, but locking the door behind me wouldn't do much good if you have the key now, would it? Besides, I need the key to the padlock."

His smile widened, obviously impressed. "Bravo, my dear."

He pulled the keys from his pocket and tossed them a foot in front of him, splashing as they landed in the standing water.

"Nice try, Jacob. I reach for the keys and you take the gun from me."

He shrugged. "It was worth a try."

"I may seem very weak to you, but I am not stupid. Now kick the keys into the hall."

He did as he was told. Abby got out of the chair and backed out of the room. She kept the gun trained on him as she scooped up the keys. Continued watching him as she backed down the hall to Jacob's office, locking the door behind her. Jacob was seconds behind, fists pounding on the door.

"Open the Goddamn door!"

The rage in his voice chilled her to the bone.

She knew she didn't have long before he broke it down. She hurried to the cabinet, pushed open the hidden compartment, and groped for her purse. She tried the closet door, but it was locked. Something hit the office door as she fumbled to find the right key. In a panic, Abby fired a shot into the closet lock. Missed. A second shot hit her mark and the door swung open. She hesitated. Returning to the cabinet, she sat the gun on the shelf before reclaiming her purse. She stared at the shoeboxes for several seconds before lifting the lid. Tossing the useless keys and phone, she emptied as much cash as she could into her oversized purse. Slipping the strap across her neck so it was draping her body, she hurried to the closet.

She tried to lock the door, but the bullet had destroyed the mechanism. Climbing the stairs, she groped for Jacob's keys. With trembling fingers, she unlocked the padlock and pushed open the flap. Breaching the opening, she slammed the hatch closed behind her. Only then did it occur to her that she'd left the gun on the shelf when she returned for her purse. She could hear Jacob spewing profanities from below. He was in the closet. She stared at the floor hatch, his last obstacle before he reached her. Looking around, she saw nothing by way of a weapon. She had no way to protect herself.

Acting purely on instinct, she pushed the heavy trunk over the opening in the floor.

"What are you doing up there, woman? Come on; move whatever that is out of the way and let me in. You know you can't get out of the attic without my help. Not in your condition. What are you going to do? Jump out the window? Not likely. See, you need me. You've always needed me."

She plopped onto the trunk, hoping her added weight would be of assistance. She had to keep him away. She wiped the sweat that trickled down her face. The attic was stifling, her head throbbing from the heat. She looked towards the small window, considered opening it, but fear kept her glued in place. Jacob's voice grew quiet and remained so for so long, she wondered if he'd finally given up. Minutes ticked away. Had he left the house?

No sooner than the thought had entered her mind, a pounding sound against the attic opening made it perfectly clear that Jacob was still in the house. Even more worrisome was the force of the hammering. Clearly, his anger had intensified.

"ABIGAIL!" Jacob seethed. "This has gone on long enough. You've had your fun, now open the door! Abigail? Open the Goddamn door! You fucking bitch, you just wait until I get my hands on you. I'm going to send you to hell with the rest of your family! Only this time, I am going to do it myself. I'm going to take my time with you. Make you beg me for mercy. I like it when you beg Abigail. You think this is a game? You think I won't find you? You have no place to run. You are mine! Mine...do you hear me? I waited for you. You've always been mine! You came to me willingly. You knew your destiny. Do you remember? You will always be mine! Now open this fucking door!"

She pressed her hands against her ears, trying in vain to drown out his words. Words that held a glimmer of truth. She had been the one to come to him. Stupidly, she had been the one to rush into marriage. How could she have been so blind to his faults? Because it had been he who'd been playing games. Using the tragedies in her life to collect her soul. Tragedies he had created, she reminded herself. Yes, but he was right, it was she who had given it willingly. She was as much to blame for her current situation as he. If only she'd waited, maybe she would have seen his true colors. Maybe...

Shots rang out. Two in quick succession. Abby shrieked, pulling her legs to her chest as the bullets penetrated the floorboards just inches from her feet. She was sobbing hysterically now. How could her life have gone so terribly wrong? She could hear him grunting as if he was pushing against the opening. She sat on the trunk for some time, still afraid to move, wondering if there were any bullets left in the gun. He would grow quiet, then scream her name menacingly, assaulting her with vile threats. In the moments between his ravings, the attic was eerily quiet. A sauna, the heat causing her pulse to drum against her temples, but the room was dry and she was alone. She felt a flicker of movement within her womb. No, she was not alone.

Time seemed to stand still. She had no idea how long she had been locked in her impenetrable fortress. Her vision was getting fuzzy, thoughts coming jumbled. Jacob's voice drifted out of the fog. "Abigail? It's pretty warm in the house. I imagine that attic is feeling even worse."

"Yes, yes it is pretty hot up here," she replied.

"See, I knew it. I can help you, Abigail. Just open the latch and let me up so I can get you out of there. You would like to get out and into the fresh air, wouldn't you?" he asked softly.

"Yes, I would." She shook her head, trying to collect her thoughts.

"Good, just move whatever is in the way so that I can get to you and our baby," he encouraged.

The baby. Her baby. Not his! The thoughts were coming more clearly now. He was trying to trick her. "You are not going to get anywhere near me. Or MY baby. Ever!"

He laughed menacingly. "Ah well, it was worth a try."

Once again, the attic grew quiet. It was another long stretch before she heard his voice. When at last he spoke, his voice held panic instead of anger. "Abigail, the water is getting pretty deep down here."

Cautiously, she went to the window and peered out. The house was an island, as was the house next door and the one beside that. She wondered where the water had come from and how long it would be before it reached her. Opening the window, she breathed in a fresh intake of air. While warm, the flowing air offered a welcomed relief from the stifling room and helped to ease the pounding within her head, even if the murky smell was not all that pleasant.

More time elapsed before he spoke. This time, he seemed resigned.

"Abigail? Even if I'm not here, they will find you. It is the way things work. They paid good money for the child."

"They who?" she questioned, returning to the trunk.

"Not at liberty to say. Confidentiality clause and all of that, you know. Unless you die in this house with me, they will come after the child."

"They are not getting my baby!" she repeated with more conviction than she actually felt.

"It's inevitable, my dear." This time his voice sounded muffled. "Abigail, this is it. Looks like you've won this round. I'll see you in hell! Abby?...A...b...bb."

Silence ensued.

She nearly wavered, wondering how she could let a man die, for surely that was what she was doing. But she knew Pearl was right, this was the only way, neither she nor the baby would be safe as long as Jacob was alive. A chill ran through her. If Jacob's threats were true, would she or her baby ever be safe?

Fear gripped her as she sat listening for any hint of life, or sign of the danger that might still exist. She strained, but heard nothing more than the sound of her own breathing, and the house creaking as the water continued to rise. There was no pounding. No clawing. No vile threats. Those sounds had finally subsided.

Murky water began seeping through the floorboards where the bullets had penetrated. As she stood, her heart pounded so hard she was afraid it was going to burst from her chest. Her once loose top now clung to her sweat-drenched body.

Cautiously, she gave the large wooden streamer trunk a feeble push. Pausing for a moment, she held her breath and listened once more. She jumped as a loud noise echoed within the attic. Hearing the sound again, she relaxed, realizing it was coming from outside. Within the house, all was still quiet. She turned her attention back to the large trunk, giving it another push. It was heavier than she remembered, making her wonder how she had gotten it over the opening so quickly just moments before.

Bracing herself, she gave it one last shove, finally revealing the hinged flap that lay nestled safely in the confines of the floor. She stared at the water-soaked hatch for several moments, half expecting Jacob to push it open. When that did not occur, she held her breath and reached for the handle. Cautiously, she lifted the flap and peered into the murky water below. Abby let out the breath. The water, no longer met with resistance, began rising upward. Startled, she released the door, sending the warm water upwards, foul-smelling droplets cascading over her already soaked body.

Seeing the water reminded Abby that she was not yet out of danger. Desperate, she sprang into action. Traveling the few short steps across the damp attic boards, she peered out the window.

"HELP!" Her cries were met with silence.

Not having any other choice, she eased backwards out the narrow window. Holding fast to the top of the windowsill she managed to pull herself up and out onto the protruding roof slant of the front porch. She thought about the path Kevin had taken, but lowering herself into the murky water was not an option. Where would she swim to? Trembling, she turned her attention to the roof.

As she climbed, she looked down into the still rising water. A wave of nausea rushed over her. Swallowing deeply, she closed her eyes, hoping that would quell the bile in her stomach. The stench of the muddy water did nothing to ease the turbulence that now raged within. Turning her head, eyes brimming with moisture, she gave in to the desire to heave, retching so powerfully that she lost her footing. Frantic, she clawed at the hot shingles, feeling the burn of them scraping through the thin layer of her drenched shirt as she slid helplessly toward the rising water.

Suddenly, the toes of her shoes came to an abrupt stop against a board just above the gutter. The water was rising so high that for a brief moment, she reconsidered the short drop into the murky water. She could swim, but for how long? The sight of a water moccasin gliding past the house atop the water stopped her cold. God only knew what other unseen dangers lurked beneath the surface. Her only hope was to reach the top of her roof, although she still did not know what she would do once she got there. Taking a deep breath, she carefully made her way to the top of what was left of her home.

Looking around at the vast waterway littered with rooftops and floating debris, Abby was quick to realize her ordeal was far from over. Water was everywhere. Several nearby homes were fully submerged. Others, like hers, had water quickly approaching the bottom of the attic dormers. Water the color of coffee with extra cream spanned as far as the eye could see. In the distance, she could see people sprinkled on rooftops, heard their panicked cries, desperately pleading for someone to come save them. But no boats were in sight. No rescuers within earshot.

Once again, she contemplated diving into the murk, but shook off the thought. Swimming was not an option, for even if she could get past the snakes, where would she go? Exhausted, Abby sank helplessly onto the blistering shingles. Lying on her side, she pulled her knees into her stomach and wrapped her arms around them for protection. Clasping her hands together and chilled from shock, she lay there on the sweltering rooftop, rocking back and forth. Her mind retraced the events that had taken place over the last few hours. How could she have done that, left him there to die? Once again, the baby inside of her moved, reminding her. It was almost as if the child was thanking her for saving its life.

Tears streamed down her face as the water began to roar. The sound was deafening within her ears, swirling as if ready to engulf her. The wind had picked up, adding to the thunderous roar of the waters. Abby, now in the clutches of deep shock, refused to let go of her protective cocoon. Just when the roar was at its loudest, Abby felt hands on her shoulders. He was alive, had come for her, come once again to threaten the life of her unborn child! Screaming, Abby struck out, both fists hitting their mark. Like a wild animal, her claws came out, striking and pounding, ripping at the man who threatened her, threatened to steal her baby within. She swung again, but this time, her attempt was stopped in midair. The roar of the water continued, but this time, a sound cut through the roar. She tried to free her hands, to no avail. What was that deafening sound? Abby felt trapped; she couldn't move her hands. Something had them and would not let them go. Through a haze came the sound again, only this time, Abby realized it was a man's voice shouting at her, no, not at her, to her, trying to reach through the foggy confines of the shock that engulfed her.

"Lady, stop fighting me," he was saying. "Ma'am, I am Petty Officer Gomez with the United States Coast Guard. It is okay. You are safe now. Is there anyone else in the house?" the voice asked more clearly this time.

Abby blinked; the fog was lifting. Safe, the voice had said. She was safe. Letting her arms relax, she looked up. It was only then she realized the roaring sound was not from the water, but from a helicopter hovering overhead.

"Is there anyone else in the house?" the man repeated, shouting over the deafening sounds of the bright orange and white helicopter.

Abby looked down at the water that was nearing the rooftop. "Yes...my husband," she stammered.

She blinked back tears.

"My husband is still inside. He didn't make it into the attic," she said, voice trembling.

Petty Officer Gomez looked at the water, which by this time was nearly to the eaves of the roof. As if realizing there was no hope, he extended a single finger to the flight crew above to let them know they were only taking on one extra passenger.

Understanding the meaning, Abby wrapped her arms protectively around her stomach, watching as the basket was lowered.

"Actually, there are two of us," she whispered quietly. "I'm pregnant."

A Special Note from the Author...

To the victims, help is only a phone call away... Please make the call!

Each year thousands of people go missing. While it is mandatory to report a missing person under the age of 18, it is not, in many states, mandatory to report the disappearance of an adult. NamUS is a searchable database which was set up to help identify some of those missing adults. In many cases there is nothing to go on except a sketch of what the person might have looked like, in other cases there are clear, and concise pictures, yet the person still remains unidentified. NamUS, the unidentified persons database plays host to thousands of unknowns, working tirelessly, to help them find their way home. http://www.namus.gov

It is estimated that 1.2 million children are trafficked each year.

Call the National Human Trafficking Resource Center

1-888-373-7888 or text BeFree (233733) to report sex trafficking, forced labor, or to get help

Every 9 seconds in the US, a woman is assaulted or beaten.

One in every four women will experience domestic violence in her lifetime.

An estimated 1.3 million women are victims of physical assault by an intimate partner each year.

Eighty-five percent of domestic violence victims are women.

Historically, females have been most often victimized by someone they knew.

Females who are 20-24 years of age are at the greatest risk of nonfatal intimate partner violence.

Most cases of domestic violence are never reported to the police.

U.S. National Domestic Violence Hotline at

1-800-799-7233 and TTY 1-800-787-3224.

http://www.ncadv.org

ABOUT THE AUTHOR

Born in Louisville, Sherry A. Burton was raised in the small town of Fairdale, Kentucky. Eloping December of 1980 with a Navy man while still in her teens, she has spent all of her adult life moving from state-to-state totaling over thirty-two moves in her thirty-three years of marriage. Sherry can attest first-hand to the fact that a whirlwind marriage can indeed last. Sherry credits her frequent moves and long separations to her ability to feel her characters' desire to find true happiness.

Sherry has worked as a private nanny and is a certified dog trainer. She is the mother of three adult children and has six wonderful grandchildren. Her hobbies include reading, walking, Pilates, and spending time with her "friends" — which is how she refers to the characters she creates. She believes in daily affirmations, positive energy and feels that karma will have the final say.

Sherry A. Burton currently resides in Chesapeake, Virginia. Sherry's books include *Tears of Betrayal, The King of My Heart, Somewhere in My Dreams,* and "Whispers of The Past (a short story)." Sherry has several other books in the works, including a sequel to *Tears of Betrayal.*

A versatile author, Sherry writes children's books under the name Sherry A. Jones.
http://www.sherryajones.com

To check out her blog, please go to:
http://www.sherryaburton.com

To follow her on Facebook:
http://www.facebook.com/pages/Sherry-A-Burton-Author/136542383031597